PRAISE FOR *The Practice of Deceit*

"The story practically spills into your lap as you turn the pages . . . A lot of wicked fun." —ALAN CHEUSE, *All Things Considered,* National Public Radio

"A psychological thriller . . . filled with ulterior motives and insights on complicated relationships." —*New York Times*

"A literary page-turner, as suspenseful as it is smart, rich in surprising twists." —STEPHEN MCCAULEY, author of *The Object of My Affection*

"A rare find: a psychological thriller with plenty of spot-on psychology in addition to the usual thrills. It's smart entertainment by a very smart writer." —*Chicago Tribune*

"Benedict's characters . . . are marvelously alive. [She] juxtaposes the aggressiveness of the law with the sweet ambiguities of therapy in fascinating, often funny ways." —MOPSY STRANGE KENNEDY, *Improper Bostonian*

"Benedict's psychological thriller will make for the perfect read . . . The genuine suspense is a bonus." —*New York Daily News*

"A smart, sexy, subtle, suburban thriller." —*Book Sense*

"Entertaining . . . [a] clever reworking of male-female roles."
—*USA Today*

"This tightly woven psychological thriller is a journey for the reader . . . with plenty of surprises and insights along the way."
—*St. Louis Post-Dispatch*

"Highly recommended . . . a suspenseful and provocative look at the intricacies and dangers of intimacy with the wrong person."
—*New Mystery Reader Magazine*

"Ms. Benedict is a gifted writer, a fluid and intelligent wordsmith who knows how to keep the reader ⟨...⟩ ⟨...⟩ *eyard Times*

"One of those rare bo⟨...⟩ thebibliofiles.com

"Intelligently written ⟨...⟩ —*Publishers Weekly*

D1113841

BOOKS BY ELIZABETH BENEDICT

FICTION

Slow Dancing

The Beginner's Book of Dreams

Safe Conduct

Almost

The Practice of Deceit

NONFICTION

The Joy of Writing Sex:
A Guide for Fiction Writers

THE PRACTICE

of

DECEIT

Elizabeth Benedict

A Mariner Book
HOUGHTON MIFFLIN COMPANY
BOSTON · NEW YORK

FIRST MARINER BOOKS EDITION 2006

Copyright © 2005 by Elizabeth Benedict
ALL RIGHTS RESERVED

For information about permission to reproduce selections
from this book, write to Permissions, Houghton Mifflin Company,
215 Park Avenue South, New York, New York 10003.

Visit our Web site: www.houghtonmifflinbooks.com.

Library of Congress Cataloging-in-Publication Data
Benedict, Elizabeth.
The practice of deceit / Elizabeth Benedict.
p.   cm.
ISBN 0-618-56371-7
1. Conflict of interests — Fiction.   2. Attorney and
client — Fiction.   3. Scarsdale (N.Y.) — Fiction.   4. Married
people — Fiction.   5. Suburban life — Fiction.   6. Women
lawyers — Fiction.   7. Divorce — Fiction.   I. Title.
PS3552.E5396P73 2005
813'.54 — dc22   2004060914
ISBN-13: 978-0-618-71051-5 (pbk.)
ISBN-10: 0-618-71051-5 (pbk.)

Printed in the United States of America

Book design by Robert Overholtzer

MP 10 9 8 7 6 5 4 3 2 1

THE PRACTICE

of

DECEIT

Could you escape from a divorce the way you could from a marriage? Was it possible to get a divorce from a divorce?

—PAULA FOX, *Borrowed Finery*

AUTHOR'S NOTE

This is a fictional story set in many real places. I have used the actual names of towns, streets, hotels, schools, universities, government agencies, and newspapers, but in every case, the characters who inhabit them and the situations that take place in them are invented.

I am enormously indebted to many experts for sharing their professional insights and experience. Abundant thanks go to Dr. Lee Birk, Arthur Bloom, Mark Bomster, Katharine Conroy, Dr. Stephen Dolgin, Finale Doshi, Richard Fatigate, John H. Galloway III, Stephen Gillers, Philip Hersh, Cynthia Jabs, Isabella Jancourtz, Daniel Loreto, Charlie Peters, Michael Schlesinger, and Donald Smith.

This is for Elly, Evelyn, Deena, Carol,
Judy, Judy, and Mom.

Women Who Need Too Much

THE REASONS I fell in love with my wife, Colleen O'Brien Golden, on December 30, 1999:

1. Chemistry.
2. Biology.
3. Seismology.
4. Elocution.
5. My deadbeat dad.
6. Her broken heart.
7. The milky breasts that covered it.

I will stop at number seven, lucky seven. My luck seems to have run out, just when I thought I still had so much to draw on, and here I am, in a holding cell in the Scarsdale Police Department on the corner of Tompkins and Fenimore. It's a building I go by nearly every day when I take my stepdaughter, Zoe, to preschool or pick her up, sometimes both if I can work it into my schedule. What a lucky SOB you are to live here, I often say to myself when I see the boxy, two-story brick structure roll past me, lucky to have landed in a town where the police don't have enough to do most days of the week. Sure, there are incidents now and then, including that hostage situation last month. But day to day, week to week, the cops have it easy in our picturesque village, celebrated for its stellar school system, its mock Tudor mansions, the sales at Zachys Wine and Liquor, where you can sometimes pick up a case of St. Emilion for $189, and our seventeen thousand well-heeled, well-behaved, college-educated residents. Many of the women can tell you the best places to buy chanterelle mushrooms, and the men to play golf, not only in Scarsdale but in the Berkshires, Amagansett, the Outer Cape, and the coast of Maine. The crime report is a feature of the local paper, but fifty-one weeks out of fifty-two, teenagers driving under the influence comes in way ahead of grand larceny. Not many places like that left, I would say to myself, and gaze at my darling stepdaughter, who has her mother's green eyes and her mother's soft strawberry blond hair, ditto her charm, and, alas, her temper, whether we were talking about how to tell if it's today or tomorrow, where goldfish go when you flush them down the toilet, and how it happens that Peter Pan doesn't grow up. She's four and a half years old.

I imagined there were only offices here, nothing like the holding cell I'm in now, or the booking room I just came from, where they took off my shoes, my belt, my watch, and asked if I ever thought of killing myself. "Never, until you showed up at my door." Would they put me on a suicide watch? They took two mug shots, three sets of fingerprints, and did a DNA swab of my tongue with a Q-Tip. Even those were a relief after the throttle of the handcuffs.

"Can you loosen them?" I had said in the back seat of the police car, my arms tied behind my back, as if I were a bull about to be de-balled. "I tore my rotator cuff last year, and my chiropractor says I'm not supposed to stress it."

Silence.

"I don't know if you heard me, but shoveling snow last year, I ended up with a torn —"

"We heard you." They don't get judged on their manners, these guys.

"If you loosened them just a little —"

"All you bastards who can't keep your hands to yourselves say they're too tight." The driver's accent was heavy Brooklyn, as thick as a slice of Sicilian pizza. "That's the point."

"I'm innocent," I said. "Does everyone say that too? You know who I am, don't you? The shrink you called to keep the kid from killing his old man at the end of August. They wanted to name a street after me — and now I'm a felon?"

No answer from the front seat.

No one wanted to name a street after me, but I thought it would get their attention. I needed to find a joke in this somewhere. Bastards like me? My right shoulder blade felt as though it were being jabbed with an ice pick, and I needed to take a piss.

This was not a joke.

This was not a social call.

Two sounds you never want to hear: the serrated metal against metal of the cuffs locking and the jail cell door clicking shut behind you.

My new identity: B0307. My arrest number. Could they make an exception for me and add "Ph.D." to it? I've been seeing patients since 1982. I'm Dr. B0307, Ph.D. What seems to be your problem? Depression? Anxiety? Uncontrollable rage? Smoldering rage? Is your husband a schmuck? Do you want to kill your deadbeat dad father with his own gun because that's the only way you can get him to pay the bills? Does your kid want to drop out of Scarsdale High and flip burgers at Fuddruckers? Is your maid addicted to Botox? Come on in. Have a seat. Sorry the wood's so hard. Take a piss if you like. There's no water in the bowl because they don't want me to dunk my head in there and drown. Did they take my watch because they think I might kill myself with it or because they don't want me to know how slowly the time passes behind bars? Will I be arraigned today or spend the night here? Will the judge set bail or send me to the real jail in Valhalla, next to which this place will seem like the Marriott? In myth, Valhalla is a hall where slain heroes are worshipped. I wonder if the Westchester Department of Corrections gets the irony.

I have no idea what time it is. There is a video camera against the wall, across from the cell, and it is trained on me: Eric Lavender, Ph.D., neighborhood shrink, with a minor specialty in the problems of teenage boys. The cops called on me late last month when fourteen-year-old Jason Cummings took his father hostage with the old man's handgun, in the house where he, the father, was living with his girlfriend in the Edgewood section of town, and I spoke to him on the phone from a house across the street. I'm dynamite in a crisis. I'm Sam Spade with empathy, Al Pacino with a New Age bedside manner. The kid put down his gun and walked out of the house with his hands on his head and his Tommy Hilfiger shorts halfway down his butt. Five minutes later, dear old dad was ungagged and untied from his chair and arrested on the spot for failing to pay child support for two years. Last I heard, Dad is still in Valhalla, overdosing on irony. The turning point in my conversation with Jason, the point at which I knew we were home free, was when I told him that I had had a deadbeat dad myself.

I poke my arm through the bars to see if I can reach the phone, which is bolted to the wall next to the camera on a tightly coiled cord that reminds me of one from my mother's old kitchen, the place she lived before the nursing home. I've already made two phone calls with the cops' help. Places like Scarsdale, you get more than one. What else do they have to do all day long? I phoned my sister, Pru, and the lawyer she found for me, Lily Lopez. She'll be here any minute. A little architectural oversight, that the prisoner can reach the phone through the bars! Hah! My desperate fantasy. I don't know who else I'd call if I could. Sandy Lefkowitz — and tell him I'm a felon? I mean, *alleged.* My new favorite word. What were my old favorites? *Insight. Transformation. Possibility.* I'm talking to the walls. I'm waving to the cops through the video cameras. Losing what's left of my mind. Losing my children. My freckle-faced Zoe with her collection of teddy bears, and my own flesh and blood, the glorious Sarah Rose, the wonder of my forty-eighth year on earth. Daddy probably won't be home tonight, honey, but I promise I'll never leave you. Solemn promise, little one. Tiny angel. Beautiful snowflake.

CHRIST. I cannot begin this way. Sarcastic one minute and full of self-pity and mawkish emotion the next. On the phone, Lily Lopez, Esq., told me to collect my thoughts, pull together the key events that led me here, so she'll have a story to tell the judge. She said to keep my emotions out of it. Now I see why. At least she believed me when I explained the charges; Pru must have filled her in on what's been going on. Or maybe that's what criminal lawyers always do: put on a show of believing the client's story. Whichever it is, I'll take it.

"You ever been arrested before?" she asked me.

"No. Never."

"Married before?"

"No."

"How long you and your wife been together?"

"Almost three and a half years. We have a daughter who's two and a half, and Zoe, my wife's four-and-a-half-year-old."

"Your sister saved my son's life. I'm taking this case, because, I'm telling you, these *pinche mujeres* in Scarsdale —"

"Don't take it as a favor to Pru. If you want to do her a favor, find me a lawyer who wants the case."

"No, you don't understand. I'm psyched, Eric. Some of these women in Scarsdale, with their *movidas* and their face-lifts and their yappy little dogs. We've seen this movie before."

She was jumping to a lot of conclusions — my innocence, for one — and she was no smooth-talking Scarsdale attorney like my wife. She had a tough-sounding New York accent with a Spanish tinge. "What are *movidas*?"

"Moves. Manipulations. What Scarsdale types pull when they want to keep living in the big house without the hubby. They don't even want him in the room over the garage anymore. That's when they learn how to work the system. When you're that rich —"

"If you want to rant about Scarsdale, Ms. Lopez, I'll find myself a lawyer who isn't so —"

"I'm just talking, Eric, blowing off steam. My acupuncturist is out of town. Forget I mentioned it. I'm on good terms with one of the detectives over there, Detective Lawson. I'm bringing you a computer notebook in half an hour so you can collect your thoughts. Makes my job a little easier for tomorrow, and they won't give you a paper and pencil because you might hurt yourself. Focus on the facts. Try to keep your feelings out of it. Dates you remember, conversations, events. Let's see, it's almost four. Lawson's good about getting you in to see a judge, because rich people aren't used to waiting, even when they're in the clinker, but it's late. You might have to spend the night. Sorry about that. If I don't get a call from the station, we'll meet in the morning before the arraignment. When that hearing is over, I want you to be released. I don't want to see you shipped to Valhalla in handcuffs. You're not one of those men who can't type, are you?"

"I can type. That's nice of you to bring me the computer."

"This is not about nice. I'm bringing you the computer because I'm good — and I hate to lose."

"Even better."

"And because your sister saved my son's life."

IF I WERE a religious man, I would say that my sister, Pru Lavender, M.D., does the Lord's work: fixing what's broken inside the hearts of tiny babies, valves, arteries, ventricles. She's one of two pediatric cardiac surgeons in all of New York City, one of two doctors who operate on the hearts of newborn babies, which are the size of a small plum. I am in awe of Pru. So is half of New York — though it still pisses me off that she got into medical school and I didn't. And that she does the manly, macho thing of cutting people up and sewing them back together, while I do women's work: talking them through their problems.

We have a complicated but not too fractious relationship. Pru is, in so many ways, the superior sibling. She balks when I mention it, but we both know her balking is politeness, not an argument with the truth. I am two years younger than she is, and when I got rejected from all six of the medical schools I applied to, she was a good big sister and tried to make light of it, to interpret these denials as information about me rather than a judgment. "You're destined for other things," she said, "like getting a good night's sleep once in a while. Like not spending the next ten years in school." I'm not unhappy to have ended up doing what I do, but it still stings sometimes that I didn't make the grade.

Did it work out that way because the women in my early life were so present and the man so much trouble? That's the theory of the poet who takes groups of men into the woods to bang drums and helps us get in touch with our proud, warlike selves. The poet claims that we men suffer from not getting "enough father," that since we no longer learn trades from our male elders, our primary relationships are with the women who raise us — and we learn to please them by becoming like them. Not enough father? When I was a kid in Teaneck, New Jersey, I thought I had too much goddamn father, even though he worked sixty hours a week — and took off for California when I was twelve. When he was home, he was always yelling. My mother's pocketbook was a mess, my sister left her shoes in the living room, I got a D in geography and my hair was too long, another sign of my overfeminized urges. All you had to do to ignite a blowup was put a seventy-five-watt bulb into a sixty-watt socket. My mother learned to cower, I learned to fight with him, and my sister, two years older and obviously smarter, did all she could to pass for perfect. These days, she speaks Spanish with the Puerto Rican mothers and fathers of her patients, French with the Haitians, and Upper East Side English with the gringos. Her office walls are covered with snapshots of babies magically restored to life because of her fine motor skills.

Did I mention that she is a lesbian? Did I mention how aware of this I am when I think of her? It's not that I disapprove, only that I wonder whether it was a case of nature or nurture. I wonder what effect, if any, our father's behavior had on her sexuality, in the same way that I wonder what effect his behavior had on me in general. My wife would tell me to quit wallowing in the past. She would tell me what her deceased mother always told her: *You won't get anywhere in this world worrying about what already happened.* Can I blame my father for my having married a woman who does not believe that our past holds the key to the rest of our lives?

She must be the only woman in Scarsdale without a shrink. She's got more important things to do than dredge up the past and complain about the present. *Les femmes de Scarsdale* call me when they want a sensitive man to talk to. They call my wife when they want a divorce. Until recently, I thought only the husbands in Scarsdale were *movida* masters, those alpha males with their stock options and their offshore girlfriends. They weren't men I had much feeling for from a distance, and they weren't my patients. Their wives were. Some of their wives still are.

When I am with them, I am empathic and supportive, and I do my best to help them through their sorrows and loneliness, which they feel as acutely as the poor and the middle classes feel their heartache. But I am tired of the way they whine about their interior decorators, their children's SAT scores, the two wrinkles that have shown up on their foreheads, and the new Saab, which has more problems than the old Jaguar. I call them the Women Who Need Too Much, and I vow to tell the next one who calls that I am not taking new patients — but you can't tell much from a phone call, and I cannot afford to turn down work. But I know I'm not the therapist I yearn to be when I recall an old *New Yorker* cartoon of a woman on a beach saying to a man: "I do think your problems are serious, Howard. I just don't think they're very interesting." Of course there are exceptions. The oddballs, misfits, newcomers, the older women who've had their careers or raised their children, lost their husbands to death or divorce, and possess real wisdom. And I like working with the teenage boys who are sent to me by their frustrated parents or the high school psychologist. Usually they need more discipline, less money, fewer tutors. I often think the best therapy would be to ship them to Manhattan, where smart, restless teenagers have things to do besides drink, drive, and rebel against the narrow ambitions of their self-satisfied hometown.

And then there is Sandy Lefkowitz. A patient in a league of his own. Poor bastard.

I've lived here barely three years. After I took up with Colleen and she wanted me to leave Manhattan and move into her house in Scarsdale, I resisted, punted, tried, as men often do, to change the subject. But when she got pregnant, after we'd known each other for four months, the conversation changed. Did it ever. I was forty-seven and she was forty-one. She had one child and I had none. Earlier in my life, I'd have pressured her to have an abortion — never mind the politics, keep your laws off my body, and all that. But I wasn't such a cocky son of a bitch at forty-seven, and Colleen was different from the women I used to date: stable, self-sufficient, a woman of the world, a warm, loving mother, and eager to be with me but not in that clingy, hectoring way that usually emerges soon after the initial blush of lust. I don't mean I decided that first night that I wanted to marry her. God, no. I was a hard-core bachelor, but by the time I actually made the decision to marry her, leave the city, and move to Scarsdale, all of which, I admit, was prompted by the pregnancy, I had convinced myself I was finally ready for a serious woman, a family, the house she already owned, the child she had already given birth to, and this one of ours who was coming. And once we were all together, I was shocked at how this family — my family — took hold of me, cradling me in varieties of love I had never felt before.

My patients in New York had been artists, designers, writers, medical researchers, community activists. I fancied myself a confidential Charlie Rose, talking to deeply interesting people about what mattered most to them. Dream on, Dr. Lavender. I wasn't talking cutting-edge architecture with them or about Middle East peacemaking. I was talking about absent mothers, insane ex-husbands, cybersex, cigarettes, and obsessions with Princess Di both before and after her death. Still, I loved what I did and the people I worked with. But when the workday was over, I indulged my politically incorrect cravings for women, as they say, young enough to be my daughter. I dated them one at a time, not in small groups and not behind each other's backs. You couldn't have accused me of being a two-timer, just a guy who had, well, a short attention span and a commitment phobia.

I told myself that I took care of people for so much of the day that when it was over, I needed someone to take care of me. Someone young, energetic, preferably buxom. There was nothing secretive about it; I took them out, these lovely specimens, introduced them to my friends — what friends I have — and tried not to notice the suppressed disapproving scowls when I would show up with yet another Brandy or Consuela or Misaka. Whatever their origins, my girlfriends tended to be actresses or dancers or aspiring account executives at BBD&O and McCann Erickson. They read the occasional Oprah novel, fashion magazines, and *Modern Bride,* with no encouragement from me. I wasn't exactly slumming. I'm a bright enough guy, but all the great books I'll ever read I read in college and graduate school, and my musical tastes are straight down the middle: Bob Dylan, Bruce Springsteen, Mostly Mozart, the Brandenburgs, a little cool jazz, a few show tunes.

To a degree that surprised me, they liked to quiz me about textbook-aberrant behavior and about my unhappy childhood, thinking, once they heard the stories, that this was the way to my heart. But they would soon find out that it was not my heart that ruled my appetite, and there would often be tears, theirs, a dramatic departure, phone calls in the middle of the night, a dozen e-mails, clothing to be sent for, and so on and so forth. Once, there was a suicide threat, which shook me up for months and should have sent me looking for a smart woman my own age. But it didn't. The acquisition of personal insight isn't exactly a plane ticket, passage to a distinct destination. Sometimes it's more like a cloud: a beautiful thing you can see but not put your arms around. And the next time you look, it's gone.

My friends gradually stopped fixing me up with the interesting women they knew, and I gradually stopped bringing dates to my apartment. I had paraded too many past my doormen and was afraid one of them might turn me in to the Children's Defense Fund. That's a joke. They were all well over the age of consent. But I never knew what to say once they started asking about "the outlook for our future." The present was all I could handle. Amanda, a friend from graduate school, dared me to go back into therapy to find out why I seemed stuck, why I kept repeating the same old scenarios. I had some ideas — Mom and Dad and the misery that was their marriage — and was on the verge of calling an old therapist when two things happened that altered my life.

One. My father died suddenly, in Los Angeles. The deadbeat dad I had mentioned to Jason Cummings.

Two. On my eighth day there to settle his affairs, the day I scattered half of his ashes into the Pacific Ocean — keeping the rest for Pru, who had already returned to New York — I met Colleen.

I have said almost nothing about her. It's not that I don't know where to start. Told from here, from this hard bench that is both bed and chair, table and couch, inside walls and bars painted a dark gray like a grim parody of jail, the story has a different ring than it would if I could tell it from the desk in my office. Told from here, who would believe I'm innocent? Where, I wonder, did our troubles begin — or were the seeds always present in our marriage?

If I had had a better role model in my father, I might be able to do the manly thing and stick to the facts. But as a therapist, I deal in feelings the way bankers deal in money. As a man accused of molesting his stepdaughter, who is four and a half years old, I am livid. The charge: "Forcible touching," Lily Lopez told me. "Touching her genitals in a sexual way," she explained as I shuddered with rage. Why avoid my feelings? They're the only thing they can't take from me, the way they can take my children, my practice, my reputation. They will try to build a case against me, but they know and I know it will be built of air, of smoke, of the cards that make up the house of cards in which I have been living.

2

White on White

Are first looks instructive? Should I have perceived everything I have come to know the instant I noticed her by the elevator in the lobby of the Mondrian Hotel? It was the second-to-last day of the twentieth century, and I had just walked into the building on Sunset Boulevard, carrying a plastic supermarket bag of what was left of my father's charred remains, about the heft of three apples. I planned to bring the bag to my room, come downstairs for a swim, and think about when to call the airline to book a flight back to New York. The woman by the elevator was striking and shapely, altogether different from the anorexia nervosa specimens that roamed the lobby. And she was reading the *New York Times* folded up in quarters as though she were a straphanger on the subway instead of a guest in this spare, postmodern palace.

It was my eighth day there, a story in itself, how I ended up sitting shiva for my father in a hotel so full of sunlight, bright white walls, fresh orchids, and playful white furniture that I felt guilty thinking a single sad thought. It was my sister's idea; she had made the reservation soon after we learned our father had been found on the kitchen floor of his apartment, fifteen blocks from the hotel. It did not look like foul play; the autopsy revealed a heart attack. We could have stayed at his place for nothing, but neither of us cared to. It was as difficult to be close to him in death as it had been in life. We agreed about that, but when I arrived at the Mondrian, two days before Prudence, I thought she had made a mistake. I should have known better; my sister does not make mistakes. She explained that it was close to Dad's apartment, she didn't want a hotel that looked like a funeral home and didn't want to feel any more deprived by the old man now than she had while he was alive. *I don't care how much it costs, I'm not going to stay in a stately gloom box or a cheap motel. Feel free to go somewhere else if you want.*

I loved the hotel and hated it and loved it again, and the ambivalence I felt about every aspect of it, including the expense, echoed my ambivalence about my father, before and after his demise. The concierge's perpetually sunny smile infuriated me because I wanted my mourning acknowledged, but the swimming pool never failed to soothe, and the view at night of the L.A. basin from my lonely window took my breath away. I stayed even after Pru left for New York, three days before I met Colleen. I'd intended to leave with Pru, but there was a problem with the lease to the apartment, and an extra day turned into two days and then three. Each extra morning, I woke up intending to move to the Holiday Inn down the street and save a small fortune, but by check-out time I had done nothing. Some part of me felt liberated pissing away so much money on dumb luxury even though there would be nothing to show for it when I left, nothing to lay claim to except an anecdote. What the hell. The place made me feel like a movie mogul, like a filthy rich geezer walking the first-class deck of an ocean liner, the wind at my back, an adoring starlet waiting in my cabin. Not having enough money had always been an issue in our family. Once my father left and the business he started in L.A. went belly-up, child support payments ended and my mother's meager salary as a secretary was all we had. Those were the days before the deadbeat dad laws; we could rely only on our anger, our industry, and an occasional check from my father's father, who did not have much to share. Our mother worried about money all the time, even once Pru and I made enough to send her something every month. Now she was beyond worrying, she was in la-la land, on the la-la-land unit of the nursing home near Pru's apartment in New York. She always knew who Pru and I were and had a motherly smile and a kiss but quickly disappeared into another world once the smile faded.

The elevator door opened and the lovely woman reading the *Times* stepped in and moved to the panel of lighted buttons, turning to ask what floor I wanted. Her cheeks were lightly freckled and a head of thick strawberry blond hair brushed her shoulders. She was five-six or -seven, with an athletic build, square shoulders and full breasts beneath her white cotton top. Black pants, womanly hips. No rings on her fingers that I could see. I had been studying her as we waited for the elevator. Maybe she was forty. I wasn't bowled over, not knocked out, but there was something to appreciate, something solid, sturdy, pretty. I wasn't on the make, just looking. Window-shopping, one of my patients calls it.

"Twelve," I said.

She pressed the button and lowered her eyes to the newspaper again. I should have been looking straight ahead at the door, but I found myself staring at her, and when she felt my gaze in that tiny space, she looked at me, puzzled at the attention. "My father," I said, by way of explanation.

"Excuse me?"

I raised the grocery bag to show her that something sat heavily at the bottom of it, something that might be sand. "He died last week. These are his —" When I saw her eyes tighten and the rest of her flinch, moving back an inch or two, I let up. This was what I hadn't tossed into the ocean at Santa Monica Beach first thing that morning, when it was only the early-morning runners and bicyclists, the homeless people, and me. Was it permissible just to feel relief that he was gone, to feel, simply, that I no longer had to blame myself for not caring enough? "His dentures. I'm sorry, I've been so . . ." I was flustered and embarrassed I had spoken at all.

"I'm sorry," she said. "How did he —"

"Never mind. I didn't mean to bother you. I've been talking to the walls." Since Pru left I had barely spoken to anyone. The elevator stopped abruptly and the door slid open. She saw we were on the eighth floor and skittered past me but turned around, holding her arm against the slot, to keep the door from closing. Poor woman was in the midst of a condolence call with someone she'd never laid eyes on. "I hope you'll be all right."

"Thanks." I stepped toward the panel of numbers, wanting her to walk away because I didn't want the temptation to make a move. Unseemly, holding my father's ashes, to invite her for a drink. At eleven in the morning. She looked at me with squinty-eyed sympathy. I could see she didn't know what to say. I was lonely. That's all I could say with certainty, but not to a stranger. "You're kind to be concerned. I'll be fine."

The door started to shut, and I thought that would be that, but seconds later a hand jabbed into the empty space and seemed about to be crushed by the sliding panel. The motion made the door jerk open and she stood in the hallway looking in at me, her eyes hard on mine. I'd venture to say that we were both startled by what she had just done. "Are you free in an hour? Do you want to have lunch at one of the restaurants downstairs? If you're talking to the walls, well — I'm better company than that. My name's Colleen. What's yours?"

YEARS FROM NOW, when my daughter, Sarah Rose, dreams the home movie of her parents' meeting and courtship, it is exactly here that she will cry out, "Daddy, Daddy, don't do it. Go straight to LAX and board the next plane home," wanting to spare us everything that lies ahead, including, paradoxically, her own birth.

But I did no such thing. I stayed on at the Mondrian because of the lunch invitation and the dreariness of my apartment in New York and because I had broken up with a girl named Gaby Goldberg three weeks before and had no one to ring in the new millennium with the following night. Gaby had called me a "selfish prick" for breaking up with her right before New Year's, and she was right. But if I'd stayed with her through the holidays, that would have suggested a feeling for her that I didn't have and couldn't fake. I'd had a patient, male, who did not start dating anyone new between early November and February fifteenth, because he didn't want the weight of the holidays plus Valentine's Day. It was like a long period of Lent: no women. I wasn't as organized, as defensive, as careful. I played it by ear — and ended up with the Gaby Goldbergs of the world enraged at me. Rightly so. I stayed in L.A. because I did not want to be reminded of the selfish prick I could be in New York. Because if I were going to be alone on this big millennial New Year's Eve, I'd rather be alone in a strange city than in the place I had lived for twenty-five years. And why leave the maid service, the swimming pool, the sunlight? I had no appointments with patients for three more days, and the therapist covering for me had called only twice. Things were under control. And now they were looking up.

I went to my room and lay down, hoping to make up for some of the sleep I hadn't had that morning when I'd woken at dawn. But I'd had too much caffeine and couldn't unwind. Time for a swim. Second-best thing to a nap. Waiting for the elevator again, I got spooked: thought I saw my old man in the mirror. Hairline receding, the pores on my nose too deep, bags under my eyes. No longer young. What were they doing with me, my sweet young things with their firm breasts and lovely bottoms? One of them had told me that I was "just good-looking enough." At first I was insulted, then I studied myself and decided she was right. Five-ten, medium frame, black hair, dark brown eyes, a straight Roman nose, nothing special except an empathic countenance and good teeth. I swam in college, ran track, tried boxing; I was a jock before sports were popular. Now I had a tire around my middle and my hair was falling out.

They fancied me a fortuneteller, my young ladies; they thought I could see into their souls because I know the difference between depression and schizophrenia. They had an idea I was deep because I didn't work at Salomon Smith Barney. Or maybe I had them all wrong. Them and myself. Isn't this what women always want to believe is true of men — that we are more complicated than we are? I tried to look at myself as though I was not the man in the mirror, as though we had never met. Could a stranger tell by looking that I would probably never marry, never have children? I had reached the age of no return, the age of no second dates with women who know that a man over forty-five who has never married never will. I turned to try to see my profile. White T-shirt and my baggy navy swim trunks that could pass for shorts. I might be mistaken for a middleweight boxer. If I lost a few pounds. Pow. Pow. *My father is dead,* I said into the mirror. I wanted to feel it land on me like a cinder block, crushing me with grief. I wanted to ache, to have that cottony disoriented feeling you have after someone has died. I wanted to miss him, but I didn't. The man I had been angry at for most of my life was gone. Was the anger still there? Or only the cavity in my body where it had lived all these years?

This was my version of sitting shiva because I knew no other, had been raised with no religious education whatsoever. We were Jews without a congregation, Jews back in the day but not now. It was like knowing my grandfather had come to this country in 1901 from Odessa: a historic detail of no particular relevance anymore, except that it sometimes still induced a lingering low-grade dread, a premonition that one day all of us secular Jews will learn again, the hard way, that a Jew by any other name is still a Jew, that we will be made to pay for our heritage whether we were bar mitzvahed or not. When the door opened on twelve, I suddenly remembered my lunch date. Or had I been thinking of her all along, trying to imagine how she would regard me? Just good-looking enough? The elevator was empty.

*   *   *

IN THE WATER, the phone doesn't ring. There is no e-mail. No pager. And I can't feel the clanging of my loneliness or my sorrow at feeling so little grief. Bouncing around at zero gravity must be like this: another medium entirely. When you're a kid, the water is the place where you can hold up your mother in your own hands as she lies on her back. The water bestows superhuman powers. In the middle of my third lap I felt a familiar clutch around my heart: anxiety. The ashes I had tossed into the ocean that morning. The father who had left us when I was twelve and Pru was fourteen, sold his foundering business in the Garment District — costume jewelry, fashion barrettes, makeup pouches — and went to L.A., accompanied by a woman who'd worked in his showroom. She left him when his business failed and set him on a path I learned to mimic, except that I was wise enough to avoid duplicating his multiple marriages. He had a series of short-term wives and a string of girlfriends in between. A series of short-term sales jobs and short-term women who did not mind supporting him until he no longer seemed like a good investment. He had died alone. There were separate messages on his machine from two women, Jackie and Eileen, who sounded as if they were his age. They hadn't heard from him and wondered how he was. We looked everywhere for their last names or phone numbers, but nothing turned up.

Pru and I had gone for years without seeing him, but he stayed in touch by phone and mail, and we did our part but without much enthusiasm. He and I never had an easy relationship, but I eventually learned, in years of therapy, to let go of my own anger. But maybe mine, like his, never entirely left me. Or I turned it against myself instead of toward the world, which is what women often do. For partners, I chose women who, at some level, I knew would not stick around or whom I would not want to stick around. I had made certain to avoid my parents' mistakes. And I was alone now too.

My mind was so clear in the water. The steady movement of my arms, my legs, the sun full on my back. I flipped over and let the warmth rain on me as I extended my arms in a modified backstroke. I kicked and stroked for five or six more laps and pulled myself up and sat on the edge of the pool. It was a small pool surrounded by wooden chaise longues lying flat on the ground, no legs, and each plumped up with a full-length pillow that covered the chaise. I idly looked for Colleen and found myself staring at a woman on a chaise across the pool. The only thing I recognized was her strawberry blond hair, almost metallic in the sunlight and mostly concealed by a hat. Her eyes were hidden behind a huge, dark pair of sunglasses, a Jackie Onassis–style masquerade, and her head covered with a droopy white hat with a broad brim that flopped over her ears. A shawl encircled her shoulders — and her arms encircled a baby at her bosom, its mouth in a position that corresponded to her left breast. It could not be the same woman. I dropped back into the water and began to swim toward her. It would be easy enough to settle this.

"Hi, Eric," she said, when I surfaced on the other side, at her feet. "I thought that might be you." This wasn't where my midday fantasies had been leading, to a nursing mother. So she was a Good Samaritan, wanting to look after me in my mourning, but otherwise engaged. Oh, well. A message from the God I did not believe in, that you're not meant to pick up women while you're sitting shiva. Okay, boss, I get it.

"Hi, Colleen." I pumped up my energy for this conversation. There weren't enough Good Samaritans in the world, never enough. It wouldn't kill me to have lunch with a married woman. People who talk to the walls can't be choosers.

"This is my daughter, Zoe."

"Hi, Zoe."

"The water looks delicious."

"It is. How old is Zoe?" She was not a newborn, that much I could tell.

"Eleven months, getting a little too big for this meal ticket. It's not the most convenient way to give her breakfast, lunch, and dinner, but I've become a whiz with the breast pump, especially at the office."

"What kind of work do you do?" What would I guess? Real estate, banking, something that involved money. She had a tailored, monied glow. Perfectly painted toenails and fingernails to match. The long shawl covered her shoulders and fell across the baby's torso and Colleen's own pale pink shorts. Nothing lavish, nothing flashy, but a look that said she knew how to put herself together.

"I'm a lawyer. I have a general practice in New York. Scarsdale, to be exact."

Just as well she was unavailable. It's not that I have a reflexive disdain for members of the legal profession. I am less judgmental than many on the subject; my clinical training has contributed to that muting of criticism, of prejudice. I try not to judge based on all the usual identifiers, because one thing therapists know is that we're all in pain, we all have the capacity to feel lost, afraid, abjectly vulnerable. Even a sociopath. Even a trial lawyer. What's the joke? It's ninety percent of the lawyers who give the other ten percent a bad name. No, my gripe is not that they're pernicious but that they're argumentative. The women, I mean. Not so my Brandys and Tiffanys. They might pout when they don't get their way, like little Lolita herself, but they don't thrive on controversy, they don't want to turn every utterance into a mock trial.

"I take it you're not," she said, but it was difficult to read the tone of her remark because so much of her face was concealed behind the sunglasses, and there was still this rather large infant pressed against her breast. This was not a situation I came across much on the Upper West Side of Manhattan, the publicly nursing mother who had led me to believe she was an ordinary Single White Female. "Sorry to disappoint you," she said.

"Not at all. Don't be silly. Forgive my distraction. The last few days have been — difficult. You're right, I'm not a lawyer, I'm a psychotherapist."

"Oh, one of *those*." She smiled and I took the smile to mean that she was gently making fun of my profession because of my response to hers, my thorny, complicated silence. "Is it true that you get into that line of work because you've got so many problems of your own? People say that all the time — that shrinks are crazy — but that can't be the primary motivation, can it?"

I got what I deserved, a combative answer, but nothing I couldn't handle. I was amused that she had found a way to get to me. "I haven't met anyone yet who doesn't have problems. It's just a matter of how we act them out and how much they get in our way. I don't think therapists have more problems than anyone else, but we're more in touch with that aspect of ourselves. What about your husband, is he a lawyer too?"

"I don't have a husband."

"Oh. I imagined that since you have —"

"Yes, a baby."

"And you live in Scarsdale."

"Not all shrinks are crazy and not all nursing mothers in Scarsdale are married."

"Touché. So, what brings you to L.A.?" I could have asked why no husband in the land of nuclear families, but we needed a softer surface to play on after our bumpy beginning, and I was just getting used to the idea that she was not the person she appeared to be.

"Vacation. I usually go to Italy, to Venice, but this year, with the baby, I wanted something easier on me. And there are a few artists out here whose work I like. I have an appointment later today at Bergamot Station, the power station they converted to galleries. Have you been there yet?"

"No, I've been consumed by my father's affairs. Does this mean you're an art collector?"

"Small *a,* small *c.* I buy things I like by people you've never heard of, which means I can afford them. When I want to invest, I buy securities or real estate. The art I buy is for art's sake." This was certainly a change from my youthful girlfriends, whose collections were confined to Kate Spade handbags and designer condoms. I was about to ask where Zoe's father was when Colleen raised her arm and called out, "Graciela, I'm over here."

A small, pretty Asian woman appeared across the pool, heading our way, smiling, her teeth especially bright against her bronze skin. It was hard to tell whether she was thirty-five or forty-five but easy to discern the nature of their relationship. Colleen disengaged the baby from her breast and quickly draped her over her shoulder, patting her back and urging her to burp. Graciela picked up the cloth bag of baby accessories at Colleen's feet and asked how the little one was.

"She's absolutely perfect," Colleen said. "This is Eric, my lunch appointment. We bumped into each other down here. Eric, this is Graciela, my dear friend and life preserver." There was some fussing with the baby, whose face I could finally make out, but what can a bachelor say — or see? Most babies are cute and most of their mothers love them. I'd be lying to myself if I said I could recall precisely how Zoe looked that day. She looked like an infant but not a newborn. Pudgy cheeks, drooly smile, soft, unblemished skin. What struck me was seeing a tiny hat of her mother's strawberry blond hair on her little head. There was a changing of the guard, and moments later Graciela and the baby were gone. It was exactly the hour our date was to have begun. Against the odds — including her status as a nursing mother — it felt like a date, especially as we walked across the patio and took seats at the outdoor café. It wasn't until we sat down that Colleen took off the sun hat and the dark glasses, revealing the luminous green eyes it had been too dark to see in the elevator. She was suddenly present and quite lovely. "I suppose you're wondering where Zoe's father is."

"It crossed my mind, but it's none of my business."

She leaned forward and focused her eyes on mine; she seemed about to tell me a secret. "He left me while I was pregnant," she said softly, so softly I was not sure I had heard her. "We'd been married for ten years." She coughed, sat back in her seat, and picked up the menu, as though she was flustered and wanted to change the subject.

"I'm so sorry. That must have been a shock."

She nodded without raising her eyes, as though the news were still reverberating in her. As though she were still trying to believe it. I could not take my eyes from her face, but I was startled when she looked up suddenly. "A student," she said in that same soft voice. "He left me for one of his students."

"Good Lord. What kind of . . . did he know you were pregnant when he —"

"Of course. Have you eaten here? I think I've tried everything but the squid. The Thai chicken salad with basil is very good. Please don't look at me that way. I've had a long time to get used to this, as painful as it was. My mother always said that you can't fix the past, so don't spend your time trying."

"That's one way to think about the past. But I'd be out of business if it got too popular. Where does your husband teach? I hope not in a high school."

I was pleased that she smiled at my question; when she did, her eyes sparkled in a way that convinced me she could be lighthearted. She signaled for the waiter and within seconds a small man appeared with a handheld computer, ready to punch in our order.

"He's a law professor," Colleen said. "She was a law student."

"Did you know her?" She shook her head. "Is there a law school in Westchester?"

"This was in Boston. Zoe and I moved to Scarsdale recently. I couldn't bear Boston any longer, after the humiliation and the —"

"Were you already a member of the New York bar?"

She nodded. "I went to school in Boston but moved to Albany when I got my degree. That didn't work out, so I headed back to my hometown."

"How did you pick Scarsdale? I'd think it's an impossible place to set up a business, unless you've got roots there. A community that's so stable and inbred." I was thinking about how difficult it would be to uproot myself after twenty-five years in the same place. Leaving clients, contacts, friends, my sister.

"I had a friend from Boston with a practice who invited me to join her. She'd just lost her partner to breast cancer, the woman who'd invited her into the Scarsdale practice in the first place. It's an unlikely place for two girls from South Boston to end up, but we've managed to keep the wolves from the door so far."

"Does he see Zoe much?"

"Bob? We agreed he would see her one weekend a month, since he's there and I'm — we're so far apart. We'll look at it again when she gets older. But truth be told, he isn't living up to that."

"Can't you take him to court?"

"My feeling is: Why should I compel a man who doesn't want to see his child? That's not the kind of father she needs."

"You have a point."

"My lawyer has been talking to his lawyer about this, to see whether there's any middle ground, but so far . . ."

"I didn't know that lawyers had lawyers."

"We try to avoid it, but when a man is as temperamental as he is . . . I say two words and he blows up. He's impossible. I can't believe we're talking about him. Tell me, do you do any forensics? I sometimes consult psychiatrists about my cases. Use them as expert witnesses. What a fascinating field."

"You do criminal law?"

"Family. Estates. Wills. The occasional adoption. A little divorce. I've just finished a book to help women through the process.

I like the variety, like helping people with the difficult passages in their lives. It can be quite a privilege."

"A privilege?"

"To be in people's confidence. To help them resolve conflicts, settle an estate, figure out how to leave their affairs in order."

"Of course."

"Don't tell me you think we're all ambulance chasers? Or are you still smarting from my remark about therapists and their problems?" All of this was said playfully, through a sly smile, and I had to say that I was enjoying our sparring.

"All I meant is that I'd never considered the law one of the helping professions."

"I think of it as a problem-solving profession."

"That's refreshing, that you have that attitude. You hear of a lot of lawyers who want to settle everything with a lawsuit."

"That's the easy way out," she said. "A skillful negotiator is a valuable commodity."

"That's refreshing to hear too."

When the food came, I added the delicate textures and flavors to the unexpected pleasures of the afternoon. When she asked me what had made me decide to become a therapist, I told her about my famous sister, which led to a discussion of my angry, deadbeat dad of a father, and eventually I wended my way around to the breakup with Gaby Goldberg three weeks before. Colleen had confided in me about her husband leaving her; no reason for me not to share a confidence too, though I left out Gaby's opinion of me. "Now you know everything about me," I said. Except that the last woman I shared my bed with called me a selfish prick. Nobody's perfect.

"One thing I don't know is when you're flying back to New York."

"I have an open return. I was supposed to leave with my sister a few days ago. Earlier today I was going to call the airline and —"

"It sounds like you don't have plans for dinner tonight." She mentioned a restaurant in Santa Monica I had never heard of and asked if I would join her. Two hours before, when I'd noticed her nursing on the deck of the pool, my accepting would have been unthinkable, but by then, over coffee and flan and confessions of middle-aged failings and furies, there was no other answer but yes.

CLICKING SOUNDS. Creaks. Footsteps. The Mondrian was white on white. This place is gray on black. Through the bars I can see the solid steel door I came through as it swings open, being pushed now by a policeman who is carrying a key ring as big as a fist and something that looks like a thin gray book, gray to match the color scheme. He stands at my barred door and slips it into the food slot.

"Someone brought this for you. She wasn't your lawyer so we couldn't let her in. There's a note." It's taped to the object, type-written, the note exposed so that anyone can read it. But it isn't a book, I know that the instant I touch it.

> Dear Mr. Lavender:
>
> I am Lily Lopez's secretary (Rita). She asked me to bring this to help you collect your thoughts. The arraignment is tomorrow morning because Lily had an emergency with her son, who fell off the jungle gym at daycare and is in the ER, but will be okay she said when she called (4 stitches), and her partner, Bernard, is in court today.
>
> The "on" button is on the right. It's the circle inside the circle. When the screen lights up, click on the typewriter icon and you will be in a word processing file.
>
> Lily will be here tomorrow morning at 8:30.
>
> Sincerely,
> Rita P.

I press the on button and the screen lightens until it is orange and then it fills with icons. I do as Rita instructed. I am in a word processing file within seconds, but my thoughts surge and swirl; they are not still long enough for me to collect them. What did Colleen tell Zoe and Sarah Rose about where I am and when I would return? They don't need me to collect my thoughts, they need me to pick them up and hold them and tell them there's nothing to be afraid of.

The screen is white like a piece of paper, and my fingers begin to move fast over the tiny keyboard, but my thoughts collect in a form that will be of no use to Lily in my defense or me in my effort to stay sane in the midst of this madness. Of no use to anyone, but I cannot stop.

Dear Sarah Rose —

I don't know if you will ever see this, and I doubt you should. But when you start to wonder, when you get to the age when you ask your mother whether it was love at first sight when she and I met, the day before the calendars changed from 1999 to 2000, I am sorry to have to tell you that it was not. It was curiosity at first sight, intrigue, and a dose of reluctance. But love was not far behind, and that love led to you. There was never a second of hesitation about my love for you, from the moment you were born to now, and that will never change. Please believe me, littlest one, darling angel.

With oceans of love from,
Your Dad

Dear Zoe, dearest child who is not entirely mine but whom I love as though you are —

Your biological father has forsaken you and left me to do his job. What kind of man is this? My own father at least had the decency to stick around until I was twelve. It's not that I mind, dear one, being your dad, but I'm not sure I'll have the job indefinitely. In fact, I think I was just fired.

❧ 3 ❧

Seismology

In the middle of our wild mushroom raviolis that first night, the earth moved, as it does every so often in California, and something shifted between us.

Before that moment, which lasted fifteen seconds, we were eating our appetizers by an open French door on a Santa Monica street as pristine and unreal as a movie set. The air was warm, dry, and smelled of grilled garlic. Colleen had told me about the art galleries she had visited that afternoon and was now telling me about the book she had just finished writing with a journalist she knew in Boston. On one channel of my brain I was trying not to look at her breasts and wondering whether she would let me put my lips to them when we returned to the hotel. I hoped she wasn't still mourning the loss of her husband, wasn't carrying a torch for him. She hadn't said a word about him all through dinner. On another channel, I noted her work habits, her organizational skills, her industry: divorce, new baby, new town, new law practice, she collects art, and she finds time to write a book? File this away in case our fling has legs: she will not have time to cling to me. She gets a gold star for that.

"My book is more of a handbook, really, for women dealing with divorce," she was saying, "to guide them through the challenges, like the husband who hides money in offshore accounts or transfers deeds to business properties when those should be —"

At that moment, the table began to shudder, the plates on it, the silverware, wineglasses, and forks, fell all over the room, pinging and shattering as they hit the tile floor. Three or four people ran for the open doors and banged into others who were trembling in place. Colleen and I gaped at each other, hands flung out to keep our dishes from sliding. We shook in our seats, or was it the seats that were shaking? Paintings quivered and fell from nails on the walls. None of us screamed — because we were holding our breath. It was over in a matter of seconds. Fifteen, maybe twenty? You could hear loud sighs, choruses of "Jesus" and "Omigod" and "Are you all right?" Everyone, not just the waiters, began to pick things up from the floor, a gesture of common cause, solidarity. Salt-shakers, bread baskets, slippery plates that had held olive oil for dipping, piles of broken wineglasses. All at once, cell phones began to ring, a cacophony of electronic bleats and tones that must have been playing all over town.

"Zoe," Colleen said and began rummaging through her bag. "I can't find my cell. There must be a pay phone somewhere. What if the hotel —"

"Where you staying?" said the woman at the next table. In an instant, we were a community in crisis, reaching out to our neighbors, California-style.

"The Mondrian."

"That's solid. Don't worry. This was nothing. Ninety-four was a cyclone. That was Tarzan lifting up your bed and hurling it across the room with you in it."

Colleen turned to me, eyes wide with apprehension. I countered it with calm, though I was shaken myself, not with fear but memories. Frantic calls for days to reach my father after the quake in 1994. His apartment was a mile from the epicenter. My mother asked me how he had fared, when her mind was still intact. Even my sister, who went for years without speaking to him, panicked at the thought that the earth had swallowed him up whole. It hadn't, but his building cracked in two and he had to move.

"We'll be fine," I said to Colleen.

AS WE WALKED to my car across Ocean Avenue, with its Rockette-like lineup of towering coconut palms, I took her hand. On another night, after another dinner, it would have been a romantic gesture, a touch of foreplay, an invitation. But that night it was purely tender. We were survivors. I squeezed her hand and she squeezed mine back. At the car, I folded her into a hug, and she drew her arms around my back. She was a sturdy package with a strong back and breasts that ballooned against my chest. I was certain this would be a sweet night.

THE QUAKE, which turned out to be a 3.7 — no serious injuries; minor damage to stoplight timers and chandeliers — had flung us together, cracked our prim social inhibitions and our carapaces of immortality. The earth rumbles and we're swapping stories with the woman at the next table. Our forks skitter to the floor and suddenly the notion of our being lovers — even for the night — is not such a hard sell. The quake shook things up and tilted us closer together. It gave us an urgent, well-defined, but still traditional role to act out: she, the mother, was afraid for her child, and I, the hunter, the warrior, could protect and comfort her. The wound of her husband leaving her was distant, but our mutual quake was fresh, an injury we sustained together. And my having seized the lead in taking care of her made it easier for her to console me, later that night, in my peculiar, my peculiarly detached, mourning.

She came to my room after she checked on her family, but there was more talking than there might have been on an ordinary night. She seemed more tentative than she had during dinner, before the quake, which, I'm sorry to say, only made me want her more. "Isn't the view amazing?" she said, moving toward the vast wall of windows. "We see the same thing from our room."

"It's better in the dark." I flipped off the overhead and joined her at the edge of curtains, drew an arm around her shoulder, and felt her move into my embrace. When she did, I held her for a moment and then reached with one hand for her bottom, her clothed bottom. I wanted just to touch it, to feel it in my palm, but she turned schoolmarmish on me and abruptly moved my hand to her waist.

"Let's just look at the view." She maneuvered us to the window, the glittering valley of lights. It is something to behold, the vast Los Angeles basin, black backdrop with a yellow glow, some of the strokes of light so thick they seem painted by de Kooning with an electric crayon and others as faint as gold dust. It was mesmerizing, an entirely different sight from the upright Manhattan skyline, which is sharply etched, obdurately vertical. The valley oozes yellow light as far as the eye can see.

"It's something, isn't it?" she said. "Five million people."

We stood facing the window chastely, her arm around my waist and mine now around her shoulder.

"And at least that many cars," I said. This was becoming a parody of a seduction. I was not used to women who were so uptight. Especially those who had issued lunch and dinner invitations.

"It's such a long way from the East Coast," she said. "Do you ever think about living out here?"

"Fleetingly. The way I think about owning a sports car. It would be fun, until I got tired of it. What about you?"

"It's daunting to think about starting over again."

"Your husband —" When I said that I could feel her flinch and turn to me. "He didn't want to reconcile? A lot of men have flings, but when push comes to shove they're not willing to abandon their families. Especially when there are young children."

For a long moment she was silent. "I learned late in the game that I hadn't married one of those men." She said this matter-offactly, not harshly, not bitterly, and I was struck by the lack of bitterness. "But even if he were more agreeable, he's in Boston and we're in Westchester now."

"Did you say you'd grown up in Boston?"

"I think I did." Her arm tightened around my waist and I could feel her turn into me, giving up her reserve. She tipped her face to me, inviting a kiss. "South Boston."

"You don't have an accent." I complied, kissing her lightly.

"Good. That was my plan. My husband gave me elocution lessons. I was a very determined student."

"Talk for me the way you used to."

"You don't want to hear that." She drew her arms tighter around my torso and pressed her hands all the way down my back to my buttocks, doing to me what I had tried earlier to do to her: another invitation, a serious one, and a sure way to halt my questions. I was compliant. My cock complied. The rest of me was not far behind. I walked her backward, in little steps, to the foot of the bed.

"I suppose I should take off my stockings." She reached down to the hem of her skirt and hiked it up, plucking at something.

"Don't tell me you're wearing real stockings."

"But I am."

"A garter belt too?"

"How else would I hold them up?"

For a moment, I couldn't speak. This accessory was as surprising as the earthquake, as startling as seeing her breast-feed her child by the pool. Why had she been so nervous before if she had this up her sleeve — or down her leg?

"I hear men like this sort of thing," she murmured.

"I can't imagine who told you."

"Word gets around."

Bing. Bing. Bing.

When we were half-undressed, when our shirts were off and her breasts were bare, and one of them was cradled in my hand, I did what I always do, what I like to do, as much as I like any part of this . . . endeavor? There must be a better word on the formal side, short of *intercourse*. The sex act. The sexual endeavor. Neither sounds like fun. Making love? Why does that sound archaic to me? I picture Maurice Chevalier in a crooning black-and-white seduction, the Eiffel Tower just over his left shoulder; or myself as an eleven-year-old boy, finding in my parents' one bookcase *A Modern Marriage Manual* and this sentence I have never forgotten: "While it may take a new wife some time to adjust to the demands of making love, she may eventually come to feel great pleasure in the act." The language problem comes up when I talk to my patients, and it can be tricky. Often I use the expressions they use, though I try to steer them away from the most vulgar, unless there is context for it that needs reaffirmation. When he first walked into my office the third week of August, poor Sandy Lefkowitz barely had any language left for talking about sex.

What I did that night: I lowered my head and put my mouth around Colleen's engorged nipple.

Had I never done this?

Of course I hadn't. None of my nubile Brandys or fourteen-karat Tiffanys could offer such a nipple, such a feast. It was a taste I'd never be able to remember having tasted. It was bittersweet. It was slightly sour. Thicker than what comes in a carton. It was delicious.

She cradled me and suckled me and held me in the most exquisite embrace of my life. It would have been enough had she said nothing, but soon she was whispering as she fed me: "Poor lamb, I can see how sad you are even though you're trying not to be, because your daddy died." With her nipple between my lips and her child's milk filling my mouth, I did something that astonished me: I choked when she said the word "daddy." I had called him nothing except his first name or "fuck face" or "asshole" since I was fourteen; I was Jason Cummings — though I had not yet met him that distant night. I was Jason except I had never had the satisfaction of expressing my feelings at gunpoint. Now I coughed and had to pull away from her tit, and, as I sat up to keep milk from pouring into my nasal passages, she kept whispering to me, "Poor lamb, poor Pooh, poor dear," and she didn't let go of me, she was so utterly tender just then.

All of this happening at once, in a matter of fifteen or twenty seconds — it was like the earthquake that way — made me shed some of my armor. Shed some of my tears. She couldn't have been sweeter. She coaxed me back down to the pillow with her, and this time she held out her breast to my mouth and whispered, "Here, this is for you."

This was chemistry, this was physiology. This was Mother Nature, Father Time, and Reason #7 that I fell in love with her.

I BANG THE BARS with my fist. I wave into the video camera. I want their attention. But this is not room service at the Mondrian.

"What do you want in here?" Creak, clang, bang. Officer Manignelli. A clean-shaven kid of twenty-eight or thirty with a nasty-looking scar beside his eyebrow.

"I have to make another phone call. Need to reach one of my patients. He was in bad shape to begin with, and when I didn't show for our appointment this afternoon . . . he's unstable and I'm afraid —" He interrupts my babbling, but I'd have kept going until he said yes.

"What's the number?" He brusquely lifts the receiver and stands poised to punch for me. For some damn reason, the number comes to me even though I have not called it often.

He hands me the receiver just as Sandy's voicemail picks up. "Sandy, Eric Lavender. I know you're wondering what the hell happened today. I had to leave suddenly, I didn't have time to call any of my patients. I'm not sure when I can reschedule." This is a complete lie. He is no longer my patient, but I need to get his attention, to warn him. "Look . . ." I lower my voice and turn a quarter turn to the dark gray wall. "Protect yourself. They came for me, and they might get you next. Call your lawyer. Don't believe what you're going to hear on TV. I can't say any more right now, but I'm —" I hear a click on the line and look up. The cop had pressed the hook of the wall phone and cut me off.

"Christ. I was in the middle of a sentence." He sticks his hand between the bars, waiting for me to give back the phone on its tightly coiled cord. "What was the point of that? To fuck with me?" My voice echoes inside my head and I know I sound like a nut. God only knows what Sandy will make of my call.

The cop doesn't meet my eyes, doesn't answer my questions, just drops the receiver into the cradle and takes out his key ring, so he can let himself out of the cell block. The motion of his turning and inserting the key in the outgoing steel door takes my breath away, as if I'd been slammed in the gut. I don't double over, but I'm winded and scared, really scared, for the first time. Or maybe it's only that the shock has worn off. And I can see the bars of the cell clearly.

This is abandonment. This is what devastates children before they have the language to know what it is. Daddy is leaving. Mommy is withdrawing. Mommy is distracted. Mommy is depressed. Mommy is dead. Your brother has leukemia. Your brother has a learning disability, which means that he sees the letters backward, and that's why Mommy can't take you ice skating, because she's too busy turning around the letters for Johnny, it's a full-time job. The baby was born without a brain and that's why Mommy and Daddy are so sad, it has nothing to do with you. Daddy's mommy and daddy and Umpah and Nana and everyone else in their family were killed by the Nazis, and that's why there are so many things he won't talk about. It seems as if he's angry when you ask him those questions, but it's just that he misses them.

People pay me to help them remember, to untangle the causes from the effects, the present from the past, their parents from themselves. I try, I do my best. Quite often, almost always, core pain comes down to abandonment, whether it was sudden or protracted or ambiguous or intermittent or communicated with the back of the hand. To the child, it always feels as though the child caused it. But I'm not a child and there is nothing ambiguous about my predicament.

I don't know what time it is. I'm guessing six in the evening. The only windows are on the wall opposite the cells. They rise a few feet above the height of the cell ceiling. They're covered with black wire mesh, but I can still see that it's dusk. I'm sitting on the only place I have to sit, this highly varnished bench against a cinderblock wall. I'm looking at a sink and a bone-dry toilet made for a midget. Taped to the wall that faces me is a paper sign in a plastic jacket:

IF YOU ARE SICK OR INJURED NOTIFY ANY OFFICER.
HE WILL MAKE THE ARRANGEMENTS TO
HAVE YOU TREATED BY SCARSDALE VOLUNTEER
AMBULANCE CORPS OR TRANSPORTED
TO WHITE PLAINS HOSPITAL EMERGENCY ROOM.

They mean transported in handcuffs.

It's the twenty-fifth of September. My stepdaughter, Zoe, started pre-K three weeks ago. Did I mention that she calls me Daddy? She has no idea that I'm not her real daddy, because she has had nothing to do with him. When it first began, Colleen asked if I thought it was healthy, wearing my psychologist's hat, for Zoe to call me Daddy. "If her real father ever showed his face around here," I said, "he could claim the title, but until he does, I don't think there's much harm in it." Why shouldn't the available men fill in for the absent fathers now and then? We had even been talking about the possibility of my adopting Zoe, once Colleen accepted her ex's total lack of interest in his child. But that was before all of this happened. I mean, before Sandy Lefkowitz walked into my office on the third Monday of August.

I mean, of all the shrinks' offices in all of Westchester County, and he had to walk into mine.

4

And So It Began

BEFORE COLLEEN, I lived and worked in an underdecorated, third-floor, prewar two-bedroom on 87th Street and West End Avenue, where my walls were lined with bookcases, my various diplomas, and an oversize print of *The Unicorn in Captivity* tapestry from the Cloisters, with all of its obvious imagery. I had a good practice based on the fundamentals of talk therapy and augmented by an assortment of techniques that have become popular in the last fifteen or twenty years: some play therapy ideas adapted for adults; some relaxation techniques that I am pleased to see are endorsed by Harvard Medical School's Mind/Body Institute and that I use with patients suffering physical pain, trauma, or anxiety.

My second bedroom was my office; the view from that wide set of casement windows was of the high-rise across the way and of the street below, doormen, dog walkers, taxis, and the rest. No great vistas, no light shows, no bleeding chemical sunsets over New Jersey. Don't ask how many of my girlfriends wanted to try their hands at redecorating and arrived, after five or six dates, with catalogues from Pottery Barn, Restoration Hardware, and God-only-knows-where.

All that has changed. I now see patients in the custom-built cottage behind Colleen's art- and antique-filled eight-room Colonial in Scarsdale, a short walk to the train station and equipped with marble-topped gourmet kitchen, Filipino nanny, part-time Polish housekeeper, wine cellar, five-zone heating and AC, built-in Jacuzzi in the master bath, and fourteen closets that light up the instant you open the door. In the two-room office-cottage that Colleen had built for me in record time, I see my patients by the glow of a skylight as they pour forth their troubles from my new leather armchair or the padded table in the second room. At her insistence, the floors are covered with Turkish kilims and the walls with etchings and several ornate Venetian papier-mâché masks like those in our living room and in the girls' bedrooms.

How did this happen?

Colleen is the answer. Colleen, with her milky breasts and her daughter who calls me Daddy. Colleen, with her sorrowful history and her blazing feminist ideals to help women and children suffering at the hands of so many deadbeat dads, a cause near to the throbbing heart of my inner child. Once she got through suckling me that almost New Year's Eve night, I learned that her appetite in this area, too, is prodigious. Soon I would discover that her tastes ran from the mock maternal to those of the college-educated enthusiast. We always had a very good time in bed. That first night, she told me she had been starved for a man's touch, that her husband's infidelity had made her physically numb for many months. "I could barely take care of Zoe, but Zoe was all that kept me going. The worst is over now. Coming to L.A. was part of my recovery. Pampering myself, staying at this hotel. Inviting you out to dinner. It was difficult for me to do."

"You'd already invited me to lunch. You'd already stuck your arm inside a closing elevator door. Was that difficult too?" My tone was lightly mocking. I was enchanted by her nerve, intoxicated by her tenderness.

"I'm never that impetuous. I don't know what came over me."

"I'm glad it came over you, whatever it was."

Here's what I thought that night: She's vulnerable but not pathetic, not needy. She's not — in that dead-on term that did not exist when I was a young man — high-maintenance. Not a whiner. She wasn't aspiring like my unseasoned Brandys; her real life was under way, with all of its scratches and dents. Like the rest of us at forty or forty-five, she was something of a used book: intact but a bit battered around the edges. I suppose I was myself, even though I didn't have a difficult ex or a child to show for it.

"I don't want to leave you, but I should go back and check on my daughter. It's best if I sleep there." She got up and began to dress in the semidarkness.

"You haven't said a word about your childhood."

She looked up abruptly. "Wearing your shrink hat, are you?"

"I'm piecing together what I know about you as you start to leave. Sorry. It's an occupational hazard."

"See if you can fly back to New York with us tomorrow, and I'll regale you with stories of stealing ankle bracelets and Pez dispensers from Woolworth's with Clare Flanagan. Didn't you say you had an open return?"

AND SO IT BEGAN, the sensual seesaw that became our life together. It was not difficult for me to begin spending weekends in Scarsdale or inviting Colleen and Zoe to my place in Manhattan for Saturdays and Sunday afternoons. They usually traveled with Graciela, who baby-sat when we wanted time alone for galleries, museums, dinners out. On a long weekend when Graciela was on her annual trip to Manila to see her children, Colleen squirreled herself away in my office with the proofs of her divorce book that was about to be published, and I looked after Zoe on my own, for as long as I could manage. Looking back, I divide that time into two segments, each lasting for two months.

The first two months were, as they can often be, blissful, fueled by novelty, surging hormones, the universal chemistry of falling in love. What surprised me was not that I could fall for Colleen, although I continued to be startled and relieved by how mature she was compared to my other girlfriends. It was my affection for Zoe that caught me up short — and hers for me. I had held a baby here and there, and a toddler on occasion, but this baby clung to me when I picked her up. This baby stared at me as I held her on my lap and threw herself against my chest and cried when I left the room. Was it that simple? I loved her because she loved me? I loved her more when I saw her mother looking tenderly at the two of us pushing a rubber ball back and forth across the floor. I would say to Colleen, "Why didn't anyone ever tell me how much fun this was?" "Because you were waiting for us to come along." I don't remember when I first told Colleen I loved her, but it took awhile. I started with the euphemisms: *I'm crazy about you. Mad about you. I adore you.* One day *love* slipped out between *I* and *you,* and I remember thinking when I heard myself say it: This isn't so difficult. I might get used to it. The only times I can remember quarreling in these first two months were when Zoe's waking in the middle of the night interrupted our sleep and made us cranky the next day. There were not many such days, but we were both quick to apologize for a harsh word or a snap judgment.

I got a different sort of glance from the doormen who'd witnessed my youthful dalliances. My neighbors on the third floor, when I met them at the elevator, looked pleased by my family-style entourage. When I took Colleen and Zoe to meet Pru and Bea, her partner of five years, we had a lively brunch in their apartment ten blocks from mine on West End Avenue. I was so besotted with Colleen and Zoe that my usual anxiety about seeing my sister and her lover — Insecure Kid Brother Visits Brilliant Sister combined with Straight Guy Not Sure What to Make of Lesbian Love — fell by the wayside.

Pru and Bea were, as they always are, lovely hostesses, welcoming, gracious, and informal. They seem made for each other, but their differing styles belie the match. Pru is a wiry, petite, fifty-two-year-old fireball with close-cropped blond hair who wears red high-top sneakers, black jeans, and an assortment of T-shirts that all contribute to the impression that she is much younger than she is. Bea is larger, older, grayer, clothed in baggy cotton clothes festooned with startling scarves, big jewelry, velvet vests — and she had a husband and children in a past life. Pru, I would say, tends toward the intense and Bea toward the witty and wry. Pru toward a youthful look and Bea toward elegance in an old-style Upper West Side way: no hair color, no lipstick, a lot of tenacity, warmth, and confidence. She is in her midfifties and works as the graphics editor for a tony lifestyle magazine. She and Pru grow herbs in planters on their patio, strip and repaint old furniture they find on the sidewalk, and favor upscale eco-vacations to rain forests, fjords, and remote coral reefs.

That morning with Colleen and Zoe, I was not wondering, as I often do, about the two of them — the mechanics, the politics, what Bea's children think — nor about My Sister the Distinguished Surgeon. Where does she get the courage to cut into those tiny babies, and where did she get the idea she could do it in the first place? I sometimes look, foolishly, at her fingers for clues, yet I know the explanation resides elsewhere, perhaps in the sinew of her nerves. That morning I was preoccupied with showing off my new family.

Over our second cups of coffee, Colleen and I told the story of how we'd met, trading segments in musical fashion, and later Colleen explained that she hoped we would travel to Venice together before too long. That inspired Bea to tell stories of having traveled with her own children when they were small, back when Bea was living a very different life as a married woman. Her children were now women in their twenties, one of whom had recently married. Pru and Bea each hugged me on our way out, whispering a version of "Good going, they're great." Zoe, I felt, was evidence of my true reform. I was like an addict who had not only renounced drugs and booze but cigarettes too: a sturdy professional woman almost my age *and* a child!

During the second two months — did I make this distinction at the time, or is it only now, looking back? — Colleen seemed to have a shorter fuse, even on days following nights when Zoe had slept straight through. She was in a foul mood one Friday night and finally told me that she felt a migraine coming on, and that she got them once or twice a year. She had some pills that usually helped but didn't that night. After that first migraine, she seemed to let her guard down and was more openly cranky on a regular basis. She didn't raise her voice much; the anger was more in the intonation, the aggravation, the putdown. "Graciela, how many times do I have to tell you to pack the baby's clothes like this?" "For God's sake, Eric, don't hold her that way. What are you trying to do to her?" "No, I *don't* want to see a movie about a guy with amnesia." "Didn't you think about what would happen if you gave her all those M&M's? You might as well pour sugar down her throat."

I blew off the first few remarks, not wanting to rock the boat, but the crack about the candy went too far. "I gave her three M&M's, Colleen."

"And now look at her. She's manic."

"She's happy."

"So now you're the big expert on children?"

"I don't appreciate being scolded." When she didn't answer, I waited ten seconds to be sure: "Did you hear me?" She darted across my living room to keep Zoe from crawling down the corridor to the bedrooms. Of course she'd heard me. I had raised my voice to her for the first time. A moment later, with Zoe wiggling in her arms, Colleen shuffled back to me, her eyes slightly downcast.

"I didn't mean to snap at you, I'm sorry."

"Did your parents fight a lot?"

"I wouldn't call this fighting."

43

"I wouldn't either. I'm just curious."

"You're always asking about my parents and my childhood."

"Always? I've asked three or four times, and you've barely said a word except that you grew up in South Boston and your parents are both gone. My sister asked me about your family, and I didn't know what to say."

Zoe suddenly yanked on Colleen's hair so hard she squealed and our attention shifted. But ten minutes later, after she put Zoe down for a nap, Colleen announced, in a voice that sounded peeved, that she would give me a short history of her family. "I grew up in the projects in Southie — South Boston — with six brothers and sisters. Two brothers died from drug overdoses when they were teenagers. I became the oldest and had to take care of everyone, including my mother when she got sick. My siblings, most of them, got pregnant or started getting girls pregnant when they were sixteen or seventeen. Sometimes they got married, sometimes they didn't. I have dozens of nieces and nephews and grand-nieces and -nephews. Now they start having kids when they're fifteen. At Christmas dinner you feel like you're in a home for unwed mothers."

"Do you see them often?"

"Before my father died three years ago they always invited me to Christmas and Easter and their kids' Communions, which were every other week. But since he died . . ."

"Should we go visit them? Have they met Zoe?"

"God no. They resent me for getting out, for having money, having good taste. My father always bullied them into inviting me. They wouldn't have bothered otherwise."

"Didn't you take care of them when they were younger?"

"Yes, indeed. But that's the kind of people they are."

"I'm not sure I understand."

"Selfish. Ungrateful. I was close to one of my sisters, but we had a falling-out a few years ago."

"I'm sorry, sweetheart." It was curious that she talked about them as though they were a monolith, a single entity that spoke with one voice. "It must be painful. And your poor brothers who died."

"I've had a long time to get used to all of it."

"Now I see why it's so hard for you to talk about."

"Don't feel sorry for me."

"I don't, I just —"

"My mother had two mottoes. 'Keep your Irish up' and 'Don't wallow in the past.'"

If she had let me explain, I'd have said that I *felt* for her. In that first conversation I would not have alienated her by suggesting she talk to a therapist, as much as I thought it would help her to work through some of this pain, instead of burying it. Keeping your Irish up is hard work. Ignoring a lifetime of anguish takes its toll. When she grew more comfortable with me, I would encourage her.

IT MUST HAVE been a week later when we accepted a second invitation from Pru and Bea for dinner at their place. I was still eager for them to approve of Colleen, so I didn't notice at first that Bea was subdued. She usually asks questions that show she remembers the previous conversation, but that night she let Pru do all the asking and most of the talking. During a lull in the conversation as we ate the main course, Bea looked from me to Colleen and said, "I'm sorry I'm a little out of it tonight. My daughter Jenny, who got married a year ago, called me just before you arrived. She suspects her husband is involved with another woman."

"What makes her think so?" I asked.

"An extra late night or two. A distance she hadn't felt before."

"Has she spoken to a lawyer?" Colleen asked.

"Heavens, no. She hasn't even confronted him. She's just begun to feel suspicious. She was embarrassed to even tell me about it."

"She'll need to talk to a lawyer. Is she in New York State?" Bea nodded. "It's still a state without no-fault divorce, so she'll need grounds, if it comes to that. Adultery is the easiest to prove. You don't need testimony from therapists, you don't need police reports. If you don't have incriminating letters or e-mail, you can hire a private investigator and get a photograph without —"

"Colleen, I very much doubt she's thinking about divorce at this point," Bea said. "She and her husband are seeing a couples' counselor, and Jenny is going to bring this up at their next meeting."

"I've learned that it helps to be prepared for whatever comes up," Colleen said kindly, looking at Bea. "It can't hurt to talk to a lawyer."

I could see that Bea wanted to disagree but that she restrained herself. I had never known her to be quick to start a fight or even to confide as much as she had about Jenny.

"What if her husband goes into their therapist's meeting and says he wants a divorce?" Colleen said.

"I would be very surprised indeed," Bea said. "I'm not convinced that he's doing what Jenny thinks he is. He's an art student and a puppy dog of a young man. They may be having their problems, but I —"

Colleen's arm shot out across the dining room table, two business cards protruding from between clenched fingers. Bea stopped in the middle of her sentence and was polite enough to take a card from her. Colleen offered the other card to Pru.

"If Jenny wants to talk to me," Colleen said, "I'd be happy to talk to her. On the house. Any time. As a public service, I like women to know what they're up against."

"I didn't realize this was your field," Pru said. "Eric said you had a general practice."

Bea was examining Colleen's business card and I could see her jaw had tightened. So had mine; it was as though Colleen had told an off-color joke, showing herself to be too crassly litigious for my sister and Bea.

"General," Colleen said, "but with an emphasis on family matters."

I had to smooth over this crater in the conversation, but what came out was more evidence of Colleen's interest in this subject. "She just finished a book about women and divorce," I offered. Until this outburst, I'd been proud of Colleen's industriousness, given the hardship she had just endured: abandonment by her husband. Of course she was sensitive to this situation. I had mentioned it to Pru on the phone soon after Colleen and I met but was not about to remind her or Bea of it now. Bea's reaction to Colleen's shotgun analysis had spread over the table like a jug of spilled milk.

"What about women and divorce?" Pru asked her.

"It's just a little handbook, nothing spectacular. General information if you're contemplating a split. It's the old story; women and kids still get the short end of the stick. I know what happened to you and your brother — and your poor mother. Things have changed since then, but not nearly enough." Colleen turned her head to address Bea. "Women have to stick together at times like this. Jenny can call me whenever she wants to."

I could see Bea struggle with how to respond, or maybe I can see the struggle on her face more clearly in retrospect. She said "thank you," but there was a moment's hesitation before it came out of her mouth: "thank you" without the warm smile that can accompany those words, "thank you" for a gift of dubious value.

"The sauce on this veal is divine," Bea said to Pru.

"I used Tellicherry peppercorns and basil."

And so the conversation took a turn — something of a hairpin turn, not a smooth, seamless shift in direction — to the subject of spices, cuts of veal, the virtues of shellfish, the best places in Little Italy for clam sauce. It was painful to listen to us, straining to converse about the particulars of food. Afterward, as we walked back to my apartment, I tried to talk to Colleen about everyone's reaction to her talk of divorce, but she insisted she was only trying to help.

"I wasn't looking for business," she said. "I was offering my services, for free."

"Maybe it was more a matter of timing," I answered. "Lawyers make people nervous. Bea probably wants to dismiss the idea that her daughter is in enough trouble to need one."

"Your relatives would rather go to shrinks than lawyers," Colleen said, "and mine would rather go to priests."

She had never mentioned this to me, but I didn't have the energy to embark on another investigation into Colleen's difficult family. One of these days, she would come around and tell me more. Or she wouldn't. As it turned out, Jenny's husband was not having an affair. He'd been secretive because he'd been planning a surprise party for Jenny's thirtieth birthday.

IT'S ONLY NOW, looking back, that these exchanges loom so large. At the time, each felt like another of the small, bright stones in the growing mosaic of our life together. I could enjoy our little family as much as I did partly because I knew I would escape to the quiet of my own apartment on Sunday nights and to the familiar problems of my patients Mondays through Fridays. When Colleen occasionally made a reference to the future or to the possibility of my moving to Scarsdale, I nodded or said "uh-huh" or waited a moment and talked about something we planned for later that day. The only forward-looking references of hers that I encouraged were of a trip to Italy she wanted to take later in the year. It seemed far enough away, in time and space, not to make me feel claustrophobic — and who doesn't like dreaming of Italy? In general, my own past and hers were the places I yearned to explore, but I couldn't press it on her often. She would call me on the contradiction — that I liked talking about the past, but not the future. Nothing slipped by her. Yes, I was crazy about her. Had even told her I loved her. But that did not mean I wanted to stitch our lives together in a permanent weave. In those first four months, I was happy with our arrangement the way it was — part-time fatherhood with a full-time nanny and tender, sexy weekends — and, as far as I knew, as far as she let on, Colleen was too.

5

Testing

THE LITTLE STRIP from the drugstore tester was pink or blue or whatever it is that means yes, positive, pregnant.

She told me as I opened my eyes to meet hers as she squatted at the side of the bed. "I couldn't wait for you to get up, I was so excited." It was early Sunday morning, a week after our dinner at Pru's.

Her smile made me smile, but when she turned and went into the bathroom I felt my face go flaccid. She had prepared me for this possibility the night before as we got ready for bed, announcing as she massaged cream into her face that her period was a week late and that she had bought a tester to use in the morning. "I thought you'd been using your diaphragm."

"I have been. Sweetie, it's an accident. But I thought it would make you happy."

The word dangled in the air, hung mysteriously like a spider spinning a web whose filaments are so fine you cannot see them. All you see is the bug twisting in space, defying gravity. "Happy?"

"Don't you remember you said you wanted a brother or sister for Zoe?"

"I said what?"

"We were in the toy store in the village a few months ago, and you said how nice it would be for Zoe to have a sibling."

I tried to picture the toy store and the moment, and what I said came back to me, but not as she had related it. "I believe I said, 'Do you ever think about having a brother or sister for Zoe?' I remember distinctly that you didn't answer me. I assumed you didn't want to talk about it."

"Let's talk about it now."

"Colleen, where I come from, we have that conversation before we get pregnant. It's called 'family planning.'"

"Is that so? Where I come from, we don't, in case you got the wrong impression of South Boston from hearing about my brothers and sisters and their thousands of children. Irish Catholics aren't big supporters of Planned Parenthood."

One instance when she had volunteered information about her past — and I would just as soon not have been reminded. We each stormed around the room silently for a few minutes, getting into our pajamas, brushing our teeth, and finally Colleen sidled up to me and said sweetly, "I don't talk about my brothers who died, but maybe they have something to do with why it makes sense to me to have another baby, even though we didn't plan to."

Poor darling, I thought, to be remembering the dead brothers she never spoke of. I had wanted that so much — for her to wade into the waters of her past — and now she had. "The least I can do is bring two children into the world, to make up for their deaths. My mother was a tough cookie, but she was devastated when they died. I'd never seen her so emotional. None of us knew what to do for her." That was all she said, but I felt she had broken through to a kind of openness that I hoped would continue. Maybe having another child would encourage her to reconnect with her family. I might be able to bring it up in a week or two.

But the next morning after the pregnancy was confirmed, I pulled the covers up over my head and dreaded having to remove them. Did she realize she should give me some time alone, to get used to this? How would I integrate these two realities? Or was it three? That I cared for her. That she was pregnant with my child. That I was not the marrying kind. Wasn't that obvious? Couldn't she tell by the date of my birth, the decades in which I had managed to elude capture?

Slowly. That's what I would tell my clients. You integrate them slowly. You need patience. But where does that come from when the nine-month clock has already started ticking? Fake it until you make it: a piece of twelve-step wisdom that one of my patients bequeathed to me. I am as good as the next man at faking it. She was not asking me to go to church and fake religion, fake faith or piety. Was this easier or harder than that? I pulled it off. Or Colleen noticed and didn't call me on it. She kept her Irish up, decided to wait for me to come around. I spent the day in a cordial retreat mode, a pose I'm afraid that I've mastered. I was affectionate and cheerful and stayed close to Zoe, to dissuade Colleen from talking more about the pregnancy. She obliged, kept things light and loose, which I thought for most of the day must have been as hard for her as it was for me. But later, as we took turns pushing Zoe on the toddler swing set in the nearby park, I had an insight about Colleen: She's not a woman who has to talk about the relationship all the time. She has a temper, God knows, but she can also be remarkably cool-headed, even distant. Holding her tongue did not seem to be the psychic hardship it was for most of the women I knew. She must have had to hold it plenty when she was a kid, with half a dozen siblings, a bully for a father, and a mother who taught her to tough it out.

I did my best that Sunday, and she was smart enough to let me go back to the city that evening without a scene, without extracting a pound of flesh, without, that is to say, a proposal of marriage.

I TOOK THE Metro-North train to Grand Central and went immediately to the pay phone and called my sister. It hadn't entirely hit home that there was a person, a potential person, taking shape inside Colleen. What hit me hardest was that I had to make a decision about the future. I couldn't keep riding the wave of this two-days-on-and-five-days-off family. End the relationship or enter it fully, headfirst, more or less forever. I couldn't very well do what her loathsome ex-husband had done, could I? Walk out on her when she was pregnant? Was there an option here I couldn't see? Surely the goddesses of infinite possibility, Pru and Bea, would have an answer for me.

Pru invited me to dinner, which she said would be ready in an hour. I said, "Can I talk to you now? I'm kind of in a bad way."

"Sure. What's up?"

I said I was thinking about marrying Colleen and wanted her opinion, though I didn't mention the embryo, my microscopic Sarah Rose. "Would you think I was nuts if I married her?"

"Don't tell me she's pregnant." My sister saves babies' lives, but she is not sentimental. She is sensible, direct, sometimes altogether too blunt, especially when talking to me. I am not the parent of a patient, not one of the nearly hysterical people she deals with all day long whose feelings she has to be mindful of. I am her kid brother. A whipping boy, an old tennis ball she can bat around with impunity.

"I didn't say that."

"But she is, isn't she? That's why you're —"

"What do you think of her?"

There was a pause in which she was doing too much thinking. "She's a lawyer."

"You don't subscribe to that kind of prejudice, do you? There are plenty of lawyers who are perfectly —"

"Did you hear how fast she wanted to get Jenny into her office? She didn't want to wait —"

"We talked about it afterward. I told her she sounded overeager. She said she was just trying to help. She pointed out that she was offering her services for free. I know how it sounded. She was trying to make a good impression, but it came out clumsily. And you have to remember that her husband left her while she was pregnant. If there's anything she's sensitive about, it's a man who —"

"I suppose all of that makes sense."

"Aside from that, Pru, what do you think?"

"You wouldn't live in Scarsdale, would you?"

"I want your opinion of Colleen, not Scarsdale."

Again, a peculiar pause in which I imagined she must have had negative thoughts, so I was relieved when she spoke. "The truth is I don't have a crystal clear sense of her. I've met her twice. She's presentable and pleasant. I don't know her well enough to say that there's something sort of vague and guarded, but that's the feeling I get. Bea has it too. If I knew her better, I might say she seems unknowable."

I wanted a ringing endorsement. My sensible sister's blessing. When I didn't get it, I fell into the trap I had landed in before, blaming her lack of enthusiasm for my decisions on her lesbian lifestyle. What does she know about straight women? I thought, and hated myself, briefly, for thinking it. What does she know about what goes on between men and women? About the tangled nature of our attraction? Women with women — that was a drama I didn't pretend to fathom.

"That's just one dyke's view," Pru said into the silence, "because I know that's what you're thinking. Don't deny it. I know exactly what that silence is about. Maybe I'm wrong. About your girlfriend. Being unknowable isn't the worst thing in the world. It just means you have to work a little harder to figure out who she is. Or something like that. You're the shrink. I'm just a mechanic with a scalpel . . . Eric, are you still there?"

I was still there, but not in one piece. Not because Pru wasn't crazy about Colleen but because my sister had nailed me. It was as though she had x-ray vision. Maybe they all do. Women. What do we have to counteract that, to level the playing field? The big jobs? The big money? The almighty cock?

"Eric, say something."

"She's pregnant."

"Shit."

"She was using a diaphragm. She's Catholic. Or she was."

"Any chance she belongs to Catholics for a Free Choice?"

"Pru, we're not talking about abortion. I'm not talking about it." I was speaking softly, in a pay phone off the main waiting room of Grand Central. "I'm thinking of going ahead with this. I wasn't going to tell you this when I called. I just wanted your read on her. I got it."

Now it was her turn to be silent. Her turn to write off this impasse to the mysteries of our differing sexual preferences.

"So we'll see you for dinner in twenty minutes?" she said finally.

"I'm sorry, I think I'll pass. But thanks."

"Anytime. You're always welcome."

Our politeness was painful, but it was fine to leave things like that, frayed but not broken. Cordial. Respectful. This was our middle-aged sibling dance: we did not have to fake our feelings, but we knew better than to let them rip.

I turned away from signs pointing to the subway and went outside. It was a beautiful late-April night, I was wound up and decided to walk home, across 42d Street and up Broadway. About two miles. It gave me a chance to think. It was a mild night, dusk when I began to walk. I wanted to be enveloped in darkness, but Times Square annihilated the distinctions between night and day. The sidewalks were always mobbed, the lights always on, the billboards screaming with things I would never buy, the marquees with shows I would never see. I walked as quickly as I could through the crowds but tried to see the place as though I were a tourist, there for the first time. It was magical, unruly, awash in lights, headline news, money, someone else's idea of ambition. As I passed a bodega on 52d Street, a line from a tinny song on the radio spilled out to the street and made me smile. *When the moon hits your eye like a big pizza pie . . .* Why did I care so much about the sounds and textures of the city that night? Why was I taking inventory? By the time I reached Columbus Circle, night had fallen and my mood was somber. If a patient were in this situation, what probing questions would I ask? Would I ask him to draw a picture of his feelings or pick up the doll he most identified with at the moment? Would I dare offer a course of action?

I don't think of myself as a therapist who gives advice, though I know I have on occasion, when it seemed appropriate. I try to keep it general enough so that the patient makes his own decision, so that I cannot be held accountable for a plan that goes awry. But I do try to steer people in the direction of keeping their options open. Don't run off with a woman you've just met. Don't liquidate your retirement account to buy a sailboat. Protect yourself.

As Lincoln Center came into view, the broad plaza, the angular, warehouse-like buildings that looked so stylish thirty years ago, I realized what I was doing that night, and what I would do with the dilemma before me. I was saying goodbye to New York. It would take a long time to say it properly, it would take many months, but this was a beginning. I could do it in stages, commuting at first to try it out. I walked fast and then slowly, trying to imagine traveling every day at rush hour. Not an enticing prospect. "Commuter Dad" was not an identity I wanted to share with my father. I stopped to look at the tables of used books the guys sell on 72d Street, $2 for paperbacks, $4 for hardcovers, and I didn't stop at Fairway to buy olives or bagels or half-and-half for my coffee in the morning. I was not going to share my thoughts with Colleen just yet — this woman my sister thought was unknowable. I was beginning to know her. What she had told me the night before about her brothers and her mother after they died was a turning point, a bold invitation for me to come closer. How would I meet it? Would I be bold myself or meek? Would I be a strong man banging a drum in the woods or the frightened, feminized commitment-phobe I saw every day in the mirror?

I had to build in a safety valve for myself, whatever I did.

I would make the transition slowly and keep the apartment I owned, sublet it, and move in with Colleen, not because I wanted to be in Scarsdale, but because if I moved to her house, instead of bringing her to mine, I would always have the option to leave.

The idea came to me as I turned off Broadway and walked toward West End. My doorman, Enrique, nodded and wished me a good night. It was only as I passed him that I saw the plug in his ear that meant he was listening to the ball game on a radio in his pocket. "Who's winning?" I asked. I had no idea who was playing what. I knew it was basketball season.

"Chee-cago. I don't know what's wrong with Duncan tonight. He can't shoot straight for cheet." He meant "shit." He can't shoot straight for shit.

But it looked like I could.

Forty-seven years old and I was about to become a father.

❧ 6 ❧

The Family Man

B<small>Y THE TIME</small> Sandy Lefkowitz walked into my office almost three and a half years later, I was a full-fledged Scarsdale family man with two small children, a wife on the board of the Scarsdale Women's Club, a Home Depot Visa card, a refrigerator covered with photos of my kids, and a chic, shingled office-cottage behind the house, where I treated my bevy of high-functioning patients.

How did it all come to be? Through the efforts of the extraordinary Colleen, whose efforts, I believed until recently, were motivated by love for me. I was certain, for the first time in my life, that the love we made was real, and that the laughter in the dark was too. You can't fake *that,* can you? I knew her interest in me wasn't financial because she had more money than I did. For once, I welcomed a woman being in love with me, or what seemed like love, what she said was love.

She hired a contractor who could build the cottage on an accelerated schedule. She designed its interior and exterior and sweated every detail — and prevailed in every dispute with me over how it should look. She introduced me to the high school guidance counselors who led me to my teenage clients, and once I had moved she somehow arranged for a reporter at the local paper to write a full-page piece in the lifestyles section about my eclectic mix of treatments: "New Village Therapist Uses Dolls, Crayons, and Massage to Fix Old Problems." The article got a few things dead wrong, oversimplified others — and the headline made me sound like a flake. But the telephone rang and *les femmes de Scarsdale* were curious. Once they arrived, they were comforted to see my Ph.D. diploma from Columbia, in part because it made explaining the expense to their husbands easier, for those whose health insurance didn't pay for psychotherapy. Having just moved my practice from New York City didn't hurt my reputation either.

Looking back on the early weeks and months when I was commuting from the city, winding down my practice there as the cottage went up and Colleen's belly began to swell, I find I want to remember the sweetness of what I felt, the power that lured me to dismantle my life and reassemble it in Scarsdale. I want to remember how solid the ground felt beneath my feet, how full my heart was, the way Colleen cradled me in her heavenly breasts, and the sensation of Zoe napping on my stomach as I sprawled out on the couch listening to Thelonious Monk while Colleen put together an Italian meal from one of her lavish cookbooks. I kept thinking I would grow tired of the domesticity, the constant company, the chaos of parenthood. I was afraid I would wake up next to her one Saturday morning and want to flee. But I liked being tended to and needed by Colleen, and I loved being loved by Zoe.

I'm tempted to airbrush the rough spots and bitchy outbursts, to glide over our arguments, skip the awkward moment when I asked her to marry me and she said that I sounded as if my heart wasn't in it, and I insisted, uncertainly, ambivalently, that it was. I'm tempted to forget the quarrels we had about the cottage. We fought about what would go on the floors and the walls — and Colleen always prevailed with her kilims and the masks that she loved to buy in Venice. She also insisted the cottage be two rooms; I said one was enough. "You simply can't have your massage table out there in plain view," she said. "Unless you're a massage therapist, having it in the main room will make people around here nervous. This isn't Marin County. Put it in the second room, and you won't have to answer any questions."

"You make it sound like I do something illicit with the table."

"For all I know, you do. But that's beside the point."

"It most certainly is not. You don't really mean that, do you? Freud had a couch in his office. So does every psychoanalyst in the world. The massage table is an updated version of that."

"Look, no one in Southie even knew what a shrink was. I don't know what they'd have made of you, with your dolls and gizmos. People aren't really so different here, when it comes to that."

"For God's sake, Colleen, leave it be. Leave the whole goddamn thing. Forget the cottage. I'll rent an office down the street."

"Oh, sweetie, don't take this so seriously. I've just had a hard day, Zoe's back molars are coming in and she's crabby. Just like her mother. You know I think what you do is marvelous, helping people all day long."

She insisted. I eventually relented.

Were the squabbles significant? Should I have read more into them? I thought it was healthy that we could fight, a positive sign that we could air our differences. And I came to see that her instincts were sharp. "You'll see," she'd say. "The room will be beautiful. You have no idea how important it is to your future patients that your office is gorgeous. But if you really don't like it after it's finished, you can put your unicorn up again."

She was right; it was beautiful. The women loved it. A good number of my clients wanted to see me twice a week — not because of my rugs and wall hangings, of course, but they helped put this particular client population at ease. And so, frankly, did the doll collection that took up two of the lower shelves of the built-in bookcase. Unlike my patients on the Upper West Side, all of my women clients here were mothers and had an instantaneous reaction to the playthings which never ceased to interest me. The dolls got them to talk about their daughters, the daughters they wished they had, and the relationships with their actual daughters that they yearned to have.

Such musings touched me differently, more deeply, than they had before I had my own daughters, before these phrases became my own: *the mother of my children; the mother of my daughters.*

One matter the mother of my children and I agreed on from the start was how we would marry. Late one night in her kitchen, as we cleaned up from a late dinner, she surprised me by saying that she had no interest in a wedding: "I'd be perfectly happy to go to city hall with Zoe and out afterward for Chinese food."

"You don't want to invite your family?"

"They're the last people I'd want to be here. Do you want to invite yours?"

"We could elope and not tell anyone."

"That would be fine with me. Would it disappoint you?"

"God no. I'm glad you're so sane about it. I've never heard anything about planning a wedding that made me want to have one." That was true and so was this: as a lifelong bachelor, the last thing I wanted was to be at the center of a spectacle that celebrated my capture, that asked me to parade my commitment on my sleeve. Better to slink off to the privacy of city hall and be done with it.

COLLEEN MANAGED to hit all the right notes with me, or enough so that I could dismiss the off notes without much internal conflict. And Zoe was there, with her mother's huge enticing green eyes — and her nanny nearby — to be doted on, embraced, swung into the air, read to, fed, and entertained. She was not my full-time job, and I imagine it would have been harder to love her so thoroughly if it had been. I plead guilty to needing time away from her, but once I moved in completely I was astonished at how much space she took up in my emotional hard drive. When I was with her, I worried about her welfare; when I was away from her, I worried too; when I spoke to Colleen, we parsed every gurgle and analyzed every bowel movement. Dwelling on my past and what I could learn of Colleen's became a relic, like a stamp-collecting hobby I had outgrown.

I had become one of those insufferable People with Children; and worst of all, Privileged People with Children. During Colleen's pregnancy, I found myself becoming another archetype, one you hear much less about: the Man Turned on by His Pregnant Wife. I desired Colleen intensely — entering her in the later months from the side or from the back — and she accommodated me with enthusiasm. I was so infatuated with the particular swellings and radiance of pregnancy that nearly the only women I paid attention to on the street were those with child. So much for the slender voluptuaries of my past.

When Sarah Rose was born, our lives became infinitely more hectic and proceeded with an internal structure that left little time for reflection, improvisation, or much of anything else. Were we happy? We were as happy as we needed to be. When our biological connection to each other was made manifest in Sarah Rose, we were delirious, and that delirium lingered, as it is meant to do. I found myself studying Sarah Rose's face as though I were an art historian with the *Mona Lisa,* assigning every square centimeter of her to either Colleen's or my own genetic influence. Sometimes Colleen's temper was shorter than it was at other times, but I'd learned to ignore her outbursts, the occasional nasty retort. I told myself it was that time of the month or she hadn't had a good night's sleep or she was under stress at work. For every snotty remark, there were days of affection, the squeeze of my arm as she passed me, her lips against my back as I fell asleep. When a crying child woke us, we often said "Oh shit" in unison. "You'll miss her when she goes to college," Colleen mumbled during one of those sleep-deprived nights, and I remember being touched beyond words, at the thought of the long life together we had embarked on.

Once Sarah Rose began sleeping through the night, our moods improved. Once we spent August together in a rented house on the Cape, we decided we wanted to do that every summer. Once we had Sarah Rose's low-key first birthday party and agreed to resist the Scarsdale instinct of hiring Ringling Brothers for the day, I'd have sworn that we were partners in the same marriage. We were, in those days. I'm sure we were, until things started shaking loose with Sandy Lefkowitz not too many weeks ago.

I have a dozen patients whose marriages are as dull as dirt, whose kids are acting out, whose eighty-five-year-old parents are wearing diapers. Next to all of that, my life and my marriage looked pretty good. One part of it that stayed good was our sex life. Sure, there were dry spells, but we managed to find each other's toes under the covers more often than People with Children usually do. On occasion Colleen would say to me over dinner, with the kids at our elbows, eating from the ends of our spoons and forks, "Got any plans later?" and I did all I could to arrange the rest of the evening accordingly. Mornings, by then, were out of the question because one or both of the kids liked to crawl into bed with us at daybreak, and we were gloriously happy to have them there.

We had grown accustomed to our routines, and there was not one we liked more than spending August on Cape Cod. This past summer, we came back ten days shy of the full month because Colleen had to prepare for two trials. The third Sunday of the month, as we drove into Scarsdale, tanned, sunburned, the car crowded with dirty laundry, damp towels, and fussy kids, my beeper went off — the start of my acquaintance with Sandy Lefkowitz. My answering service was paging me. When I phoned in, I heard: "A Mr. Lefkowitz wants you to call him. He said he phoned fifteen therapists from the yellow pages and everyone's on vacation for the rest of the month. He said it was an emergency."

✄ 7 ✄

Sex, Money, Intimacy,
Trust, Children

I REACHED Mr. Lefkowitz soon after we arrived home, when I could steal a few minutes in the small office off our bedroom. All he would say at first was that "it was a family matter."

"Your message said it was an emergency. Are you hurt, physically?"

"No."

"Are you in danger of hurting yourself?"

"It's not that kind of emergency."

When he wouldn't say what kind it was, I took it to mean he was not in imminent danger and told him I had time the following morning.

He arrived in wrinkled khakis, a navy blue short-sleeved polo shirt, and grease-stained running shoes, worn down at the heels, an outfit you might wear to clean out the basement. Was he a runner, or a former runner? He wasn't lean, he wasn't stylish. His hair was thick, auburn, peppered with gray, his mustache droopy and his posture too; his left hand remained locked in a loose fist, until about halfway through the session, when he unlocked it and splayed the fingers, which seemed to trigger a deep sigh. He looked to be forty-five or fifty, which is to say, my age, and the combination of slovenliness and extreme tension, which I could see in his jaw, his eyes, in the way he held his shoulders, struck me. And I don't believe I'd ever had any patients who'd picked me cold out of the yellow pages. Why would they? There's no big, splashy ad in the "Psychologists" section, just my name and the phone number.

"It's hard to talk about" was one of the first things he said, just after he sat down on the couch across from my chair.

"You said it was an emergency."

"It felt like that when every shrink was away until after Labor Day. If one gas station is closed, it's okay. Or two. But if every single one is closed, you start to panic."

"Because you're running out of gas."

"Right. Yeah, I guess that's what was happening."

"I'm glad I was here to get your call."

It was a while more before he spoke again. I took out my pen and began to take notes, to try to put him at ease. "Why don't I get some basic information. What's your full name?"

"It's about my son," he said.

I waited for him to continue, but he got quiet again. He looked worn around the edges and tired, as though he didn't sleep well. It wasn't a Scarsdale presentation; even the gardeners here look fresh-faced, starched, ready for church.

"What's your son's name?"

"Jack." Then he clammed up again for ten seconds. "I don't know if you've had any experience with this." Another pause, eyes averted. "He's kind of withdrawn. Sometimes I wonder if he could be gay."

"How old is he?"

"Ten."

It seemed young to worry. Might Mr. Lefkowitz have been talking indirectly about himself? He'd say a few words, shoot them out of his mouth like BBs, and shut right up again.

"Why are you concerned about this right now? Did something happen?"

Medium-long pause before he answered. "His mother."

"What about her?"

"She's distracted. She's distant. From him."

"Is she distant from you too?"

"I guess you could say that."

"How's your relationship with your son?"

"I try to be there for him, because she's not. Well, she is there, because I'm at work. I'm an architect in the city. Ursula goes through the motions, but she acts bored and put-upon. I don't know. Maybe she has a boyfriend. Maybe she's like one of those men with two different families. I help Jack with his homework and put him to bed and sometimes I fall asleep in the other bed in his room. At nine o'clock." More silence. Slumped shoulders. Depression, probably. Deprivation: emotional, sexual. He didn't need to spell it out. She sounded depressed, too. If the two of them were, Jack was probably not far behind.

"Why don't we go through some of the basic information. Your wife's name is Ursula?"

"Ursula Higgenbotham." The surname caught me up short. It wasn't one you come across often, not around here. And not married to a Lefkowitz.

"Does she work?"

"She did until a few months ago. She got laid off. She was the office manager at a vet's office in the village. I thought she'd spend time with Jack now that she's got so much of it on her hands."

"Any other children?"

"Just Jack. Ursula had a few miscarriages before that. It was a difficult pregnancy. She had to spend the last three months in bed."

"Was it a normal birth?"

"Yeah. For the first year, he was all right."

"Then?" I looked up to see how he was doing. He'd sat back in the chair and seemed to be breathing more easily, though these were clearly difficult questions, and I had the feeling he had not spent much time in a therapist's office.

"He developed a cough that turned into pneumonia. He was in pediatric intensive care. That's a place you never want to be."

"What do you remember about it?"

"Waiting. Not knowing. The machines, never being able to figure out what the lights and the squiggles meant. It was a foreign language with no subtitles, no translations."

"How was your son when he left there?"

"Fragile."

"Is he still?"

"No, he's more — normal, regular. He's a good student, he's got friends, a few."

"Has something happened recently that makes your life more stressful?"

"I've got a short fuse at work. Friday I blew up at my assistant because she'd misplaced a blueprint. A really nice kid. Woman. Smart, supertalented. Seventeen little gold hoop earrings. I counted once." He traced a line around the rim of his ear. That detail seemed to relax him; he almost smiled. "She just graduated from Pratt. She started crying. It was a blueprint for a stairwell in a nursing home. I blew up over nothing. Then I went home and tried to talk to my wife."

"About?"

"The state of our marriage." He rolled his eyes — more emotion than he'd shown yet. "And my wanting to take a trip with her. I said we should go back to London and see the new British Library. Or go to Bilbao in Spain. I told her I was thinking of taking flamenco lessons like a guy in my office. I'm not really, but I wanted to see if she was listening."

"What did she say to your ideas?"

"Zip. Looked at me like I was nuts."

"Have you talked to her about your concern regarding your son?"

He shook his head.

"What would you say are some of the issues you and your wife are struggling with, besides your son?" What is it writers say?

There are only two stories: someone shows up; someone leaves. Shrinks will tell you there are only five problems: sex, money, intimacy, trust, children. No, six: add "parents," as in in-laws, Alzheimer's, inheritance. And of course they are all related, as intertwined as the rules of grammar.

"Money," he said, right on cue. "She grew up rich in Greenwich, Connecticut, and thought I'd become a big shot, a Philip Johnson, I. M. Pei, Frank Gehry. Instead I'm a line architect. I'm like a book editor. There are a lot of people who can do what I do."

"You're hardly an unskilled laborer."

"I make ninety K a year. That's minimum wage in Scarsdale. We're a charity case. I told her we should apply to become one of the *Time*'s Neediest Cases at the end of the year. She didn't think that was funny. She worked for the last two years and stopped complaining, but since she got laid off —"

"What part of town do you live in?"

"Edgewood. The slum of Scarsdale." It's the most modest of our five neighborhoods, the area behind the Catholic church on the Post Road, but the only difference I can see is the minimal distance between houses, unless you're talking about some of the Versailles-type mansions up in the hills. "Our three-bedroom with study and finished basement is worth seven hundred K. I don't know if this is related to anything, but a month ago a very pretty architect in Atlanta put the moves on me at a conference on structural design innovations. What the hell did she want with an old married guy like me?"

Infidelity. I left out number seven. How could I have forgotten that? Yes, it's related to sex and trust but not synonymous; you don't get many illicit lovers who come in with sexual problems they want to work on.

"How did it make you feel that this woman wanted you?"

"I thought she needed a new prescription for her contact lenses." Silence. A slight smile. More of a smirk.

Poor guy, wound as tight as a — a Higgenbotham. As tight as a Puritan preacher. As unaccustomed to the format as my sullen teenage boy clients, who have one-word answers to all of my questions, who make me feel like a machine that spits out tennis balls. Sandy had called fifteen of us from the yellow pages, pleading for someone to listen, and now he was tongue-tied. His obvious discomfort with the elemental transaction — he talks, I talk — made me want to try one of my standard body-mind exercises with him, if he was willing. He seemed not to have noticed the two shelves of dolls in the corner bookcase, and there was no point calling his attention to them.

"Sandy, would you mind trying an exercise I sometimes do with new clients?"

"What is it?"

"We'll go slowly. Close your eyes, uncross your legs." He did one, then the other. "Rest your palms on your thighs, wherever they're comfortable." So far, so good. "Do you remember the woman at the conference looking at you?"

"Yeah."

"Can you picture her looking at you?"

"Sort of."

"Do you remember what you felt when you noticed her looking?"

"I thought she was looking at the guy behind me."

"But when you realized it was you, how did you feel?"

"Self-conscious."

"Anything else?"

"I don't know. Guilty."

"Can you recall another time you felt guilty?"

"I can recall a hundred times. A thousand."

"In any of those times, is there a place where you remember feeling the guilt in your body?"

His eyes popped open and glared at me. "In my body? You're

not some crystal-headed weirdo about to light a stick of incense, are you?"

"No crystals, no incense. I have a Ph.D. in clinical psychology, but I'm eclectic in what I do. I trust you've learned a few new techniques for yourself, or the only buildings you'd build would look like what, the Parthenon? Fifty years ago, people thought the best way to examine your inner life was to lie on a couch five days a week and talk to a guy who didn't talk back. And they thought a good diet was red meat, canned peas, and iceberg lettuce. One of the trends I follow is body-oriented psychotherapy. Freudians used to talk a lot about 'psychosomatic illnesses,' physical illness caused by psychic stress. Body-oriented therapy picks up where that idea left off and asks us to use the body as a metaphor for the unconscious." When he didn't say anything or make any noticeable faces for ten or fifteen seconds, I decided to press a little further. "Does that seem reasonable to you?"

He shrugged but did not seem angry.

"Do you mind if I ask why you shrugged?"

"I don't know why."

"What does a shrug mean to you?"

"What kind of bullshit is this? A shrug is a shrug."

"What if it could talk?"

"Oh, Jesus."

"What would it say?"

"'Get me the fuck out of here.'"

"Out of here, this office?"

"Out of my life."

I winced at the pain I knew he felt, but I winced silently, internally. I have been trained to keep it quiet, but when a client suffers, especially someone who has tried so hard to keep it to himself, I feel it deeply.

He closed his eyes and drew his hands into fists in his lap.

"Can you tell me about making your hands into fists just now?"

"You think I want to hit you?"

"I have no idea. Do you?"

"You're trying to get me to say that I want to hit you."

"Sandy, I'm looking at your hands clench, both at the same time. I don't know what it feels like to *you*. That's what I'm interested in."

He opened his eyes suddenly and peered at me. "This is a bunch of crap. I want to talk to you about my wife and my son, and you want to talk about my fists. You're so fucking calm."

"And what are you?"

"The opposite."

"What does that look like, the opposite of calm?"

"Not this again."

"All right. What does it feel like?"

"An explosion."

"What does that look like?"

"Red and fiery."

"Has it hurt you?"

"Of course."

"Where?"

"Everywhere."

When he said nothing more, I let us listen to the absence of speech, for fifteen or twenty seconds. I noticed all the deep breaths he was taking, the sounds of his sighing. "Ask me some questions," he said. "I thought that's what shrinks do."

"Okay." I wasn't sure whether to ask him about his breathing or his wife, didn't know which would upset him less. I wanted to leave him with some relief. The hour was almost up. "Can you remember a happy time with your wife and your son?"

He began to nod and his eyes fell shut. His mouth started to curve into a smile. "After Jack got better, Ursula's mother gave us a vacation to London. We stayed at Claridge's and walked everywhere with Jack in a pouch on my back."

His eyes were still closed, his breathing steadier. I didn't want to break the spell, but we had to finish. He opened his eyes and looked at me through squinted lids. "How did you do that?" he said.

"Do what?"

"Calm me down."

"I like to think we did it together."

He gazed around the room as if he hadn't seen it yet, as if he were just coming out of a trance and not sure where he was. I waited a few beats. "Would you like to make another appointment?"

"You think I should come back? You think this could work?"

"I think it already has. By your choosing to come here. By asking for help."

"You've got an answer for everything, don't you?"

"Why don't we talk about what that means to you next time. If you'd like to come back."

"What about tomorrow?"

I reached for my book and remembered he'd begun by talking about his son.

"That doesn't mean I'm nuts, does it, to come two days in a row?"

"I think it means you have things you want to talk about."

"An answer for everything," he muttered, but our time was up and I chose not to engage him on that point.

That's how it was with Sandy for the first few sessions, a lot of silence, challenging, testing the limits, sudden shifts between defiance and curiosity. It's not an unusual way to begin, though Sandy was more skeptical, more hostile, than most. But I was touched by him from the start, his wrinkled clothes, his droopy mustache. Most of my current clients are women, and it isn't difficult to get them to talk or pick up the dolls or tell me where in their bodies they feel their jealousy most acutely. The problem is that I'm not always interested in what they have to say. Sandy, on the other hand, for all of his abruptness, tormented silences, his elliptical answers, his cluelessness, his inelegance — it wasn't just that I liked him and wanted to help. I don't know if I was aware of it that first day or whether it came to me later but with such force that it seems I had known it from the start. There is no other way to put it: I was going to have to rescue him. That's the sense I had, although I did not yet know from what.

✣ 8 ✣

The Bullets Are Real

W HEN WE MET, Colleen had recently finished the handbook she had mentioned during our first dinner, and it was published six months later. *Your Fair Share! Women and Divorce* is now in its fifth printing, exceeding the modest expectations she and the publisher had when it appeared. I've leafed through it two or three times: part motivational pep talk — yes, there is life after divorce, but it's up to you and your lawyer to make sure it's a good life! — and the rest practical. How to pick a lawyer. How to decide the grounds for your divorce. Telltale signs your husband has hidden assets. Where to look for them. What to tell the children. When to initiate legal action. It's decently written and laced with snappy case studies in which ingenuity, sleuthing, and a bit of legal know-how pay off.

Soon after it came out, a spate of high-profile splits led to Colleen's appearance on two national TV gabfests, to talk about what happens when Mr. and Mrs. Ordinary hang up the matrimonial gloves. Against all odds, after the second show, the book made a brief appearance on a national bestseller list and on a popular women's Web site that can turn a new book into a runaway hit without a penny of advertising. Such was its fate.

When the book showed up on the *Times* bestseller list, I expressed my admiration. "I don't know how you found time to write it in the midst of a divorce and a new baby."

"I told you, didn't I, that I got some help from a journalist friend in Boston? I'd been taking notes and making outlines for a long time, but I could never figure out how to pull it all together. She whipped it into shape in three months, a little while before we moved here."

"How much did you pay her?"

"Actually, we bartered."

"Really? What was the swap?"

"She helped me write my book and I helped with her divorce."

"Ingenious. I didn't know lawyers did that."

"We don't, usually." There was a rough edge to Colleen's comment, and I could see she was not eager to keep talking about this. But I was curious.

"Didn't she want her name on it?"

"At the beginning, but by the end she decided she didn't want to be pigeonholed, you know, as a writer, as someone who only did handbooks. I insisted on thanking her in the acknowledgments. I think that was enough for her."

"It might be nice to send her a bonus. I had a patient in New York who hired a ghostwriter and then the book they wrote became a major bestseller and the ghostwriter sued him for more money."

"What did you advise your patient?"

"I wasn't his lawyer, and I don't make a habit of giving advice."

"What happened?"

"They settled. My patient gave him a chunk of money, I can't remember how much it was."

"I hadn't thought about it, but I'll take it under advisement. You're always so considerate, dearest."

I filed that conversation away until our recent troubles began. In fact, I rarely gave the book any thought, except when Colleen was on local TV discussing it, and soon after, when I'd see her cornered by women at the community swimming pool or the gourmet store, near the bins of $5 baguettes and cookies shipped in from East Hampton. The stories she came back with were hair-raising. Husbands who'd run off with the *au pair*, with a business partner's daughter, and one who vanished with the high school Russian teacher's Ukrainian boyfriend. You don't realize until you get deep into it that there are so many bad apples and deadbeat dads in Larchmont, Eastchester, and right here in Scarsdale.

It was because of one of these dads that my office phone began to ring at the end of my third meeting with Sandy, the last week of August. I had gone a few minutes over our time when I heard the answering machine emit a series of clicks that told me a call was coming in. I ignored the noises until the third call in as many minutes. Click stop, click click. By then, Sandy and I had made an appointment for the following week. The fourth round of click-stops began. "Sounds like someone needs to reach you," he said and crossed the room to let himself out. When I heard the door shut behind him, I grabbed the phone.

"Turn on the TV," Colleen's voice said into my ear. "That boy's mother is my client."

"Let me go into the house. Are you all right? Keep talking, I'm on the portable. You're at your office, aren't you?"

"Yeah. I'm a little flipped out." She sounded as though she were talking between clenched teeth, clenching to keep her composure, which I could hear had been shaken. "And the phone hasn't stopped ringing. I told the cops you might be able to help out."

"Help with what?" I was racing across the lawn, taking note that, as far as I knew, both our children were safely in the house with Graciela. As I entered the house through the back door, I could hear their noises — notably Zoe having a temper tantrum — but they sounded far away, across the house or upstairs.

Within seconds, I turned on a small TV we keep in the kitchen. The word "LIVE" flashed across the screen, over a shot of a small brick Colonial house with a modest lawn. An instant later, a close-up of the house front, a bay window whose yellow drapes were tightly drawn, and the TV station banner, SCARSDALE HOSTAGE CRISIS, blaring across the bottom. A frantic voice-over: "There is still no word from anyone inside the house, but the Scarsdale police — wait, wait. We're being instructed: the police have just told our crews that for safety reasons, we must remain more than five hundred feet from the house."

"What the hell's going on?"

"A teenage boy is holding his father hostage at gunpoint inside the house," Colleen said. "He fired a shot an hour ago. The father's girlfriend escaped through the basement. She isn't hurt. The cops are looking for a shrink to talk to the kid, but everyone they use is on vacation. They've got a detective who's been trying to call the house, but they think someone who's not a cop might —"

"Who'd he shoot?"

"A neighbor heard glass break, so there's a chance the shot just hit the window. They want to get the kid on the phone, but he's not picking up. They can use a bullhorn to talk to him, to tell him to answer the phone, but so far he's —"

"Who's your client?"

"The boy's mother. In her divorce. The dad is eighteen months behind in support payments. He's living in his girlfriend's house. The mother's getting eviction notices, the kid's flunking summer school. Can you do it, can you talk to him? I told the cops you're great with boys like this."

"I have no training in hostage intervention. None."

"Honey, they've been calling shrinks for an hour. There's my other line. Hold on." I heard her talking to someone else: "I've reached him. I have him on the phone. He'll do it. Where should he go? Okay. I've got that. He'll be there."

"Colleen, for God's sake. What the hell did you tell them about my qualifications?"

"Eric, go outside and wait on the curb. They're sending a patrol car for you right now. They'll be there in two minutes. There's a whole police setup across the street from this house, and they'll brief you on —"

"What do you mean speaking for me when —"

"Don't wimp out on me, honey. You can do this. I've got the boy's mother on the other line, and she's losing it. They'll be there in two minutes." That was it. She hung up on me, another click in my ear.

It seemed I'd only turned around and gone back to my office to put a sign on the door — APPOINTMENTS CANCELED DUE TO EMERGENCY — when the unfamiliar swell of police sirens closed in on the house. I ditched the paper and pen and ran out to the curb, hoping I could get away before Graciela saw the patrol car and panicked. Its back door swung open, and I leaped in just as she appeared in the front doorway; the car sped off within seconds.

"I need to call my wife and have her call our nanny to tell her what's going on so she won't worry."

We raced through the still streets, quieter than usual because the news must have permeated the village during the hour I'd been talking to Sandy Lefkowitz about the state of his marriage. Or I imagined the calm because we were going so fast, moving at such a clip, sirens shrieking, the car cutting corners and surging ahead as though it were rocket-propelled.

By the time I got off a few-second call with Colleen's secretary, we'd turned onto a side street whose small brick and Tudor houses stood cheek by jowl. Already, the lawns seemed thick with strangers. Strangers, I saw now, with video cameras and microphones. I realized I hadn't had time to collect my thoughts, ask the cops questions, think about what I was supposed to do. Noise crackled on the police radio, static, numbers, street names, phrases like "the suspect is" and "roger" and "where the fuck" and "ask him again" and "over and out."

"What's the kid's name?"

"Jason Cummings."

"I'm not sure what you want me to do, but I —"

"Get him out of the house ASAP."

Before I could say more, we'd pulled into a driveway with two other patrol cars already parked there, and a swarm of reporters milling around cheerily as though this were a story about an Easter egg hunt, not a teenager with a handgun and a geyser of rage. It was August, hot, and humid. I saw beads of perspiration on every forehead, Texas-size sweat stains on every shirt and blouse.

"We're operating from this house. The perp's house is across the street and down two. Go in through the garage. Fast."

Three steps in, and I was standing in the middle of somebody's kitchen, the cops pushing me in deeper, toward the back, not the front, of the house, into a clean-cut Crate and Barrel living room, where everything matched. There must've been a dozen people there, cops in uniform, detectives in suits, two or three women in civilian clothes holding clipboards whose jobs I couldn't guess, and cell phones ringing like bird calls in the rain forest, a hundred different tweets and trills. I was following one of the cops who brought me here, but he couldn't find the person he was looking for. I could see him casting glances around the room. I followed his gaze and recognized a familiar face. But he was out of context, way out. Sandy Lefkowitz by the kitchen door? He saw me and negotiated the mob between us. It had all happened so fast, I realized I'd last seen Sandy seven or eight minutes ago in my office. The cops needed an architect too?

He cocked his head and directed me to a quieter corner of the room. "What are you doing here?" he asked.

"They called me in to talk to the boy. What about you?"

"This is my house. I was on my way to the train station after our appointment, and my wife called me. They wanted the house directly across the street, but no one was home so they came here. I just walked in the door."

"Jesus. What a mess. For them. For you." I wanted to apologize to him for ending up here, in his living room, uninvited. Twenty

79

years doing this, and I couldn't remember when I'd ended up in a patient's house. I'd paid a few condolence calls when the child of a patient had died or the spouse of someone I'd seen in couples therapy. But nothing like this, when the relationship was new and unproven. And no place where I hadn't been invited. The danger was that it might spook Sandy to allow me to see him up close so soon. He'd told me today that his wife hadn't slept with him in years. Didn't offer how many, but the point was that it could be measured in years, plural, not months, and not one year to the next, but many such years. Getting to be a habit. All of that was going through my mind at lightning speed — I read somewhere that there are ten million electrical currents surging among brain cells every second — when a short brunette with a pixie haircut and enormous eyes appeared across from Sandy and announced, "I'm going to get Jack out of camp." This was his wife, this was Ursula? She was bosomy and a bit overweight, had big brown Liza Minnelli eyes, and dressed entirely in stretchy black clothes that she might wear to an exercise class.

"What for?"

"It's not safe."

"He's safer there than he is here."

"No, he's not," she said and spun the other way and out through the kitchen door. With that name, Ursula Higgenbotham, I had expected a willowy WASP in an outfit from Talbots.

"Doc?" A hand grabbed my elbow, and I was pulled away from Sandy, a relief for both of us. A man in a suit, not a uniform. "You an M.D.?"

"Clinical psychologist."

"I'm Detective Lawson. We're trying to get the kid to pick up the phone. We've got a quiet room here with a phone setup." He escorted me down the hall on the first floor to a spacious room, everything in it white with black accents, like musical notation, the keyboard of a piano, a very striking look. As neat as a hotel room. A sleek black phone on a bright white desktop. A bare drafting table, slanted, in the corner. A few framed photos on the walls: a stone church, a Gothic cathedral, a Japanese house that looked like it was made of paper. No people. Art and architecture books on the spanking white bookcase, every book straight up, bindings flush with the edge of the case. Sandy's study, as polished and tidy as he was slovenly, suggested that the dissonance in him was not confined to his marriage. I was relieved, for his sake, that they hadn't taken me to his bedroom.

"We've got someone outside with a bullhorn telling the kid to pick up the phone when it rings. We got him to pick it up before, but he said he doesn't want to talk to a cop. If we get him to pick up, you introduce yourself. Your name. You live in Scarsdale. You want to talk to him. Find out if anyone's hurt. If not, distract him. Lure him out. Whatever it takes to —"

"Are you Colleen's husband?" The voice was a woman's, and she had just appeared at the door.

"Yes."

"I'm Carolyn, Jason's mother. I just wanted you to know —" She looked young, not more than thirty or thirty-five, pale, blond, puffy-eyed, in short shorts and a halter top. She did not present Scarsdale. More like Yonkers. "He's not violent. Please don't hurt him. He's just stressed up to here, that's all. Our air conditioner broke, my car needs new brakes, he found an eviction notice on the door. Yesterday, the bastard picks him up for a visit in a shiny new Subaru Outback. That's what made him lose it. Don't hurt him, please. He's a good kid. I don't know what I'd do if —"

"Mrs. Cummings, time is of the essence," the detective said. "We've got to ask you to go in the other room, for Jason's sake, so that the doctor here can talk frankly to him." He turned and started to usher her out, but she shook her arms and went by herself. Poor woman. I hadn't been able to say a word to her.

"Doc, you got to get him to put down the gun and walk out the front door with his hands on his head."

"Like the movies."

"Just like the movies. But the bullets are real. So's the blood."

"He's picking up," another cop whispered. Several others had headsets on, but I couldn't tell where their wires ran. They were nodding now, pointing to me. The detective put a receiver to my ear, the one connected to Sandy's desk phone.

"Jason? Is that you?"

"Who's this?"

"Eric. Eric Lavender."

"What kind of name is that? Like purple?"

"Yeah, but lighter."

"Are you a cop?"

"No."

"A reporter?"

"Nope."

"A shrink?"

"How'd you know?"

"You think they'd put a dentist up to this?"

I suppressed a light laugh.

"This isn't funny, man."

"I know it isn't, Jason."

"You want to make some deal with me, don't you?"

This wasn't funny, and it wasn't going to be easy. A part of my brain said to me: Above all, be honest with him. Another part said: Don't bind yourself to a plan. Consider every question on its own. Listen. Don't rush. Don't be glib. See it from his point of view.

"What's the situation there, Jason? Are you hurt?"

"No."

"Is your father hurt?"

"I think he'll live."

"Is he bleeding?"

"Fuck no. He'll have rope burns. Shit like that."

This is what it means when you say your life feels like a movie:

there's been a sudden reversal, a crisis, a dramatic rearrangement of the central narrative. You always mean a Hollywood movie when you say this, not a French movie. *Scarface,* not *Claire's Knee.*

"Rope burns," I said, to see if he'd say any more.

"Yeah, rope burns."

"So he's tied up?"

"'Course. He's a hostage."

"So you must want to make a deal, too. If you're holding a hostage."

"Maybe I do and maybe I don't."

Kee-ryste. I turned and looked at the detective. He mouthed the words "Keep talking." I took a leap. "I think I have some idea how you feel. Jason, I had a difficult father too. He was a schmuck."

"No kidding," he said but with only flatness, not surprise, in his voice.

"You thought you were the only one?"

"I never thought about that part."

"Which part do you think about? Which part gets your juices going?"

"It would be kinda weird to talk about it in front of him."

"You want to pop him first and talk about it from jail?"

"I wouldn't do adult time. I'm a kid."

Was this Scarsdale talking, or was this kid a member of the Jets, the Sharks, the Crips? I didn't have the courtroom lingo to bullshit along these lines. I'm a white-collar shrink myself.

The cop signaled me again to keep talking. He must have sensed that I was running out of lines.

"Listen, Jason, if you could be anywhere now, where would you be?"

"I don't know. Las Vegas."

"What would you be doing there?"

"I don't like this game."

I didn't either, but I had no idea how to get out of it or into another that would bring about his surrender. But just about then, he made it easy. He said, "What happened with yours?"

It took a few seconds for me to get it. "My old man? It's a long story." I paused, for effect. "With a happy ending."

"You mean he died?"

I laughed. I hadn't expected to, but I was wound up so tight, so focused on getting him and his father out of there alive. Real bullets, real blood. This was not one of my bored Scarsdale housewives who wants to tell me how much she wants to fuck the guy who cleans her swimming pool. And it wasn't me with my old man, because when mine left, he went too far away for me to chase him.

"That's a good one," I said. "I bet you think your dad's an asshole."

"Total. Worse."

"A shithead?"

I could hear him trying not to chortle. We were home free. "I'm writing an article about kids who have fathers like ours. Can I talk to you sometime about your dad?"

"Not now, right?"

"Right."

"Is he going to read it?"

"Not unless he subscribes to *The Journal of the American Psychological Association.* I wouldn't use your real name either."

"Why not? It's going to be on TV."

"It might be, it might not. You're a minor. There are laws about these things."

"Am I going to jail?"

"If you use the gun, you'll probably go somewhere that feels like jail. It might be just for teenage boys, but it won't be fun."

"And if I don't use it?"

"I don't know the legal stuff, but you'll earn the respect of a lot of people. Especially me. Because I have this very deep understanding" — I paused, because I wanted to make sure he heard me — "of how pissed off you are." Another pause. I could hear him listening. "I know what it'll mean to restrain yourself."

"Hmmm." That was the sound of him considering his options. Which weren't many. I let him ponder them, I resisted the urge to say a word. Silence makes people uncomfortable; if you let it, it can act as a mirror or an echo that doesn't end.

A few minutes later, he did everything I asked him to. The police did everything they said they would. And my wife — by the time Jason walked out of the house with his hands on his head, Colleen had found him a good criminal lawyer for all the trouble he was in. It shouldn't have surprised me, but it did: there are lawyers who specialize in juvenile offenders. The guy Colleen found, seventy percent of his clients are kids. I'm scheduled to testify at Jason's upcoming trial. For all I know, I'll want him to testify, as a character reference, at mine.

THAT NIGHT AT our house, I got a hero's welcome from my wife. She had Zachys deliver a bottle of Veuve Cliquot '97 and from somewhere inside the fridge came a slab of fois gras as smooth as butter. She made a toast over the marble kitchen counter, kissed me with her mouth slightly open so I could taste the dry bubbly stuff on the inside of her lips, and said I had performed "brilliantly." The phone rang, the doorbell rang, our children were noisier and needier than usual, absorbing the tumult in the air without understanding its source. We agreed to tell Zoe that a very angry teenage boy had broken a window, which had frightened his parents and people in the neighborhood, and Daddy helped everyone not to be frightened, that's why the phone and the doorbell were ringing so much.

When the *Scarsdale Inquirer* called wanting to interview me, I knew the drill; the police had given me orders once Jason gave up and the press descended on Sandy's house. "You're gratified the episode is over and that's *it*. The kid and his father are both in custody, and you don't say a word in public."

I fed that day on adrenaline, floated on the fumes of my ingenuity. Of course I loved the attention, even though I knew I was gagged. I loved being important enough to be gagged. My sister's regular triumphs, saving the lives of those tiny, tiny babies, this must be her daily diet: painstaking work, grace under pressure, matters of life and death, adulation, honor, power, fame, riches, and the love of women.

The problem was that by the time we got the kids to bed, the fumes had worn off and I was left with two unsettling images that wouldn't go away: Sandy telling me that we were in his house and Jason holding a gun to his father's head. I had saved the day by keeping the son from pulling the trigger on dad, but there was nothing triumphal about Jason's predicament, or Sandy's. First thing in the morning, I would call the lead detective and ask him about getting Jason a shrink while he was in custody. Right now, though — I glanced at our kitchen clock as I sat alone at the table, drinking warm champagne, lonelier than I had felt in some time — it was nine-fifteen. Not too late to call Sandy. Usually I would wait for a client to call me, but what had happened that day was so far out of the ordinary that I felt I had to break some of the rules, to keep him from slinking away from our nascent therapy.

I was relieved when he answered the phone because I realized that his wife might not even know he was seeing me. But he didn't sound perturbed. He said "Hi" in a bright, welcoming way that sounded as though we were friends who hadn't spoken in a long time.

"Is this a good time to talk for a few minutes?"

"Sure. My wife is out, my son's upstairs on-line. He might as well be on Mars. He might be, for all I know."

"How are you doing?"

"I just turned on *Law and Order*, but it was too much like a home movie."

"I can imagine."

He wasn't rushing to open up, and this didn't need to be a long call, unless he wanted to talk. "I don't usually call clients unless they've asked me to, but I wanted to acknowledge what happened today and find out how you were doing, and if you had any feelings about finding me in your house."

"You and the entire Scarsdale police force. I think they're still lurking in the bathrooms."

He wasn't talking, which I knew didn't mean he had nothing to say.

"Sandy, if you want to come in before next week, I'm open to that. My ending up there — along with the entire police force — might have brought up some feelings worth looking at."

"I'm just glad it's over," he said. "I told my wife tonight that I'm seeing you."

"How did that go?"

"She didn't say much. Do you ever do marriage counseling?"

"I've done some. I've worked with couples."

"Maybe the two of us could come in and talk to you. What do you think?"

I thought it was a terrible idea. Sandy needed — desperately — to take care of himself. I could say that with more certainty having seen his study today, which represented, perhaps, an idealized or a former self: sleek, polished, talented. Yet these traits had gotten buried in the rubble of domestic collapse. "I think it's something you and I should talk about next time," I said in that calm, calculating therapist's way. "How does that sit with you?"

"Okay. Yeah, fine."

I'm sure he said "fine." I'm sure I didn't push him or pull him, but I spent some time going over this conversation once the following Tuesday morning rolled around, when, at precisely eight o'clock, I found him in my tiny waiting room with a copy of *Time* on his lap and Ursula Higgenbotham, pouting, in the chair next to him.

❧ 9 ❧

Grounds for Divorce

In an issue of *Consumer Reports* a few years back, I was surprised to find an article — amid the comparisons of refrigerators, humidifiers, diapers, and station wagons — on psychotherapy. It discussed what kinds were available, how customers rated them, and what was the best dollar value. I was amused, though not surprised, to see that people felt the best value for the money was group therapy and the least satisfying category, by a considerable margin, was marriage counseling.

It's not difficult to see why. By the time most people agree to embark on it together, the fissures are deep and wide. Once they begin doing the work, the normal therapeutic hurdles — resistance, denial, lifelong habits, character itself — are multiplied not times two but exponentially. Each client has two parents, which brings the number of competing voices in the room to six, not counting the therapist — and his parents. It's why I prefer working with teenage boys instead of married couples. Teenagers, even the most troubled, give me hope, because I know that with some work and positive modeling, they might turn a corner, and at some point they will outgrow the raging hormones and the restrictions and injustices heaped upon them. But deeply miserable married couples radiate a corrosive despair that saddens me, no doubt because it echoes my parents' marriage. Still, I have seen enough couples over the years to feel comfortable and confident about working with them. But when I laid eyes on Ursula in the waiting room with Sandy, I was speechless.

It was a bumpy session with only a single bright spot at the very end when I asked Sandy if he wanted Ursula to come to our next meeting. Despite the friction, he said yes right away. I asked her if she wanted to join him. "Sure," she said and smiled, and I remember being surprised at the smile and at the "Sure," because nothing in what had transpired earlier would have suggested either. But I chose to read her gestures as a flicker of hope, a "yes" vote for the process and maybe even for the marriage. You can't do what I do without being an optimist, someone who believes that people can change, that every insight is a personal victory, that once you accumulate a few insights, you will want to fill your basket with them and feel the glow of their heavenly, transformative light.

I can still picture Ursula that morning with her big brown Liza Minnelli eyes and her black pixie haircut, also a touch of Liza. I don't usually notice makeup on women, but hers was so prominent I couldn't help it. Her lashes were so thick they might have been pasted on, and eyeliner framed each eye entirely. I imagine she used to be cute; in my office that morning she looked tired and impatient. She wore a small diamond engagement ring next to her plain gold wedding band. It wasn't a Scarsdale stone, it was a chip of a thing, and I remembered that Sandy had told me she complained that they didn't have more money. I wondered about her family: her name put her on the *Mayflower,* but her looks suggested Little Italy.

Once they sat down on the couch — quite a few feet from each other — I turned to Sandy. Ursula's unexpected appearance had left me off balance, and I wasn't sure how to proceed. "How did you happen to invite Ursula to join us today?"

"He said it would be a good idea for Jack," she answered. "Our son."

"Is that why you invited her?" I said, again, to Sandy.

"After what happened last week, our house invaded, the shooting, the cops everywhere, I was shaken up. I told Ursula I was seeing a shrink. I said I was worried about Jack. And worried about us. I hadn't planned to, but last night I asked if she'd come with me this morning. I didn't think she'd say yes."

"Ursula, is that the way you remember the conversation?"

"More or less."

"What would you change?"

"He went on and on about Jack." She spoke in parsimonious snippets, as though she were extremely put out by having to speak at all.

"What about him?"

"Some nonsense about him being depressed. He's ten years old. He's too young to be depressed, so there's no point talking about it."

"I'm not sure I understand why you agreed to come today."

"I don't know what he's been telling you, but there is nothing wrong with Jack. I came to say that Jack is absolutely fine and doesn't need help from anyone, including him." Here she pointed, without looking at him, to Sandy sitting on her right. "Period, end of sentence."

I was seized with a fear that my annoyance with her would show. "So that's why you came," I said lamely. "It's good we got that cleared up. I'm wondering if Sandy said anything else to you that you care to comment on, about his concern for your marriage, for example."

"We've had problems for a while. That's nothing new."

"What do you think the problems with the marriage are?"

"I didn't come here to talk about them. Sandy knows."

"Since you're here, why don't you give it a try and say a few words. Think of it as a safe place to communicate."

By this time, I had little hope that she would cooperate, but I had to keep the ball rolling, and I didn't think I would get far discussing their son.

"It may be safe for Sandy, but it isn't for me."

"Is there anything I can do to make it feel safer for you?"

"No."

I turned to Sandy, who looked sadder and droopier than he had that terrible first morning. He was in a suit, on his way to the office, but he looked wrinkled already, as though it were the end, not the beginning, of the workday. "What do you feel when you hear Ursula say all of this?" It took him awhile. His mustache seemed to fall a bit more, and he looked glumly at his knees. "Sad."

"Anything else?"

"Like it's my fault."

"Maybe it is," she countered.

"I prefer to avoid assigning blame when I work with a couple, and I try to discourage my clients from doing that. It's useful to the process to start with the proposition that each of you brings fifty percent to the relationship. That each of you brings your own unique problems and —"

She interrupted me. "It's not my fault that he's a bully."

"A bully?" I said. I hadn't seen evidence of that. If anyone was a bully —

"Wanting me to come here to talk about Jack's so-called problem was bullying."

"Ursula, for Christ's sake —" Sandy began, until she cut him off.

"That's bullying," she said.

"Contradicting you is bullying?" I asked calmly.

"He does it all the time. Throws his weight around like he's the prince of Wales."

"That's ridiculous," Sandy interrupted. "That's patently —"

"He's doing it again," she said. "I don't think he could stop if he tried."

So it went. She badgered him for bullying her until I changed the subject. When I asked her about her life and her background, her answers were clipped. She'd been the office manager at a vet's in the village but had been laid off several months before. That sounded peculiar to me because people seemed to have more pets than children these days, but I simply asked if she was looking for a new job. She had been, she said, but things were quiet in summer and nothing had turned up. She'd been a dance major at Connecticut College and worked for years as a waitress and exercise instructor, taking dance classes when she could. But the whole professional dance thing never worked out. "You know," she kept saying. "You know how that is."

I was relieved when our time was up, but baffled about how to conclude. And what to propose for the future. So when Sandy said he wanted her to come back, and she smiled and said she would come back, I felt oddly triumphant. I let myself think that by the end of the session she had come around to me, to the process. In our next meeting, I would offer a clean slate and ask Sandy and Ursula to talk about their families of origin.

Simple. Straightforward. But Sandy surprised me again the following Tuesday. He showed up alone. He said nothing as he walked from the waiting room to the office, not even hello. "Will Ursula be joining us?" I asked casually, because I guessed she might be arriving late. When he shook his head and said nothing, I realized his shamed look and silence were those of a man who'd been stood up. I expected he would begin with that issue, so I was taken aback with this opening sentence, delivered before he made contact with the couch: "We haven't slept together for a few years. I guess I told you that. Three, maybe four." His hedging, his imprecision, told me how embarrassed he was by this admission.

"Thank you for telling me. I'm pleased you feel you could. I think it's a sign of self-regard that you're here, that you're taking care of yourself." He had no reaction to that. "At the end of our meeting last week, she said she wanted to come back. What do you think happened?"

"When I mentioned the appointment, she said she had forgotten about it and had scheduled a job interview."

I was reminded again why I hadn't developed a specialty in couples work: it is excruciating to see up so close how much pain married people can inflict on each other. I didn't know what Ursula needed, but to start with, Sandy needed some basic support, an assurance that there was a way out of feeling so bad about himself. He told me at the end of the session that he felt better than he had when he walked in. We made an appointment for a week later.

Those early days of September were warm, busy, and bright, the leaves still fully green, the village sidewalks crowded, the neighborhood abuzz with kids in their new fall clothes and their designer backpacks. Zoe's preschool had begun the previous week. It was an innovative, arts-and-play-oriented program that Colleen and I were excited about. We knew Zoe would have plenty of structure once kindergarten began, so we resisted the Montessori preschool that was so popular in our neighborhood of wildly ambitious parents. Sarah Rose had just begun speaking in full sentences, many of them run-ons. "Sarah wants a kiss Sarah wants a cookie Sarah wants a kitty" was among her favorites. I was preparing a talk with the high school psychologist to give to the faculty and parents, "Coping with Senior Stress in the 21st Century."

Two nights after I had seen Sandy, I had just put Zoe to bed and collapsed on the living room couch with a legal pad, taking notes for my talk, when the phone rang. It was my answering service — I give out that number on my machine in case of emergencies because I don't want clients calling the house directly — with a message for me to call Sandy Lefkowitz as soon as possible. The answering service gave me a phone number and a room number.

When I called, I reached a hotel in White Plains.

"Sandy? Eric Lavender. I just got your message."

When he didn't say anything, I asked if he was all right.

"No."

"What is it?"

"She kicked me out. She served me with papers when I got home from work. She wasn't home. Jack wasn't either. I could barely read them I was so dizzy, but one said I had to get out of the house immediately because she felt threatened by me. By me! If I go back there, they'll arrest me. I don't know how I got over here."

"Jesus Christ. Sandy, I'm —"

"She's accusing me of abandoning her. Where does she get off with that? Was that when I went out to buy groceries the other day? When I —"

"Sandy, you need a lawyer. Do you have a lawyer?"

"I just called my brother, and he's making some phone calls. A guy I work with lives in Larchmont, or lived there until his wife —"

"I'm sure my wife can find you someone. Or maybe she —" No, I thought, we had agreed when I moved here that we wouldn't share clients: too messy, conflicts of interest. "What does it say in those papers? Who's Ursula's lawyer?"

"I put them down and now I — I'm still shaking. I checked in here ten minutes ago and now I'm thinking maybe I should have stayed there, but the papers said I had to go. Here we are. I've heard about guys who refuse to leave, but maybe they didn't get that particular . . . Golden. Colleen O. Golden."

"What?"

"Colleen Golden. Donlon Golden Associates. Scarsdale."

I wish I hadn't been so stunned, because my peculiar silence gave Sandy time to ask the most obvious question — "Do you know her?" — and prevented me from seizing the moment with a deft, distracting word. "Yeah," I said to him clumsily, "yeah," all the tone gone out of my voice, so I didn't exactly give away the truth, but I also was too shaken up to be the sturdy therapist he needed. "I'll talk to her about — what I mean is I'll find out who else — I'll get you —"

"Listen to this. Are you there? 'Causes of Action: Grounds for

Divorce: One, Mental Cruelty. Two, Constructive Abandonment. The defendant' — that's me — 'refused to have sexual intercourse with the plaintiff for a period of four years and two months.' I said no to her?"

"What else does it say? Is this a letter you've gotten or is it —"

"It's legal papers. A process server came to the door, a little weasel. There's a case number. It's called *Higgenbotham versus Lefkowitz*, filed in the Family Court of Westchester County." I heard him rifling papers. "Doc, what the fuck am I supposed to do?"

"You did what you had to do," I said, though I knew that was cold comfort. "You left. You called your brother. You called me." I had no idea what to tell him. The truth was unspeakable, that my wife was prosecuting him, that my wife was in cahoots with his. I couldn't keep it a secret from him forever, though I could for right now. But I was not able to do what I would in any other case: go find Colleen upstairs and ask her for a referral.

"Honey," I heard her call down. "I need to use the phone."

I covered the mouthpiece. "I'll be a few minutes. Use your cell.

"Sandy, can you come by and see me tomorrow morning? Bring the legal papers. If you want, you can park your car in my driveway for the day and take the train to the city from here."

"What time?"

"A few minutes after nine. Can you do that?" Colleen usually left the house at eight-thirty. And if she was around, I wouldn't introduce them.

"Yeah." His voice sounded tinny, still shocked. "Yeah, I think I can."

"In the meantime, talk to people you know about lawyers. I'll see who I can come up with. It's a terrible shock. I know it is. But you'll be okay." I was talking to him as much as to myself, talking us both down from the high pitch of an unexpected betrayal. "Call me again if you need to."

"Thanks," he said, and the phone clicked off as he hung up.

I dropped the portable onto the couch next to me and sat back, feeling pulses all over my body, in places I'd never felt them. My blood pressure must have gone up forty points. I thought Colleen's specialty was deadbeat dads, helping women get their fair share from the selfish SOBs of the world. Where did poor, downtrodden Sandy Lefkowitz fit into that picture?

I had gone overboard just now, offering him help he hadn't asked for and might not know what to do with. Offering to find him a lawyer, which, without Colleen's help, would be a shot in the dark. Offering him my driveway for a parking space. Telling him to call me again. I thought of a wonderful older therapist I'd known years ago in New York, Louise Wallace, who had a sliding scale that went down to $5. Occasionally her clients were in such bad shape — they hadn't eaten in days because they were so worked up — that she put aside her professional training and made them a sandwich. She did what people needed, she didn't have a book of rules and regulations. "What's wrong with taking care of another human being in distress?" she would say. "Do we always have to draw lines and find excuses to say 'No, that's not my job' or 'No, I'm your therapist, not your fill-in-the-blank'?"

Sandy needed a lawyer. And to be absolutely kosher, he needed a new shrink, one who wasn't married to his wife's lawyer. But I wasn't going to concede that point anytime soon. My position, when it came time to spell it out, should be that Ursula needed a new lawyer, because Sandy started seeing me before Ursula hired Colleen.

"I'm off the phone," I called and began to make my way up the stairs. I wasn't sure what I would do up there, but it seemed cowardly to camp out in the living room, cowardly to feel as though I had to just because she had served some papers on a naive, unsuspecting guy who happened to be my patient.

Colleen was on a cell phone in the bedroom, leaning into a mountain of down pillows on her side of the bed. She had a legal pad in her lap and was scribbling notes. Her briefcase was on the bed next to the front section of the *Times*. Her striking briefcase, a yellow gold soft leather with large silver buckles, was another alluring souvenir from Venice. She smiled at me as I entered the room, and I was aware of deciding not to smile back. No matter. Her head dropped and her pen raced across the page. Did she look any different? Her hair was still lovely, and though her breasts had lost most of their nursing fullness, she still had marvelous legs and a cherry red pedicure that had an effect on my groin.

"Okay," she said into the phone. "I'll have Ruth type this up tomorrow and fax it to you. You should have it by noon. Good. You too." When she hung up, she looked at me and blew through her lips. "Phew. I thought that would never end."

"Anything interesting?"

"Fascinating. An addendum to a lease. Clarification for what happens if the tenant's dog craps on the wall-to-wall carpet."

"You're kidding."

"I'm not."

I flopped into the swivel armchair, not taking my eyes off her. She put the legal pad inside her briefcase and took out a sheaf of papers.

"How was your day?" I asked.

"Uneventful. How 'bout yours?"

"The usual. A little depression, a heavy dose of empty nest syndrome, a guy who's afraid he's addicted to Viagra." I wasn't sure whether to say anything about sudden divorce syndrome.

"I don't know how you do it." She was back in her briefcase, looking for something on the bottom of it. "Sit and listen to people's problems all day long. Day after day."

"Isn't that what you do?"

"I listen a little. And strategize a lot. I'd go bonkers if I couldn't tell people what to do." She took out a red pen and a manila file and opened it against her knees, not aware, I think, that I was staring at her, filtering everything she said and did now through another lens. A magnifying glass. A glass darkly.

"I get to give advice now and then," I said, thinking of everything Sandy and I needed to talk about. "It isn't all sitting there like I'm a sack of cement."

"You won't believe what Sarah Rose said to me tonight when I was tucking her in. 'Sarah wants a brother.' Who put that idea in her head?"

"She really said that? I didn't think she knew what a brother was."

"She's a fast learner. Did Zoe say the same thing to you? Maybe they're in cahoots."

That was sweet. That was a funny thought. On another night I would have smiled.

Colleen seemed to be writing a list; I could see her go from line to line, short lines, and she'd nod every now and then as though she remembered what she had to add. Was this all in a day's work, serving some decent guy with papers that kicked him out of his house when his kid wasn't even home to say goodbye to? How many times a week did she do that? Was that the same to her or different from writing an addendum to a lease about dog crap?

She looked up suddenly. "How's your little talk going?"

"My what?"

"The talk you're giving at the high school. I thought you had to finish writing it tonight."

"I think I have a few more nights. Why do you call it 'little'?"

"I didn't say that."

"Yes you did. You said 'How's your little talk going?'"

"I don't remember that." Back to her list, her occasional nods to herself. Flip the pad to a new page. More notes. Dog shit? Custody? A contested will?

"I suppose it's little in that it's the high school, not the Nobel Prize committee."

But she wasn't listening closely. "What about the Nobel Prize?"

"I'm thinking about raising my fees."

She looked up. "Really? How come?"

"What do you charge these days?"

"Two fifty is the basic rate, but we do all kinds of deals with people."

"Like what?"

She raised her head and wrinkled her face at me in a mock frown. "I've told you about all this. Don't you remember?"

"You do something with the Westchester Bar Association, right?"

"A pro bono case now and then. With regular clients, I have a sliding scale if I decide I want it to slide. A woman came to see me wanting a divorce. She said her mother's dying and she's going to inherit a lot of money. I'm willing to work something out in a case like that. I won't take all the risk, but I'll entertain proposals that most lawyers won't. How high are you thinking of going?"

"Five or ten dollars more. What do you think?" I was thinking of no such thing, I just wanted to talk to her about money and business and whatever else came up. I couldn't not talk to her to-night, I couldn't just sit there and watch her scribble when I had learned something so startling about her. Could it be Ursula's mother who was dying? No. Sandy would have mentioned it. Ursula would have too. That was too big to forget about. It was another woman in town who wanted a divorce. No shortage of women who wanted to leave their husbands.

"Why not raise your rates," Colleen said, "if the market can bear it?"

"What's the risk to you if the client's going to inherit a lot of money?"

Colleen's eyes rose before the rest of her face. I was interrupting her. I was bothering her. "If she changes lawyers before she gets her inheritance, I may not get paid. Settling the estate could take years. But CD lawyers accept liens on clients' houses all the time."

"CD?"

"Criminal defense. If you need a criminal lawyer and you have no cash, you're willing to give up everything if he can get you off, including your house."

"Would you accept payment that way?"

"You can't in a divorce because the house is usually marital property. One party can't sign it away."

She knows what she's talking about, I said to myself. She knows the laws and customs, the ins and outs. There must have been a critical bit of information that Sandy hadn't told me. That's what I said to myself as I got up and asked Colleen if I could get her anything from downstairs.

"I'm fine, hon," she said and buried herself back in her briefcase.

Most of the lights were off downstairs, except for the kitchen. Graciela's room was off the breakfast nook, and I could hear the faint sounds of a TV in there. I pressed the rheostat in the dining room and went toward the built-in bar. Colleen said it came with the house, the shelving and drawers and glass cabinet doors, but she was the one who decided to stock it with hard liquor even though we rarely drink it. We prefer wine and we don't do much entertaining. I suppose she thought she had to have it; no house in Scarsdale should be without one. A few dozen crystal glasses, a shot glass, a martini jigger, swizzle sticks. Welcome to the Copacabana. I poured myself a glass of Scotch straight up and remembered the first time I'd had a taste of it, in college. Hadn't liked it then. Something harsh and medicinal. It burned going down. I didn't like it tonight either, but it numbed me fast, like a shot of Novocain. I took another swig and felt the numbness spread. It was a good feeling. It gave me the courage to go back upstairs and stare at Colleen some more. I had this idea suddenly that if I looked hard enough,

I'd see whatever it was I hadn't seen before. I'd locate the piece of her I had missed.

That's not how it worked out. By the time I got upstairs, our bathroom door was closed and the tub was filling. That meant she would be in there for half an hour, soaking in scented water, and emerge sweet-smelling and provocative, as she often did after a bath. But that night, I had no intention of waiting up for her.

10

Sandy Lefkowitz
Is Having a Bad Day

By the time Sandy got to my office the following morning, he had already met with a lawyer in White Plains who needed a $5,000 retainer before he would do any work. Sandy said this as he thrust a batch of legal papers at me and then sat down on the couch as I positioned myself in my leather chair in my role as *ad hoc* legal adviser, a role for which I had no training and no appetite. Any minute I would give it up and give him back the papers.

I went through the five or six pages quickly, trying to pick up the most salient facts, not sure what to look for. There was a court date at the end of next week concerning the divorce complaint and another court date for the order of protection, which forbade him from setting foot on his own property. Ursula feared for her safety and her kid's. There was a statement that she did not have income or assets to pay their bills. On the last page was my wife's signature and the date: just like that, cold, impersonal, implacable. I wanted to ask what her name was doing there, at the bottom of these bizarre accusations and assertions. We had come back early from the Cape so she could get ready for a trial. She must have been preparing these papers in the days before Labor Day, when Sandy had first come to see me.

I raised my head expecting to ask him how he was doing, but I didn't need to say anything. He was sleeping. Sitting up with his eyes shut, his head cocked to one side. I thought of Louise Wallace making sandwiches for hungry clients. Was that next for me?

"Sandy."

He didn't move.

"Sandy? Are you sleeping or just relaxing?"

A moment later, his eyes squinted open and he apologized. "I didn't sleep last night. I had the TV on, the light on. Maybe I slept for an hour."

"Have you decided to go with this lawyer?"

"I don't know yet. I need to borrow money for the retainer. I should probably talk to someone else, get a second opinion. I don't know how these things work."

Truth be told, I didn't either, and the one person I could ask was off-limits.

"I don't know where she's getting the money to hire a lawyer," he said.

"Does she have a savings bank? A personal account?"

"No. A few years ago, an aunt of hers died and left her thirty thousand dollars. But she invested in some dot-com stocks when they were a hundred and fifty a share and lost most of it."

"Are her parents still alive?"

"Her mother is."

I was afraid to ask the next question. "Is she well?"

"As far as I know. We went up to Greenwich a few times in August and hung out at her pool. She seemed fine. Maybe her mother's giving her the money. She's got plenty."

His eyes twitched. It was work to keep them open, I could see that. My next patient was coming at ten-thirty. I had an idea.

"Sandy, lie down and sleep for an hour. I've got to do an errand. Take one of those pillows. Take your shoes off."

He didn't object, didn't resist; he surrendered to gravity as though we were old friends or siblings. As though he were over-come with jet lag or felled by flu. More lessons from Louise.

I RARELY had occasion to go to her office in the village, a seven-minute walk from our house. The building is an art deco complex from the 1930s, austere in a pleasing way. You are paying for loca-tion when you hire a lawyer or accountant in this building, not for frills, not for Mark Rothko in the lobby or state-of-the-art eleva-tors. The doors to each office are the quaint wood-and-glass design you recognize from old black-and-white movies, the name of the firm or the individual painted painstakingly on the milky glass in letters that will be razored off and replaced with a new name by the end of the movie.

"Eric, hi, how are you?" Ruth, Colleen's secretary, was hovering over a computer keyboard and monitor. "Long time, no see."

"Is she in?"

Ruth nodded. "She just got on the phone, for a change. How's the baby?"

"Not such a baby anymore."

"They have a way of doing that, don't they?"

Colleen, who could see me through her open door, waved me in and motioned to the chair on the other side of her desk. Her office was small, simple, and elegant, with a large window behind her desk overlooking the train station. She was writing something on a Post-it note and speaking into the phone. "I'm not available for the next — oh, let's see — three weeks. No, four. Sorry, make that six. I have back-to-back trials, then a two-week break, where I have de-positions almost every day. It's a hell of a schedule. Of course I un-derstand what the issue is. . . . What? Thirty thousand? . . . I'm not sure my accountant would come up with the same number, but it's irrelevant because I don't have the time to meet with you to discuss it until November. Can't get blood from a stone, Mr. Goodman. I'm looking at the clock and I'm already late for a meeting. Sorry about the schedule. I'll have my secretary call you if something opens up." She replaced the phone in its cradle and looked up at me. "Hi, hon, what can I do for you?"

"You have trials every day for the next six weeks? Did you forget to tell me?"

"No, sweetie. Not at all. That's just lawyer talk. My only upcoming trial is the week after next for two days."

"Lawyer talk for what?"

"I'm not ready to negotiate yet. That's all it means. Goodman's a lawyer. He knows. What's up? Is everything all right?"

I got up and closed the door. A scene from dinner at Pru's apartment came flooding back to me. Bea's daughter Jenny thought her husband might be fooling around on her. Bea was upset and Colleen offered Jenny a free legal consultation. How long ago was that?

When I turned, I could see Colleen thought something had happened to the children; her cheeks reddened, her eyes grew. I let her fear that possibility for a few more seconds than necessary. "Can you explain to me what's going on with Sandy Lefkowitz?"

"What?"

"I don't understand what you're doing to him."

"How do you know him?"

"None of your business."

"Did you get off on the right floor? Who do you think you're talking to that way?"

"I want to know what you're doing to him."

"I want to know what you're doing to *me,* barging in here like this. Are you going to tell me what this is about or should I guess?"

"Take a guess."

"For Christ's sake, Eric, I don't have time for this. I'm on my way to a meeting, so make it quick."

I had heard this bitchy tone before, and those bitchy flourishes — "so make it quick" — and they always sent a shiver through me.

They always made me wonder if one day I would get the full bitchy treatment and buck my way out the door.

"He's my patient."

"Why didn't you say so?"

"You served him papers last night when he got home from work. You kicked him out of his house without consulting him. Without letting him say goodbye to his son."

"Acting on behalf of his wife. Sweetheart, let me give you some free legal advice, and we can talk about this later. You have a conflict of interest in your relationship with him. He'll have to get a new therapist."

"Or she'll need a new lawyer. He came to me before she came to you."

"Really?" She looked down at her datebook open on her desk, the size of a large paperback book, and started flipping pages into the past. "Consultation. Ursula Higgenbotham. June twelfth. Ten A.M."

"Let me see." I took steps toward the calendar on the corner of the desk. Three months ago? Was that possible?

"You don't trust me?"

"I'd like to see it."

"You think I would invent an appointment?"

"Then it shouldn't be a problem to let me see it."

"The problem is trust. And if you're saying you don't trust me —"

I reached for the datebook and before I fully extended my hand, she grabbed the book and slammed it shut. "There," she said and dropped it on the other side of her desk.

I gaped at her for a long moment, and she gaped back, which was more frightening to me than if she had looked away. She was not going to back down. And now I wasn't going to either. "Open the book," I said.

"What has gotten into you? My God, is this the same man I

woke up with this morning? I really do think you're overreacting, sweetie. There are dozens of shrinks in Scarsdale. It shouldn't be hard for him to find someone else. Should it?" Her tone was supercilious, verging on sarcastic. We had fought before, but one of us had always relented, pulled back, stepped forward and made up with a joke or a kiss. This fight felt different. Was it because I wouldn't back down? Had *I* always been the one to give in? Not always. But this, now, was something else.

"If you want me to trust you, open the book." Yet I knew that trust would not be restored even if she did. And if she was telling the truth about the date, I would lose Sandy on the merits.

"I have a meeting to go to." She turned and reached toward the windowsill behind her desk for her briefcase. Her tone was neutral, maybe it was veering toward conciliatory.

"It'll take you half a second, Colleen."

"Here." She picked up the datebook, extended her arm, and flicked her wrist, sending it across the room as though it were a Frisbee. Pieces of paper and business cards fell out of it and cascaded to the floor like autumn leaves as the calendar hit the far wall and landed in a thud on the floor.

"Is this what you do now instead of speaking? Throw things? You and your four-year-old daughter?"

"Not quite. I've got plenty to say. Starting with this conflict of interest, which happens to be *your* problem."

"I will not give up my patient under these circumstances."

"Honey, give him up. He could sue you like this." She snapped her fingers and started for the door. "I'm late."

I took two steps and blocked her path. "You can't leave. We need to resolve this."

"Eric, I'm not Doctors Without goddamn Borders. I'm an attorney. Maybe there's some countertransference — is that what you call it? — and you can't differentiate this guy from yourself. Have you thought of that?"

"He's coming apart."

"It's been twelve hours, fourteen hours. He had a bad night. He's having a bad day. I've had a few myself."

"He didn't know she wanted a divorce."

"Now he knows."

"He's been kicked out of his house, couldn't say anything to his son. He's the one who takes care of the boy."

"Maybe he fixes him chocolate milk, but do you think he's going to quit his job and stay home with the kid — a big-shot architect?"

"A big shot? A bad day? You've accused him of mental cruelty, abandoning his wife, and —"

"His wife accused him."

"None of it's true and you know it. *I* know it."

"He can bring his version just like she can bring hers."

"He can't afford a lawyer. He's got nowhere to live."

"Sweetheart, ninety-five percent of my clients have bad days every day of their lives because their husbands ran off with the baby-sitter or the secretary or the cute young thing who just graduated from law school and left them with nothing but dirty diapers and taxes to pay and no health insurance. The women stay home and raise the kids and in ten years they're qualified to work at Dunkin' Donuts. Case in point, your mother. I'm awfully sorry Sandy Lefkowitz is having a bad day." She grabbed her briefcase by the handle, walked across the room to the far wall, picked up her datebook, and started again for the door.

"So you work on a payback strategy, is that it?" I said, finally putting all the pieces together.

"What?"

"What you're doing to Sandy is payback for all the wronged women of this world. Isn't it?"

"Oh, please. You're blocking the door. Are you going to move or —"

"By the way, who's paying her bills?"

"I don't ask. Do you ask who pays your clients' bills? You know, we shouldn't fight over this, honey. We were exactly right when we agreed not to share clients. Let's not quarrel anymore. Let's just write this off as a learning experience. And let's try to have a peaceful Friday-night dinner with the kids and a nice weekend. Graciela's got the night off." I stepped aside and let her open the door to her office. "I'll be home by six." I could see her secretary leaning over a file cabinet. How much had she heard? "Kiss, kiss, darling." The words were accompanied by two little air smacks and a fake smile that froze all the parts of me that were not already numb.

SANDY'S CAR was gone from my driveway and my office was empty. In his place on the couch was a note: "Couldn't sleep. Friend found me lawyer in Yonkers. Loan from brother came through. Thanks. Will call."

THAT WAS IT? That was all he was going to say?

My relief at his being gone imploded into a sudden fury — fury at having been swept up into the chaos of his life and the chaos of his life having erupted, without warning, into mine. How does he walk away and leave me with this mess? I looked at the clock: 10:21 A.M. What happens now? Kiss, kiss? I crushed Sandy's note and tossed it into the chic wire wastebasket that went with the chic beech-wood desk in my chic shrink backyard lair. No good deed goes unpunished. I was livid. I stood at my desk, picked up the phone, and called my sister's office. There was a one-in-a-hundred chance she would be able to take my call. I was put on hold. I held and held. Hung up before I left a message. I called an old friend from graduate school, Amanda, the one who had once told me to go back into therapy because she didn't like my taste in women. She would be honest with me and know the right answer. I would know it myself, if I weren't so goddamn angry. And shaken. If I had to give up Sandy, it was not going to be because Colleen told me to.

"Dr. Ritter speaking."

"Amanda, it's Eric."

"Lavender? I don't believe it. Hey, stranger. Still in Scarsdale?"

"Yup."

"How's everything?"

"Fine. Well, no. Not fine. You still teach that seminar in ethics for shrinks?"

"Wouldn't give it up for anything. What's going on?"

"A conflict of interest. I need some advice."

"I hope you're not sleeping with a patient."

"Oh no. That would be much too simple."

SIMPLE THIS was not going to be, for any of us.

Once she heard the story, Amanda zeroed in on a few problems. She said I had violated doctor-patient privilege by telling Colleen that Sandy was my client. I knew that already, sort of. In hindsight. Sandy's double-whammy phone call with the news he had been banished from his house and the news that Colleen was the legal eagle behind his ouster had impaired my professional judgment. I couldn't argue with that.

Next, she seconded Colleen's advice: I had to sever my ties with Sandy, regardless of what he wanted. If I didn't, I'd be a candidate for a lawsuit. Sandy might claim that treatment was compromised, that I was more interested in helping my wife's lawsuit against him than in helping him. He might claim that I violated his trust by giving her information about him, whether I did or not. The fact was, I already had.

Amanda's next opinion would eventually be a nasty surprise to Colleen. Amanda said that Sandy's lawyer would have to get Colleen to give up Ursula's case, given what had already gone on. If she wouldn't give up the case voluntarily, Sandy's lawyer would have to file a motion to force her. "It's a conflict of interest for all of you at this point, even if you give up Sandy," Amanda said, "especially after the fight you just had with Colleen. She knows Sandy's been seeing a therapist, which she could try to use against him."

Once Amanda explained all of this to me, I knew that whatever kissing and making up my wife and I might do would only define the interim between today's temper tantrum and her next one. When was the last blowup? A few weeks ago. When a delivery guy came with her dry cleaning, she had a fit because it was a day late. At least she isn't yelling at me or the kids, I remember thinking. At least it happens only once a month.

"What are you going to do later with Colleen?" Amanda asked.

"No clue."

"Buy her some flowers. Write a sweet note on them."

"Jesus H."

"You fucked up, my friend. She's got that over you. And she's right about the conflict of interest. You need to calm these waters before they get stirred up again. And you have to meet with Sandy soon too."

"I thought therapists aren't supposed to give advice."

"This is not advice, Eric. These are direct orders from your commanding officer. And don't get the chintzy ones from the supermarket that were wrapped in cellophane two weeks ago."

When my next patient, Susan Reed, arrived and took her seat, I suddenly remembered something else Colleen had said in her office that I hadn't heard before. *Ninety-five percent of my clients have bad days every day of their lives because their husbands ran off with the baby-sitter.* That meant that most of her cases were divorces. But she had always told me divorce was only a fraction of what she did. Was the ninety-five percent a hotheaded exaggeration or was there another wrinkle in this fabric I had never noticed until now?

❦ 11 ❦

I Feel a Migraine Coming On

IT WAS NOT until I put the box of long-stemmed roses on the kitchen table, uncertain whether to leave them there or put them in a vase, that I considered my choice of flower. By any other name, they would smell as sweet — and prick as sharply. My dear prickly Colleen. Oh, Lord. I left them in the box and looked again at the notecard in the miniature envelope. Did that contain some hidden hostility too?

> Dearest Darling —
> To err is human, to forgive is divine, and I know you
> are. Let's keep talking. — E.

No hostility, certainly, but not a declaration of contrition or undying affection either. Had we ever had a fight this serious, Colleen and I? I couldn't think of one.

I WAS upstairs doing a puzzle with the girls when we heard her come in a little after six that night. "Guess who just came home?" I whispered. I wanted them to run downstairs and greet her so that I didn't have to be alone with her yet. I was angry at myself, angry at her, and not certain how to repair the damage that had been done.

I needn't have worried. By the time I got downstairs, she had put the roses in a vase, cleaned the box off the table, and put in its place another box, gift-wrapped, this one with a miniature card that had my name on it. I came close to asking if she had gotten advice from my friend Amanda too. It was obviously liquor.

"Daddy, is it your birthday?" Zoe asked.

"No, sweetheart."

"I just got Daddy a present because I love him," Colleen said.

Our eyes met across the kitchen and I held her gaze, the beautiful green eyes, the embarrassed smile, our daughter at her feet, clinging to her shapely stockinged leg. "Sarah wants a cookie," Sarah Rose said. "Wants a cookie now."

"Not before dinner," Zoe said.

"Now!"

"It's not allowed!" Zoe cried.

"Who wants to finish our puzzle?" I asked.

"I want a cookie," Sarah Rose reminded us.

"If she gets one, I get one," Zoe said.

"Zoe, darling, bring the puzzle downstairs."

"Aren't you going to open your present?" Colleen asked. She took an apron from a hook near the door and covered her lawyerly black skirt.

"Does this mean you're cooking?" I opened the envelope first.

"I stopped at the market and bought shrimp to make you scampi. The answer is yes."

As she said that, I read the message she'd scrawled on the tiny blank card.

Do you have any plans for later?
XOXO, C.

I held out my arms and she came toward me. "I think I'm free," I murmured into her hair. Scampi was my favorite dish, and the card was sexy and sweet. "Did you read mine?"

I could feel her nod against my chest. "Thank you."

"Sarah Rose wants a cookie," we heard.

"Does she?" Colleen said joyfully, disengaging herself from my embrace. "We'll just have to see what we can do about that."

"Mommy, here's the puzzle," Zoe said, appearing at the table. "We couldn't find his tail."

"What have you got there? The Lion King!"

While Zoe pointed out the most difficult corner of the puzzle, I opened the gift box. A snazzy box, a bottle of dry sherry. A good idea that didn't often cross my palate, but who doesn't like a glass of sherry now and then? The air was still charged with the static from our fight, but I was touched by the gift and felt myself drawn back into the orbit of her affections. I tore off the plastic sealed around the cork and saw Sarah Rose try to hoist herself onto my lap. Zoe stood on a chair and climbed, as though she were a monkey and I were a tree, onto my back, throwing her arms around my neck. Colleen took the bottle from me, poured out a glass, and put it in my hand. Zoe squealed with delight, and Sarah Rose cried, "Pick up Sarah Rose, pick up Sarah Rose!" And Colleen began cooking. First you have conflict. Then you have resolution. Isn't this what I teach my patients? Can't it apply to me as well? Could I push everything that had happened in the last twenty-four hours with Sandy Lefkowitz out of my mind? Could I forget Colleen's indelicacies — and my own — at least until tomorrow? All I had to do was pay attention to the pulsing, thriving life in my midst, let myself be fully in the present, which was as much my authentic life as what had happened that morning in Colleen's office.

HALF AN HOUR later, this was the picture in our happy home, our happy kitchen: Colleen at the stove cooking our scampi, the girls at the table eating the plain chicken and roasted potatoes I had warmed up for them, and me singing a butchered version of "Yellow Submarine" while nursing a second glass of sherry and helping Sarah Rose keep track of the chicken still on her plate. "And we live a life of ease, eating turnips and mashed peas, in our yellow submarine, ah hah." When the song ends, I engage Zoe in a discussion of which children in her new nursery school she likes and which she doesn't. So far, she likes them all, except the boy who pulled her hair on the class trip to the petting zoo yesterday in Hartsdale. I am about to explain to her that his hair-pulling probably means that he likes her, but introducing a specific lesson in deceptive behavior, behavior that suggests one emotion but actually means its opposite, seems the wrong message to promote tonight.

Colleen turns from the stove and meets my eye across the kitchen. Her look is severe, rattled. Is she angry at what I'm saying, what I'm singing? "Sweetheart, I feel a migraine coming on. My vision is a little blurry around the edges. Would you be a dear and look for my pills? I don't want to leave the shrimp cooking while I —"

"Of course, sweets. It's been awhile since your last one. Six months? Eight months?"

"Just get me the pills, please. Try the top shelf of the linen closet, way in back. I think that's where I put them after last time. It's a prescription. The label says something about migraines."

"Sure."

As I walked up the stairs, I realized that if she did have a migraine we wouldn't have our date that night. And we wouldn't rehash our morning fight. We had a Friday-night routine, different from the usual Parents with Children scenario: we'd collapse into each other's exhausted arms and come what may. "The hell," she sometimes said on those nights, "with foreplay." At the top of the stairs, I heard a child begin to shriek the word "No!" and I knew it was Zoe. Her lungs were stronger, her will more ferocious, than Sarah Rose's. After a brief aria, the single operatic syllable was transformed into a staccato, a hail of gunfire, shooting out "no" and only "no." I started to turn around so I could help out but caught myself. Get the pills. The pills will help.

The linen closet is in the central hallway on the second floor.

The shelves are long and deep, and everything is meticulously organized and labeled except for the messy top shelf of bottles, jars, and tubes. Colleen and Graciela always seemed to know what was up there and what was necessary for what sort of pain. Where were the prescription drugs? I got a step stool from the girls' bathroom so I could reach into the back, where I saw a basket of ten or twelve little orange bottles. I made a path and pulled it to me. Painkillers for dental surgery. An empty ampicillin. Take one at meals for fourteen days. Take one at bedtime as needed. Nothing about migraines. "Take 3 tablets a day on days 5–9 of cycle to induce ovulation." Clomiphene. What was this? Colleen's name on the prescription. Date: January 20, 2000. Sarah Rose was born in November of that year. I counted on my fingers, backward from November. Minus nine months puts us at March. Colleen and I met on December 30, 1999. She told me she was pregnant on . . . when was that? Late March? Early April? The prescription was for forty-five pills. There were — I dumped them into my hand and counted — fifteen left. Fifteen pills per cycle. She took them for two cycles. February. March. Pregnant by the end of March.

"Sweetie," Colleen called from downstairs, during a lull in Zoe's shrieking, "did you find them? I'm going bonkers down here."

And I was starting, in my quieter way, to go bonkers up there: She had told me she was using a diaphragm. Told me the pregnancy was an accident. Sarah Rose was an accident. But she wasn't. A brutal exchange we had had about family planning flashed through my memory. What had I said? "Where I come from we call that family planning." Then she'd trotted out her two brothers who had died as teenagers and said she wanted two kids of her own to replace them. And I had been so damn moved by her confession! Sarah Rose was no diaphragm baby, she was a clomiphene baby. Could that be right? Were those the dates? Or was she taking the pills now?

The next bottle I picked up had the word *migraine* typed on the label. Why hadn't I found this first? I did not think of my daughter in those first, fluttering moments. I did not think, as I did later: I love her regardless. No, this is what I thought: I must go downstairs and pretend I don't know this. I talked Jason Cummings down from shooting his father. All I have to do now is give her these pills. With a migraine coming on, she's a mess anyway. She won't notice what shape I'm in.

I put everything else back and returned like a good boy to the kitchen, where Zoe now sat quietly at the table with a dish of chocolate ice cream, Sarah Rose sucked on a yogurt pop, and Colleen stood slumped against the kitchen counter with her eyes closed, her face drained of color. "I burned the scampi," she said. "I'm sorry, I couldn't handle everything." She was massaging her forehead with her fingers. "The butter burned."

What a relief that she was in such a weakened state: I couldn't rage at her and couldn't imagine her doing something as duplicitous as what it looked as if she had done. "Don't worry about it. How many of these do you take?"

"I don't remember."

I studied the label and drew her a glass of water.

"Mommy's not feeling well," I said to the girls and fed Colleen what she needed.

"Mommy, do you have a temperature?" Zoe asked.

She took a few steps to the kitchen table and plopped down in a chair, her head in her hands. "No."

"An earache?"

"No, sweetie."

"Do you want some of my ice cream?"

She shook her head, eyes still shut, shoulders drooping. If I wanted to make a joke, I'd say, She looked like I felt.

"Colleen, why don't you go upstairs and lie down. I'll take care of this."

"Daddy can carry you," Zoe said, "carry you like Wendy." Zoe loved to invoke this reference to Peter Pan carrying Wendy, and now it made Colleen laugh a little. "I think I can make it on my own," she said and hoisted herself up. As she made her way haltingly across the room and out the kitchen door, I realized three things, one sadder than the next. The first was that if Colleen had gotten this headache yesterday, anytime before the phone call from Sandy last night, I would be giving her my arm and walking her upstairs. The second was that maybe she was faking this entire episode because she could not face me either, given what had gone on between us this morning. The third was that if the migraine was real it had come on because she had no way to process conflict other than try to bury it.

"Can we watch a movie?" Zoe asked. "Can we watch *One Hundred and Two Dalmatians*?"

Sarah Rose's yogurt pop was melting faster than she could eat it, but she was determined to try to keep up. I kept my eye on it, in case it fell.

"When I was a kid," I said, "there was only *One Hundred and One Dalmatians*."

"Did they have a baby?" Zoe asked.

"I think the dogs had a puppy."

"Can we get a puppy?"

"When you get a little older." How many times had I uttered that phrase to her? Two hundred? Five hundred? Suddenly the future was a landscape with a tornado in the distance, a vista that cautioned me to shudder and recoil.

"Why not now?"

"You have to be big and strong to walk them and train them. You have to be at least eight or nine."

"When will I be eight?"

"You know the answer to that. What's eight minus four?"

At that moment, Sarah Rose's yogurt pop fell to the floor and she began to whimper. I reached down to grab it and caught sight of Colleen's yellow briefcase slouching against the wall by the table. For the first time in our marriage, I wondered what was inside it. For the first time, I decided I would look.

"Four," Zoe said. "In four years I'm eight."

I sat Sarah Rose in my lap and fed her some of the salvaged pieces of pop that had not touched the floor, which allayed her cries instantly. I looked at the clock on the microwave. It was only 7:07. It felt like 9:30, which, for anyone with small children, feels like one in the morning. Time to call it a night. "I've got an idea," I said. "*The Wind in the Willows.*" This brought forth a squeal of delight from Zoe and an abrupt sprint to the TV room; Sarah Rose slithered from my lap to follow her sister out the door and down the hall to this room that saved our lives. Colleen and I sometimes referred to it as the ER. I hated to park them in front of anything electronic, but the DVD I inserted into the player that night is a beautiful animated version of the book, with a cast of brilliant English actors doing the voices. The girls were instantly riveted. I was home free for twenty minutes, half an hour.

Like a thief in my own house, I knelt by Colleen's briefcase on the kitchen floor, not physically moving it from where she had left it when she got home. The chances of finding anything significant were slender; it was Friday night, and if she needed to work over the weekend, she would walk down to her office for an hour or two. And after our fight that morning, she would likely keep all evidence of the case away from our house. Or so I thought, so I imagined. I didn't know her very well at all, did I?

Maybe I didn't know myself, either, because as I knelt and tried to flip through her files and papers, all still in the briefcase, I made a vow to myself that surprised me: I vowed to tell anything I thought would be useful to Sandy Lefkowitz. Useful in his divorce. I wasn't going to lift pieces of paper, just find a cryptic way to pass along information he wouldn't be able to get any other way. I didn't need a lawyer to tell me I was on shaky ground. Oh Jesus, there it was. HIGGENBOTHAM VS. LEFKOWITZ, typed on the flap of the file. A bunch of photocopies, the legal filings Sandy had shown me that morning. Something that looked like a questionnaire, filled out in pen. Wife's name, address, employer, education, bank accounts. The handwriting was hard to read at the angle I was at, crouching, peering into the slots of the case. It was little, tight script in purple ink. Odd choice. Teenage girl ink. Behind it were several sheets from a yellow legal pad with Colleen's large signature scrawl, her usual blue Bic:

> inher. CT vs NY
> Mom <6 mos.
> $90K vs 0
> MH $750K
> JCK: $260

I memorized it without knowing what all of it meant. "Inheritance" was easy. In light of that, "Mom" was probably Ursula's mom, who had less than six months to live, which Sandy did not know. Who or what was MH? JCK? An instant later, the front door made noises that it was being opened and I straightened up. I had no papers or files to put back. But standing up suddenly made me dizzy. I clutched the side of the kitchen table and closed my eyes for a moment.

"Mr. Lavender?" It was Graciela. "Are you all right?" She called Colleen by her first name but had so far resisted my invitations to call me by mine.

"Fine, Graciela, thank you. How are you tonight? You're home early."

"A little early. My friend couldn't eat with me because her family had a party and she had to work for them" — her family meaning her employer — "so I ate alone. Not much to do, but I'm okay. They like that movie." She had a soft voice and a slight but undefinable accent. She had learned English in school in the Philippines and had a remarkably agile sense of the language.

"They do. How are your children?"

They live in a small town with her sister outside Manila, a boy and a girl, twelve and fourteen years old. She sees them for three weeks a year, in the vacation time we give her, paying for the trip and her salary while she's gone. Colleen had always insisted that the arrangement was fine with Graciela and had thwarted my efforts to offer her several more weeks a year. That night I felt particularly self-conscious about Graciela's sacrifice: she takes care of my children so that her sister can take care of hers.

"They're so big," she said, beaming, as though she had seen them recently. "And they fight *all* the time!" As though she is there to watch them. Then she asked, "Is Colleen working late tonight?"

"She got one of her migraines and went upstairs a little while ago."

"Should I put the children to bed?"

It was such a tempting offer, but I resisted. "Not on your night off."

"I'll clean the table."

"Thanks. Since you're here, would you watch the children for a minute? I left something in my car."

But I hadn't. I went out to our garage to call my sister on my cell phone, to be sure no one could hear me, no one could listen in. I sat in my dark car, in the dark garage, with the eerie blue light of my cell phone keypad the only light there was, except for a bright red dot above the garage door, the sensors for the remote control gizmo, that I could see in the rearview mirror.

I was prepared to leave a message, but Prudence was home.

"Do me a favor. Call here tomorrow morning and say that Mom isn't doing well and you need me to come to the city to see her."

"You can't come see her on your own?"

"Of course I can, but it would make it easier if you summoned me."

"You want me to make up a serious illness for her? You want me to put her on her deathbed? Eric, I'm superstitious about Mom, I know it's crazy —"

"It's important. I need to talk to you."

"Is everything all right?"

"It's complicated."

"Are you having an affair?"

"You're the second person today who's asked me that. Is that the only problem people have?"

"No, but —"

"That's the only problem you think *I* would have? I wish I were."

"You're not sick, are you?"

"No, nothing like that. We're all healthy."

"You better not be lying to me. What time should I call you?"

WHEN I GOT off the phone with her, I decided to call Sandy at his hotel, not to tell him what I had read in the file, but to set up an appointment for Monday, because he still didn't know who Colleen was to me, and he didn't know what that would mean for the two of us. But as I dialed information to get the number, the door from the garage to the house creaked open and light flooded the cramped space.

"Mr. Lavender, the baby's crying for you." Graciela looked surprised to find me where I was, in the passenger seat of my car, holding a cell phone.

She must have come to the same conclusion that Amanda and Pru had: that I was having an affair. I looked as guilty as hell. What else would a married man be doing in this position, at this hour, in the goddamn dark? Is there a psychic phenomenon where so many people believe you are guilty of something you haven't done that you begin to believe you did something heinous? Of course there is. There has to be. I'm afflicted with it.

Now that I'm locked up, I've got it worse. I've got it bad. You see, I'm not guilty of anything that people suspect me of, anything I've been accused of. I'm not having an affair and I didn't lay an inappropriate hand on my stepdaughter, ever. But in the days and weeks that followed that night, I was not myself. I was desperate to find out who my wife was — desperate, except for the hours and days I preferred to be in denial — and did quite a few things that stretched my idea of who *I* was. Stretched it almost beyond recognition.

✒ 12 ✒

Confusion Takes Hold

THE NEXT MORNING, Colleen picked up the ringing phone as she made a pot of coffee and argued with Zoe about having chocolate waffles for breakfast. She had told me her migraine had run its course and she had woken up feeling fine, wanting to have a low-key Saturday. My own head ached with a throbbing intensity around the temples, pressing on what felt like the back of my eyes. Life had returned, so to speak, to normal. "Hi, Pru," I heard Colleen say, and, seconds later as she handed me the phone, "Your mother fell."

"Pru, is she all right?"

I asked a few questions, feigned worry, let my brow furrow in concern. "Can it wait till tomorrow?" I asked. "Or do you think I should come right in?"

"Park in the garage in our building," Pru said, "and come upstairs. Bea and I will feed you breakfast and find out what's going on. Then we'll go see Mom."

"Let me ask Colleen if this works for her."

"Anything's fine," she said, "as long as you're back by three. Zoe's going to the twins' birthday party down the street, and I need to go to the hairdresser."

THAT MORNING I did not land where I often do when I see my sister: feeling second-rate in the presence of her first-rate self. I was just relieved to be welcomed and ushered into her apartment, which was the same vintage as my own New York apartment ten blocks north but better decorated, higher up, and sunnier. Pru and Bea led me into their dining room, whose glass-topped table was covered with brunch food for twenty people.

"Who are you expecting?" I said. "The New York Psychoanalytic Society?"

"The Hemlock Society," Bea joked. "Have a seat. Have a bagel. Have some cream cheese. The pink is caviar, the orange is lox, and I'm not sure about the green. Then move to the quiche and the prosciutto." Bea comes by her profession as a graphics editor naturally. The table could have come from a page of her magazine.

"You didn't have to do all this. I don't know where to start."

"People need to eat at wakes and funerals," Bea said. "This is comfort food. Prosciutto the way your mother used to make it."

"So," Pru said, "what the hell's going on?"

I started with the story of Sandy Lefkowitz — an abbreviated version and the pseudonym Mr. L. because I was not permitted to discuss my patients — and went straight through to my discovering the clomiphene the night before. I wrapped up by describing how I had crawled into our bed after putting the kids to sleep and lain on my back, close to the edge on my side, as stiff as a corpse.

As I talked, Pru listened with rapt attention and indulged a nervous habit from childhood that she does only in front of Bea and me: picked at the doughy part of an untoasted bagel and made little pellets that she piled on the side of her plate and did not eat. She claims it helps her listen. She's a serious listener, which makes her advice, when she gives it, all the more thoughtful. It's probably the reason I don't ask for it more often: I'm afraid that what she'll say will make sense and that I'll decline to do it anyway. Is my petulance a vestige of sibling rivalry or a purer form of male stubbornness in the face of indisputable female wisdom?

When I finished the story, there was a long silence. "That's it," I said. "That was last night."

Bea said, "Yikes."

Pru said, "So you never talked to her after the fight in her office?"

I shook my head. "She got a migraine."

"So what's next?" Bea asked.

"I'm stumped," I said. "When I called you last night, I was frantic. Now I'm just confused. Do people get divorced over things like this? I should know that, but I can't think straight anymore."

"I don't think the pregnancy trick is grounds for divorce in New York," Bea said. "It's not, strictly speaking, abuse."

"What *would* you call it?" I asked.

"Treachery," Pru said.

I turned to Bea and waited for her assessment. She shrugged, but shrugging was not in her usual vocabulary; she never seemed at a loss for words.

"Why do I get the feeling there's something the two of you aren't saying?"

Pru said, "I hate to remind you of a dinner we had here when Bea's daughter thought her husband might be fooling around on her and —"

"I remember it well."

"And Colleen was ready to haul him into court, sight unseen."

"Not quite, Pru."

"She gave us her business cards," Bea said, and I winced at the memory of them displayed between Colleen's fingers, one for Bea and one for Pru.

"It's not a crime to hand out your business card. It's a faux pas, and Colleen agreed with me afterward that it was. I know it didn't sit well with you. It didn't sit well with me either, but that's not —"

"I also don't think having a wife who's a divorce lawyer and finding out what she does to the opposition is grounds for divorce," Bea said, "but maybe it should be."

"That's clever," I said, rather sharply.

"I didn't mean it to be clever," Bea said. "I'm thinking it through."

"Eric, remember when I told you we thought she seemed unknowable?" Pru asked. I could see she wanted to change the subject, to keep Bea and me from locking horns; it was better manners for me to take issue with my sister. "We still feel that way. We see her on holidays and with the kids and she's always chatty and distant, unless she's bitching at the kids or at you. I've never heard her open up about anything. It's like we've just met."

"What does that have to do with the pregnancy?"

"We don't know who's behind the facade. What's with the masks all over your house?"

"They're souvenirs from Venice. Colleen collects all kinds of Venetian baubles. Don't tell me you think she's got a secret life because she has papier-mâché masks on the wall? That's like saying every dream about a train —"

"In answer to your question," Bea said, "it's not time to think about divorce. Treachery *should* be grounds for divorce, and I suppose if it continues, it can be. But for right now —"

"Should I talk to her about finding the fertility pills?"

"I'm not sure what you gain from bringing it up," Pru said, "except to tell her she's been found out. I assume she'd feel guilty."

"I'm not so sure," Bea said.

"*I'd* feel guilty," Pru said.

"Of course *you* would," Bea said.

"What's that supposed to mean?" I said to Bea.

"Colleen is a divorce lawyer. You just got finished telling us about poor Mr. L., who was kicked out of his house the other night with papers signed by your wife."

"Acting on behalf of *his* wife."

"I know all about divorce lawyers acting on behalf of their clients," Bea said. "All four of mine acted on my behalf, and my husband's team acted on his behalf. These people tell you what they're

going to do and then they do it. Then they send you the bill."
Once she began talking, I remembered she had had a difficult divorce, the details of which I didn't know. Bea is so good-tempered
and well mannered that she didn't invite prodding into her past,
didn't seem to need to unburden herself. And it had never come
up. "It took me five years to divorce my ex," she said. "He quit his
job as the CEO of a Fortune 500 company, moved ninety percent
of our money to a Swiss bank, and moved himself to an ashram in
India so he could pretend he had no income and wouldn't have to
support his children. And got away with it for years. To be fair, I
don't think the lawyers gave him that idea, but they sure helped
him carry it out. I went through three lawyers before I found one
who could outmaneuver him. Must've paid each of them ten
grand. There was my Harvard Law School white-glove WASP, my
early feminist who didn't believe in alimony, my Greek NYU grad
who aspired to be the white-glove WASP, *and* there was Guido
Corleone — not his real name — who got his degree from a school
on a matchbook cover and carried a handgun in his briefcase. He
was the only one who knew how to shake down my ex and his pha-
lanx of lawyers. I know all the tricks in their slimy little books."

Bea's story silenced me, both the grisly content and the fact that
I knew so little about this part of her history. "I hate to talk about
it," she said, sensing my embarrassment. "Avoid it like the plague.
The bastard ruined enough years of my life. He doesn't get another
minute."

"I'm sorry you went through that," I said. "It sounds horrific,
but, as you say, it's not fair to blame all the nastiness on the lawyers.
I see enough couples on the verge of divorce" — I thought of Sandy
and Ursula two weeks before, exuding marital misery — "and I
never have the feeling they need help stoking their animosity." As I
remembered them on my couch, I realized now that they *were* on
the verge of divorce, and Colleen and I were not. We had just hit a
rough spot. I was here to figure out how to get through it.

"The lawyers don't cause it," Bea said, "but they do everything they can to keep the pitch up, as long as there's someone to pay the bills. Mr. Tolstoy had it exactly right in that short story, when he said that in a marriage, hostility leads to conflict and conflict leads to hostility. Or was it vice versa?"

"Did Colleen ever tell you why she became a divorce lawyer?" Pru asked.

"Divorce is a fraction of what she does. She does adoptions and estates and God-knows-what-else. Don't turn it into something sinister." But as soon as I said that, I wondered again if that were really true. It might be that she fit the other cases in between the divorces. How could I find that out?

"I'm not," Pru said. "I'm just doing your thing, looking for the backstory, the motivation. Trying to connect it to what else we know about her. Have you met her siblings yet?"

"No, I told you, she had a falling-out with them."

"All four?"

I wanted to contradict her and say we got Christmas cards or phone calls now and then, but we didn't. "Not all families are —" I didn't know enough about Colleen's to fill in that blank, except that it was damaged and she'd had the good sense to stay away from them.

"What was the falling-out about?" Bea asked.

"I'm not a hundred percent sure." For the first time, my not knowing seemed like a failing, an oversight that someone with my training should have been savvy enough to avoid. "Something to do with Colleen's taking care of the family after her mother died."

"Haven't you asked her?" Pru said.

"Of course I've asked her."

"What does she say?"

I could hear myself sigh as I remembered how hard it was to get her to talk. "She's not obsessed with every morsel of her past the way some of us are."

"What do we know about her ex-husband?" Bea asked.

"Temperamental. Walked out on her when she was pregnant. Has nothing to do with Zoe."

"Who do you know who knows her?"

"What are you guys getting at? You're making it sound like she's a mobster."

"You came here to tell us she took fertility drugs when she said she was using contraceptives," Pru said. "I'm trying to figure out what it means."

"She was eager to have a baby," I said, coming to her defense. "Women spend years doing fertility treatments; it's not considered a suspect motivation." When I called Pru the night before, I had simply needed to anchor myself. When I came to see her and Bea that morning, I realized I wanted them to convince me that my concerns were exaggerated — not that things were worse than I had imagined.

"She doesn't talk to her siblings," Bea said, "doesn't talk to the father of her child, and she tricked you into having a kid. What would you say if she were your patient?"

"You don't know the whole story, Bea. It's very complicated."

"And she's a divorce lawyer. Forgive me for being prejudiced on that score."

"Bea didn't tell you that after her divorce from hell," Pru said, trying, I could see, to change the subject, "when she had to move to a tiny apartment and sleep in the living room so her kids could share the bedroom, a friend of hers told everyone that 'Bea went from high to low with style.'"

"Wit," Bea said. "It was with wit, my darling, not style. I want that on my tombstone."

"Wit *is* style," Pru said, "and you have plenty of both. And now you have money again too."

"I went from low back to high with . . . Prudence. And joy."

They reached for each other's hands and gave a squeeze, and this instant of tender connection infuriated me. What were they doing flaunting their closeness as I began to fear that my intimacy with Colleen might be a mirage?

When I think back on that brunch, I shudder, not because I began to see things more clearly but because it was where my confusion took hold. When Pru and Bea criticized Colleen, I came to her defense; but I was there that morning — lying to Colleen about why I had come to the city — because of my own doubts. It was that morning when I began to live fully in a state of uncertainty, lurching from one possible truth about my life to its exact opposite in the next sentence. I could say that I loved my wife, but I could also say I was not sure who she was anymore. It was not because of any one thing that Pru and Bea had said to me, it was because of the nature of their questions about her and the flimsiness of my answers. I wanted to be convinced that my doubts were unfounded, but I could not dismiss out of hand my sister and Bea's implied accusations.

When they held hands and gazed at each other, I knew that if Colleen and I found ourselves in that pose, the affection that passed between us might be just that, a pose, a put-on. On the other hand, I hoped that when I got home, all my suspicions would vanish, like water down a drain, and my life would return to normal.

Pru turned to me. "Should we head out to see Mom in a few minutes?"

"Have a little more to eat," Bea said to me. "Try some of the tapenade on your bagel. Give it a schmear and add a slice of gravlax."

"I'm not sure I'm up for a visit to Mom now. I should probably go home. That's where it feels like I belong. I'm sorry." I stood up, making it clear that I didn't want to be convinced to change my mind.

*   *   *

I DON'T REMEMBER much about leaving their apartment or getting into my car, but I can recall what the upper Henry Hudson Parkway felt like to drive, the road's graceful curves underneath me, the leaves that lined them just beginning to turn, dusted with bright orange and points of red. This was the way home, the road to my children, my office, my patients who needed me. I could not walk out on any of them, regardless of what Colleen had done. And maybe I was wrong. Maybe there was another explanation for the pills. What did they call that? Off-label use? When a pill for high blood pressure is used for acne. Maybe she had female troubles she had never mentioned. I took the Cross County to the Bronx River Parkway and remembered when this drive felt alien to me, remembered all the times I was not sure it *was* where I belonged.

All of that was swimming in my caffeinated brain when my cell phone rang. I had three or four exits left, about fifteen minutes until I had to walk into my house and lie to Colleen about where I had been. "Are you all right?" Pru said. "I felt terrible when you left. Can you talk?"

"I'm driving. I'm okay."

"We're both sad for you, sweetie."

"Do you think she could have been using the clomiphene for something else? Does it have an off-label use? Maybe she's done something completely innocent and I've misread the evidence."

"I've never heard of another use for it, but it's not my field."

"Could you ask around? Ask a fertility specialist?"

"Okay." She sounded tentative. "Listen, Bea and I were talking after you left, trying to figure out how to help. I know I don't have to call and tell you this, and I'm not sure I agree with Bea, but she thinks you should be on your guard."

"You think Colleen has a gun in her briefcase too?"

"In a manner of speaking."

"Great, thanks for sharing. I'll be sure to tell the kids."

"Don't hang up, Eric."

"What do you want me to say? Don't you think I feel crappy enough? I know you don't like her. I know you think I'm a pitiful heterosexual wimp stuck in a pitiful heterosexual marriage."

"Hold on. That may be what you think, but it's not what we think. We love you. We love your kids, and as long as you're happy with Colleen, we're happy."

"Don't hate her. She was desperate. Her husband left her. She wanted a father for Zoe. I could be misinterpreting this whole thing with the pills."

"Have that conversation with her, the one you didn't have because of her migraine. You'll feel better once you talk to her. I'm sorry I called."

Minutes later I came to the exit for Scarsdale and made a sharp turn onto the road that zigzagged through the village, this precious place that was now my home. This home that housed my marriage. For richer, for poorer — strike that. That was one problem we did not have. In sickness and in health. In truth and in treachery.

I turned the corner of our street and saw our stately house half a block away in the shaded sunlight, and my beautiful two-year-old daughter came into view, on her tricycle, bright yellow with hot pink handlebars, pedaling down the sidewalk with her mother at the end of our walk waiting to catch her. I could see Sarah Rose grinning and I could see Colleen squatting in a tank top and jeans, her arms extended to seem to stop her, to break her roll down the slight incline, and the look on her face was not suspicious, not treacherous, nothing but pure mother love.

I pulled up the car to the curb and called to them out the open window. "Hey, you two!"

"How's your mother?" Colleen asked.

"She's okay. Under the circumstances."

"Hi, Daddy. Look at me!"

"Zoe's at the twins' birthday party," Colleen said, "and I'm about to be late to get my hair cut. Can you take over?"

"I'll be there as soon as I park. Colleen . . ." She turned to me again, her face still and expectant. I could see Sarah Rose pedaling noisily away from her so that she could turn around and roll right back. "Should we have a date tonight?"

"You mean a date date or a —"

"A slow dance in the living room after the kids go to bed?"

"I think I'm free," she said and smiled. "I'll meet you at the foot of the stairs. I'll be the one in the go-go boots."

I smiled back, and the strangeness and certainty of my lips moving in that direction made me question the trip to New York I had just taken, made me question the doubts I had felt. I could see Sarah Rose in my rearview window, her fine hair flying, her tiny self, the genes half mine, rolling past our manicured shrubs and the home that housed this marriage — and this amiable unicorn in captivity who was her father.

THERE WAS a message on the machine in my cottage from Sandy Lefkowitz. I called him while I took care of Sarah Rose back there; she surrounded herself with the dolls from my bookcase, arranged them in an oval and put herself in the center. How blessedly simple that was, how sweet; no one else who saw the dolls had such a straightforward, uncomplicated reaction to them. "Sandy, it's Eric Lavender, I just got your message. How are you doing?"

"I'm not much of a Jew, but my grandmother used to tell me about a yearly ritual in the old country called *shlug kapores.* They'd take a live chicken and, one at a time, hold it over their heads by the wings and the legs, so it wouldn't fly away, and move it in a circle. Doing that would transfer all of their troubles for the whole year out of themselves and into the chicken. You want to know how I am? I'm the chicken."

It took a moment for me to catch up to the punch line, to put it all together and tell him how rough that sounded. After an appropriate interval I asked if he'd found a lawyer yet.

"Finding a lawyer is easy. Paying for a lawyer isn't. I'm drowning in legal bills. I won't be able to see you again between those bills and all the other new expenses I have. I can't live with my cousin forever."

"Doesn't your insurance pay for some of the therapy?"

"Twenty-five dollars a session up to ten sessions."

I needed to get him in here and level with him about Colleen; it was too complicated for the phone. "Given what you're going through, it would be a good idea to have a wrap-up session, see where you are, what you've accomplished."

"The lawyer's bills are going to kill me. I found a guy in Yonkers, I think his name's Murphy, whose usual retainer is five grand, but when he heard who Ursula's lawyer is, he said he has to charge me eight. She's a litigation freak. Never settles anything out of court that she can take before a judge. He says she's a big-time man hater. Leave it to Ursula to find someone like that."

A lawyer had said this about Colleen? Couldn't be right. He's ex-aggerating, fueling his fears with this name-calling. Maybe the lawyer said — never mind. I had to get Sandy in here. I took a deep breath. I had to be persuasive and couldn't sound desperate or beg-garly. But his comments were reverberating in me, even though they sounded implausible. "Sandy, in certain situations, I have a sliding scale. You can pay me whatever your insurance pays you." I had to address the money to get him in here, but after we met, I would drop the fee. "I have an idea or two about how you'll be able to cope with this." Did I mean that?

"You got Jason Cummings to walk out of that house without killing his father, so I know you've got some tricks up your sleeve. Do you have any time this week?"

We made an appointment for Monday evening after work, the day after tomorrow, and he thanked me for the discount. Some discount. Wait until he hears what it's all about, I thought.

I sat back in my desk chair for a moment, shaking my head

against this onslaught of information, of infamy. Sandy's lawyer had to be more circumspect than Sandy made him out to be. Of course he was. The important thing is that I got him to come in. I could talk about Colleen, instruct his lawyer to remove her from the case. That could solve his problem for the time being. If Ursula had to find a lawyer who wanted to be paid up front, the way most do, her plan could be derailed until she got her inheritance. Sandy's lawyer probably didn't say Colleen was a man hater — but he might have nailed her litigation lust. What else would you call what she did to Sandy? Communication via lawsuit. It is not the therapist's impulse; we encourage people to work things out even if they end in dissolution, not escalate them to the hilt. But that's what Colleen does. The fertility pills that she bought at the pharmacy twenty days after we met. She barely knew me. What if I'd bugged out at day thirty-seven and she was pregnant? Then there was the cottage. And the article about me in the newspaper. What else had she engineered?

I felt Sarah Rose's hand tugging at my trousers. She held tightly to the fabric, hoisted herself up to a standing position, and embraced my knee as though it were a dance partner. "Papapapa-papapa," she sang in a song without a tune and raised her arms to me. She wore a light blue corduroy jumper and matching tights, and she had my dark hair and eyes, instead of her mother's fair features. I pulled her to my lap and had the idea to stand up and *be* her dance partner, to hold her against my chest and waltz around the office, all twenty-seven pounds of her.

It was a simple Viennese waltz in three-quarter time, the only thing I knew from a hundred movies — da da da da DUM dum dum dum dum and so forth — and I clumped around the floor, hardly a leading man, but it made Sarah Rose giggle and squeal and sing my waltz along with me. "Da da da da DUM dum dum dum dum," we sang and giggled and twirled, carving out a few moments of what the poets would call ecstasy, an intense, pleasurable feeling or mood in which you have no awareness of the past or the future, a few moments in which you experience a pure connection to the present, which Sarah Rose and I experienced beyond the shadow of a doubt. Half my genes and half Colleen's. Had I lost my mind? Was I insane to think I would ever leave here, even if Colleen had had the good sense to trick me into fathering this child?

❧ 13 ❧

The Bridegroom Was a Widower

A HOUSE with two small children in it, not to mention a set of parents working full-time, has its own hyperkinetic energy, its own timetable that is always changing due to circumstances beyond anyone's control. "Chaos" is not an abstraction, or someone else's problem, but a way of life. The act of rumination — sometimes the act of reading the newspaper — calls out from a distant shore, shimmers on the horizon like an archaic sport or hobby, playing whist or building ships in bottles. Improvisation is all; you must fill the time with clever, stimulating activities, which often devolve into tantrums and time-outs. You must place limits on TV watching, sugar, and bribery, and endure your children's fevers and injuries. Calamity is always a breath away.

It came to us late Saturday afternoon. Zoe swung too high on the backyard swing at her twin friends' birthday party and fell off in her giddy abandon. Her knee collided with the sharp end of a gardening tool. Six stitches, Colleen holding her hand in the ER while I stayed home with Sarah Rose. One crisis led to another, and we missed our sultry Saturday-night date. We woke up Sunday morning with both kids in our bed, Sarah Rose begging to have Band-Aids on her knee in the same place Zoe had her bandages.

It was not until late that afternoon, when we arranged for Graciela to take the kids to a movie, that Colleen and I had two consecutive minutes to ourselves. Hoping to talk to her about our fight on Friday, I invited her to the faux diner in the village we liked to go to sometimes for coffee and pie. She said she was tired and wanted to relax with the Sunday *Times* in the living room. She had spread out the newspaper on the coffee table and taken over the couch next to it, lying down with two or three sections and a pillow to prop her up. My sister was right: there are two papier-mâché masks on the wall above her — ornate black and gold concoctions — along with a series of delicate etchings Colleen had bought in a gallery near the Peggy Guggenheim museum in Venice. The arrangement always seemed to me a sign of her consummate good taste, her knack for juxtaposing slightly hokey souvenirs with lovely, serious pieces of art. I had never looked at the masks as evidence of Colleen's hidden selves or secret lives, or whatever my sister was accusing her of. But that afternoon, the possibility lingered in my thoughts.

"There's an article about Venice in the 'Travel' section," she said. "This is perfect. I've been thinking we should go for Christmas, while Graciela goes to Manila to see her children."

"The dead of winter in Venice with two kids and no nanny. I'm not sure, Colleen."

"The only time we've gone together is when I was pregnant with Sarah Rose and that was just for a week."

"It was a lovely week, but it was June. Why don't we go somewhere warm?"

"I'll call my travel agent and find out what the weather's like at Christmas. Maybe it's milder than we imagine. I've been there into October, and it's fine. I get such cabin fever here." I watched her from a leather armchair across the room as she propped the paper against her raised knees and scanned the page. This is what she had been doing when we met, reading the *Times* in the lobby of the Mondrian. An hour later she was nursing Zoe by the pool, and I assumed this meant the obvious: that she was married; that the breast and all the rest were taken. Now they were mine. And every-thing that came with them, including her cabin fever in our mini-mansion.

She turned to me. "Do you miss your life in New York?"

It took me by surprise. I tended to ask questions about her past, not she about mine. "What makes you ask?"

"Isn't that what shrinks say whenever you ask them anything?" she said playfully.

"I have the monopoly on asking about *everyone's* past." I felt playful too. "What *does* make you ask?"

"I saw in the wedding announcements that your old girlfriend Gaby Goldberg got married. Maybe it was a month ago. I forgot to tell you."

"And you want to know if I miss her? The answer is no." But did I miss my bachelor life? Sometimes, but in the way I miss Paris. I have fond memories, and I would go back if I had no other obliga-tions, but it was not what I considered my home. "Who did she marry?"

"I don't remember. Someone who plays with large sums of money."

"That sounds about right. She didn't approve of my decorating budget."

"I didn't either, darling, but I convinced you to give up trying and come live with us."

Had she convinced me or had she conned me?

"Are you jealous?" Colleen said.

"Of?"

"Gaby Goldberg's husband?"

"God no."

"Do you miss any of them?"

"What's gotten into you? Am I acting as though I'm pining away?" I know I had felt more tentative in the last few days, but I didn't think my behavior had changed enough to get Colleen's attention; I would have to say that on the continuum of people who are self-involved versus other-involved, Colleen didn't need blinders to keep the focus on herself. I was more attentive to her moods and humors than she ever was to mine.

"I'm just curious," she said, though this seemed improbable. Now that I thought of it, I couldn't remember a time she'd asked idle questions about my feelings. Could that really be the case? "I suppose reading Gaby's wedding announcement made me wonder if you missed her."

She went back to reading the "Travel" section without further comment, leading *me* to wonder if there was someone from her past that she missed. Her husband — even though he had treated her so badly?

"Colleen, darling. Let's talk for a few minutes about what happened on Friday in your office."

She turned again to me, the playfulness and concern gone from her face. "Mr. Lefkowitz will get a new therapist. Isn't that what's required?"

"There's a little more to it. You'll have to give up his wife's case."

"I don't think so, sweetheart."

"It's been explained to me that you have a conflict of interest now too. You know too much about the husband to fairly represent the wife."

"Explained to you by whom? Don't tell me you've hired an attorney."

"I'm trying to have a thoughtful conversation with you and you're turning it into a power struggle. Can't we just —"

"A power struggle? I'm simply giving my legal opinion, which is that Mr. Lefkowitz needs a new therapist."

"Why are you so resistant to giving up this woman? Do *you* have an attachment to her?"

"Don't be ridiculous."

"Before I moved here we had a serious conversation that you initiated, saying that it would be a conflict of interest to share clients."

"We're not sharing clients. As far as I'm concerned, the matter is resolved."

"No, it's not. You're representing the wife of a client of mine who —"

"We had a little squabble and it's over. Why can't you accept that? I think I know why. Because you have to turn every issue into a psychiatric session and talk it to death."

When she hurled that barb and finished it with the word *death,* my mind automatically played a free-association word game and bounced first to the word *sex* and then to the word *money.* Isn't that my job, to read between the lines, to make connections that are not apparent to the speaker? Why hadn't I considered this before? "How many hours have you spent on Ursula's case? Ten? Twelve? Fifteen?"

"Why on earth would you care?"

"I bet she's the woman you told me about the other night, whose rich mother is dying and she'll pay you when she gets her inheritance." This was more than a good guess, but I had no trouble portraying it as one. The rest of my theory *was* a guess, but the more I said about it, the more sense it made. If I was way off base, she could defend herself. "But if you drop her now, she'll be pissed off and may not pay you when she gets her money. That's why you won't give her up. If you've spent fifteen hours on her case, you're out almost four thousand dollars."

"That's enough from you. This conversation is over." She turned theatrically to read the paper, or pretend to read it, and I winced to hear the bitchy phrasing, the imperious pronouncements.

"I don't know why you're ashamed of this, Colleen. Of admitting you're working for money. I'm actually relieved with that explanation, because I couldn't figure out why you were so insistent that you keep Ursula's case even though you know it's a conflict of interest. She probably hasn't paid you. You want to get your money. You want to go to Venice for Christmas."

"I told you, our conversation is over." I could see she was flustered and furious. Her lovely fair skin reddened as though she were sunburned; her breathing was hard, but she was trying to cover it up. For the first time since Sandy called me on Thursday night, I had her cornered, and she was not pleased.

"It feels to me like it's just beginning."

"I don't know what's come over you in the last few days." She spoke softly and did not look up from the paper, and the more she talked, the calmer she seemed. But at least she was talking, at least she hadn't fled the room. "You barge into my office, accuse me of God-knows-what, tell me how to run my business, ask nosy questions about my clients. I'm afraid to think about what you might do next."

"What's your worst fear?" It's a question I would ask a patient. She was beginning to feel like one, someone I regarded from a distance, responded to strategically, not emotionally. I could have leveled with her and mentioned the clomiphene, but I didn't want her to know that I knew until I had more information about the drug.

She turned to me, soft again, vulnerable, not in a hurry to answer. "That you'll do what my ex-husband did and leave us."

I was genuinely touched, on her behalf and on Zoe's, who had lost her father before she was born. "I don't think there's much likelihood of that," I said. Not a ringing endorsement, was it? "I'm sorry if I've been on edge. I didn't mean to frighten you. I was upset about what happened to Sandy Lefkowitz. I knew he and his wife had problems, but I didn't think they were hopeless." This wasn't a gross violation of doctor-patient; if it was a minor one, I didn't care. No harm done. No great confidences breached. I had to tell her a little of the truth, although I had no idea how much she was telling me. That's what it had come to.

"I'll consider what you said, dearest, about Ursula." Her voice was as smooth as suede. "I can't talk more about my business with her. It would be unethical." Four days before, I'd have thought her eyes were as sad and guileless as a golden retriever's, but today I wasn't so sure. "You can understand that, can't you?"

"Of course I can."

"Here." She held out a folded section of the newspaper. "You're right about Venice in December. Pick out someplace warm instead."

I walked across the room and took it from her, leaning down to kiss her forehead. "That feels good," she whispered. "Maybe later we can have that Saturday-night date we missed."

"I'll see if I can squeeze it into my schedule."

A moment later, the front door opened and the sounds of Graciela and the girls erupted into the house. Time moved so slowly when they were here, and so fast when they were gone. Colleen sat up on the couch and straightened herself, as though we'd been fooling around like teenagers.

MUCH LATER that night, feeling more exhausted than anything else, I came downstairs after everyone had gone to bed to spend a half hour reading the newspaper, which still sat in a pile on the coffee table. I pulled out the magazine and the "Week in Review," and had a sudden urge to pick up "Sunday Styles" to read the wedding announcements. Maybe some of my other old girlfriends had gotten married. I combed through the pages, but none of the names or photographs called to me, and I was about to toss the section aside when I saw a small notice, no picture, on the last page.

RACHEL WEINSTEIN WEDS ROBERT GOLDEN

Rachel Weinstein and Robert Golden were married last night at the Harvard Club in Boston, in the presence of their grown children and the bride's parents, Dr. Herman

Weinstein, retired chief of internal medicine at Mt. Sinai, and Dr. Eleanor Weinstein, a psychiatrist in New York City. The bride, 54, is a pediatrician in private practice. She will keep her name and relocate to Boston, where Mr. Golden, 56, teaches at Northeastern University's College of Law. Mr. Golden specializes in human rights law and serves on international commissions that seek to establish standards for treating political prisoners and refugees.

The bride's previous marriage ended in divorce. The bridegroom was a widower.

I read it four or five times. I must have missed a sentence. A reference. Had a line been dropped? Could this be Colleen's Robert Golden? But could there be another the same age who also teaches law in Boston? Abandons his kid and marries a pediatrician? Leaves his wife for a student and then marries a woman his own age? A widower? Had he married someone who had died since he had split up with Colleen four years ago? This was Zoe's father? Colleen had told me specifically that he taught basic courses, evidence, contracts, torts. Not a word about human rights.

I wondered if Colleen had looked through the wedding announcements earlier that day. Maybe she had when she was grilling me about my old girlfriends. But if she had seen this, she would have mentioned it, that her ex had remarried. Wouldn't she?

I looked at the clock. Eleven-thirty. Too late to wake her. I would ask in the morning.

BUT I DIDN'T. There wasn't a block of time without the kids, and, I must admit, I got cold feet. I didn't want to get into another wrangle with her. The saga of Sandy and his wife should have been simple too — conflicts of interest all around — but we managed to turn it into an international incident. I could easily find out about Golden by calling Northeastern.

When my last patient of the morning left my office, I cleared a space on my desk for a legal pad and a fresh pen and called information in Boston. Called the university, which put me in touch with the law school. I wrote the name on the legal pad, hoping I would get two numbers. The two Professors Golden. I would write one number on the top line and the second number beneath it.

1.
2.

It was simple.

There was only one. The operator was certain. I took down his number. I called the number, perhaps because I assumed he wouldn't be there, a day after his wedding. I don't know what I'd have said if he answered. There was a recording that talked about him in the third person. "Professor Golden will be unavailable until Monday, September twenty-second. If you need to reach him . . ."

The wedding announcement did not mention a honeymoon. That's probably where he was.

But where the hell was I?

This was Colleen's ex-husband. This was Zoe's father.

Which account should I believe? The wronged ex-wife's or the minuscule wedding announcement?

I flipped up the lid on my laptop and switched it on. It was the first time it had occurred to me to Google him. To Google Golden.

Hundreds of listings. Articles. Conferences. Syllabi. Op-ed pieces he had written. He was clearly renowned for his human rights work. Bosnia. Rwanda. Bangladesh. The university's Web site had a biography. He had clerked for a Supreme Court justice, worked for the Manhattan district attorney, had a stint at the ACLU, an association with the UN High Commission for Refugees. How could Colleen have missed mentioning this? Had she repressed her memories, after what he did to her? Or was she still so pissed off that she preferred to diminish him, cut down his stature, knock him off the pedestal? I knew of men like this: revered and beloved by everyone except their families. They set out to save the world but have no time for their children. I had had a patient in New York whose father won the Nobel Prize but who did not go to her high school graduation. Narcissistic bastards. It was difficult to be a great man *and* a good father. I would never have that problem. The colossal failings of Great Men. And Colleen? What could I make of her not telling me more about her ex? Not giving me a fuller picture? Maybe she didn't want to make me jealous of him, of his prominence in the big world, when my own universe was so small. This cozy cottage she had built for me in our backyard, a display case for my collection of dolls. Hardly an international stage.

I went back to Google's main page and typed in Colleen's name. I had done this once before, for the hell of it, and had come up with only listings for her divorce book, notices about her appearances on TV, and talks she gave at women's clubs. Most of the cases she worked on were not high profile. No movie stars, no big financiers. No ink.

There was a knock at my door and I realized my next client was here. I opened the door to Marion Gray, whose husband had not told her he loved her since their daughter's wedding in 1998.

"It's over," she said to me as she sat down. She was in her early sixties but had always struck me as a sixty-year-old from my grandmother's generation, gray-haired and way out of touch. She had gone to Smith and worked as a photographer for several years before becoming Mrs. John Gray, Jr. She raised three children and volunteered with every white-glove ladies' group in the village. How do we end up such dead-on parodies of ourselves, our behavior confined to a few predictable moves, our feelings scraped from a palette of three or four tired colors? "He left this letter — here, I want you to read it — on the kitchen table this morning. I called you when I got it, but your machine was on. Then I picked myself up and called every divorce lawyer in the book. I know I should have done this before now. I should have been prepared, but I've been so busy taking care of the house and my . . ." Her eyes welled up with tears.

Could I recuse myself, the way a judge can, from a case in which he has an interest? Was I allowed to tell her I couldn't talk anymore about divorce and divorce lawyers? Couldn't listen, couldn't empathize, couldn't ask a question worth shit. And what's more, I was relieved that Mr. G. had finally done what I imagine he had been wanting to do for years. I hadn't made an inch of headway trying to get Mrs. G. to open up, to want to change, entertain new pursuits, to give up her abject longing for the "useful" life she used to live. She wouldn't get on my massage table, wouldn't look at the dolls or talk about her breathing or where her anxiety or her sadness lingered in her body. When I asked if she wanted to take photographs again, she said it was too complicated for her. I'm not sure why she had continued to see me, except that my undivided attention was trained on her for fifty minutes a week.

"I'm so sorry that you have to face this now, Marion, very sorry, because I know how much you've wanted to make your marriage work. But I should tell you before too much more time goes by that my wife is a divorce lawyer in the village. Her name is Colleen Golden. It would be a conflict of interest if she were to represent you while you're seeing me."

"A conflict for whom?"

The question startled me; it seemed so obvious. "For all of us."

"Why can't you both help me through this?"

"If you became dissatisfied with me, you might try to get my wife to patch things up. Or if you wanted to fire her, you might want me to intervene in a way that's not appropriate. It's not in your interest to work with both of us. And it's not in our interest as professionals to —"

"She *was* one of the lawyers I spoke to. She told me she wrote a book about women and divorce."

"Marion, I want to be very clear about this." The situation was not identical, but I was older and wiser than I'd been before Sandy Lefkowitz. "I'm afraid that if you hire her, you'll have to get a new therapist."

"You're cheering for him, aren't you? You've barely said a word to acknowledge what happened. You haven't even opened his letter."

She was right, mostly. I assembled a sheaf of words — soothing, empathic, just what the doctor ordered — and presented them to her in a manner befitting our relationship. Equal parts support, flattery, and psychic massage. They left me feeling crappy and false. But her presence and her problems had done the trick for most but not all of the session: kept me from thinking continuously, without cease, like a Möbius strip that always leads back along the same path, about my wife and her ex-husband, and I was grateful, truly grateful, for the lull.

When Marion left, I was frantic with hunger and went immediately to the house and fixed myself a hefty sandwich, sliced ham and Swiss. There was no one home; Graciela must have been out on errands with Sarah Rose. I had half an hour before my next patient. When I heard the mail being dropped through the front door slot, I wandered there with my food, in something of a dream state, as though I had the beginning of a head cold. It was all junk and bills, and as I turned to place it on the table at the foot of the stairs, I found myself gazing up the staircase to the landing for a long moment, until I realized what I was contemplating.

It was a conflicted longing, and satisfying it might make me feel worse than I already did, but I marched anyway to the second floor. In the small room off our bedroom, I sat down in front of our clunky old computer, one I had used on occasion until a year ago, when I transferred all my files to my new laptop, which I kept in the cottage.

Even when we had used the same computer, we always had two different e-mail accounts because so much of our work is confidential. I didn't know Colleen's e-mail password, but as I sat down that day I hoped that she might not have the computer set up to need a password anymore given that she was now the only one who used it. Had she ever told me her password? Was it the same one she used for our ATM account? I punched in the series of numbers and letters I knew. No go. I glanced around her desk and the wall above it; no signs of what it might be. I typed in the children's names. Nothing. Our phone number. Zip.

On a small bookcase next to the desk was a half shelf of copies of the book she had written. What had she told me about the woman who helped her write it? They had bartered, swapped writing the book for help with her divorce? Was that it? I turned to the acknowledgments page. Her secretary. Her law partner. Her paralegal. Someone without a title. "I'd also like to express my gratitude to Catherine Franks, for her tremendous help in this effort." Could that be the journalist she had mentioned to me, the woman who wrote the book for her?

I swung around to the desk and clicked on the screen icon that would connect me to the Internet. I Googled Catherine Franks — that I could do with no password — and got forty listings. She had interviewed some rock musicians whose names I didn't know. Had written book reviews and articles for obscure magazines or Web zines, pieces about raising kids and recycling and neighborhood crime watches. But it was not easy to tell where she lived. A neighborhood called Mission Hill. Where the hell was that? I must've looked through every one of her listings. It seemed she lived somewhere near Boston, but I couldn't pinpoint where. I couldn't pinpoint much of anything except my creeping suspicions that all was not as it seemed.

*   *   *

AS I CROSSED the lawn to return to the cottage and my next patient, I had to collect myself, transform myself into a sturdy, wise man, a healer, the backyard guru with his massage table and his doll collection. The sensitive man who helps *les femmes de Scarsdale* with all their problems.

But who was there to help me with mine?

⚜ 14 ⚜

A Haunted House

THAT NIGHT at seven, when I opened my office door for Sandy Lefkowitz, I expected a shell of the man, given what he'd been through. He looked an awful lot better than he had the first time he came into my office. He was wearing a seersucker suit, smart Italian shoes, and even his posture was better. Something was different. Had he shaved his mustache? Parted his hair a different way? Not living with his wife agreed with him.

We shook hands and he sat down on the couch across from me.

"You said you had some pointers for me, how to get through this ordeal."

"Before we get into that, how are you doing?"

He rolled his eyes. That was it; he'd shaved his mustache. "I'm sleeping on my cousin's couch. I'm going half-blind trolling this Web site, divorce.com, because I'm trying to figure out what I have to do to get custody of my son. I have to be in court Thursday about the order of protection and Friday about the complaint for divorce. I haven't been fired from my job yet, so that's a disaster I can still look forward to."

"I think I've got some good news for you. Of a sort."

"What's that? I've got colon cancer, but you caught it early and I'll probably live?"

It was difficult not to smile. "Something of a different nature, Sandy. Your wife's lawyer, Colleen Golden —"

"What, she's your sister?"

I waited a moment, so it would not seem as if we were acting out a vaudeville routine. "Actually, she's my wife."

He said nothing for quite a few seconds, just gaped at me in rising disbelief and apprehension. "How long were you planning to keep that a secret?"

"It hasn't been very long. You called me Thursday night. Tonight's Monday. But the reason I didn't say anything — I wanted to be able to give you some professional counsel, and there were people I needed to consult with. This is a serious ethical issue."

"Did you know she was going to kick me out before I knew?"

"Absolutely not. I had no idea there was any connection. Neither did she."

"You said this is good news. What's good about it?"

"I can't be your therapist because I have a conflict of interest and —"

"I can't afford you anyway, so that's not exactly —"

"And Colleen shouldn't be representing your wife, either, because she has a conflict of interest, being *my* wife. Your wife will have to get another lawyer, and in the meantime, you might be able to talk to her, now that you know she's serious about a divorce. You might be able to negotiate something with her that — you might be able to avoid some of these legal bills. Lawyers sometimes generate controversy that isn't there, and if her lawyer is removed from the case, there could be an opening." I wanted to tell him his mother-in-law was dying, that Ursula intended to pay her legal bills with her inheritance, and that few lawyers besides Colleen would take her case on faith, on the promise of an inheritance. Ursula might not be able to hire another lawyer until she got her money. But I stopped short of saying that. It might come back to haunt me if I passed on a confidence I could have gotten only by snooping.

"Have you told her she has to give up my case?" Sandy asked.

I shook my head; I didn't need to mention that we had come to blows over this, that *Higgenbotham vs. Lefkowitz* was the grenade that had been lobbed into the middle of our union. Would it become *Golden vs. Lavender*? Or *Lavender vs. Golden*? "As I understand it — and I'm not advising you as a lawyer — your lawyer has to go over this with my wife. If she doesn't drop the case, your lawyer can file a motion to force her."

"How many thousands will that cost me?"

"I don't know, but it might save you a lot of money if you can —" I wasn't sure how to finish that sentence. I didn't need to, because Sandy had it figured out.

"You mean, it'll save me money if Ursula hires someone other than your wife. The litigation freak. The man hater. Now I get it. The big house in front. This cottage. I know how much it costs to build these places and keep them going. I could never figure out how you did this on what you make per hour, unless you're working sixty, seventy hours a week. You'd have to make three times —"

"Sandy, let's talk about you in the time we have left."

"Me? You want to give me some breathing exercises or some incense to take with me on my spiritual journey? What ever happened to your New Age hocus-pocus anyway?"

I could hear his anger and his disappointment, and I could imagine he held me accountable for my wife's appalling behavior, her false accusations, her kicking him out of his house and taking away his son. Look at us in our grand house with our servants and my spiffy therapy cottage out back, where I lure people in with promises of insight and recovery and end up telling their secrets to my trigger-happy, man-hating wife. He must have believed I was her accomplice — instead of what? Had I been her victim?

"Sandy, I don't know how to talk about this because I've never been in a situation that resembles this one. My wife and I don't talk shop. We don't collaborate. I don't know much about her practice, the details, and she doesn't know much about mine." I wanted to tell him I had tried to read her e-mail but couldn't crack the code.

"You might imagine our relationship differently. I can understand how you would, but —"

"Maybe all of this would have turned out differently if I'd never come to see you. Ursula might never have hooked up with her, she might never have cooked up these accusations against me. I told you she wouldn't sleep with me, and she turned around and accused me of refusing to sleep with *her*. You and the man hater must have had a helluva strategy session on that one."

"She knew nothing about your marriage from me. Nothing. And what happened legally had no relationship to your coming to see me."

"Why should I believe that?"

I remembered the datebook Colleen had thrown across her office. I remembered she told me Ursula had first come to see her in June, three months before, long before I met Sandy.

"I want to tell you something that might set your mind at ease about that, even though it's a tough piece of news. I'm telling you because it's important for you to know that I didn't betray your confidence. I don't know what took place between my wife and your wife, but I think their relationship started a few months ago."

"How many?"

"My wife told me Ursula first went to see her in June. But to tell you the truth, Sandy, I don't know if that's right."

"June what?"

"I don't know."

"You can't find out?"

"We decided not to talk about it after . . . after the initial revelation. It was too complicated."

He surprised me by standing up abruptly. We still had ten minutes. "This is too complicated for *me*." I had just told him his wife had been planning her exit, or his, for quite some time, and that was a blow; I could see it in his sudden shortness of breath, in his retreat. "I wasn't in a fog. I knew we had problems, but every time I tried to talk to her about them — wham. Instant insanity. When I invited her to come to London last month, when I was trying to save the marriage and she didn't even have the courtesy to answer me, the truth is I was relieved. I didn't want to go to London with a mannequin. I don't know how this is going to end, but it doesn't look good, does it?" He walked across the office and grabbed the doorknob but didn't turn it. Did he want me to try to stop him? "Send the bill to my cousin's. I'll leave the address on your machine tomorrow."

"We still have a few minutes, if you want to talk about —"

"There's nothing to say."

"Forget the bill, Sandy. This was my idea. I had a responsibility to tell you about Colleen." I wanted to do what Louise Wallace would have done, offer to see him for five bucks a session, make him dinner, whatever he needed, but I couldn't do that now. I had to end this or I'd be open to a lawsuit; regardless of what I did, he could take me to court for conspiring with the enemy, who happened to be my wife. Before he left for good, should I tell him that Ursula's mother was dying? What did it matter? Ursula would find another litigation-freak lawyer to do her bidding. She would express her hostility by turning the child against him or moving to another state or inventing a new batch of lies, and my wife, or a lawyer just like her, would offer a sister's helping hand at $250 an hour, dressing up the wife's petulance as a legitimate response to life with Sandy and rewriting her flimsy résumé as another piece of evidence in the long history of the subjugation of women.

"Thanks," Sandy said and nodded at me as he turned the doorknob. "Thanks a lot." His words were pointy and sarcastic — *thanks for nothing, thanks for saving me twenty-five bucks* — and I opened my mouth to say something reassuring or kind or apologetic, but my mind went blank.

When he stepped over the threshold and closed the door behind him, I don't know which of us felt worse.

The light on my answering machine was blinking as I prepared to go back to the house. Pru's message said she had news for me. She was at the hospital on her cell phone. When I reached her a moment later, her first words were, "It's not great."

"Is it Mom?"

"Oh, no, she's fine, I mean, for someone who wears her underpants on her head and thinks Eisenhower is president. It's about clomiphene. It does have an off-label use, but I don't think it would apply to Colleen. They give it to men with low sperm count who are trying to have a baby."

"Oh."

"Sorry."

"It was a nice idea." I wasn't entirely surprised. It had been my last-ditch effort to give Colleen the benefit of the doubt. "That's what happens when you put your faith in modern medicine. It's bound to disappoint."

"It really sucks," my sister said. I was touched that she was so blunt, that she had said something so kidlike, reminding me that we had been kids together. And I was relieved that she didn't attack Colleen. I suppose she didn't have to.

"You didn't really think I was on to something, did you?" I said. "Like she was taking clomiphene for athlete's foot?"

"Come on, I did the research with an open mind."

"Thanks. I appreciate it. I'll put it in the mix with what I read yesterday in the *Times*. Colleen's ex had a wedding announcement that said he was a widower human rights lawyer with a grown daughter."

"What did she say when she saw it?"

"She didn't see it, as far as I know."

"And you didn't ask her?"

"I was going to, but I chickened out."

"Did you have the talk about your fight on Friday?"

"Yeah. That's why I didn't ask about the wedding announcement. I wasn't up for another melee."

"Maybe it was a typo," Pru said, "the stuff about her ex."

"Interesting theory."

"I'm sure there's an explanation."

"There always is, but I'm starting to feel like I live in a haunted house."

"Oh, shit. That's my beeper. I need to run."

I entered our house as I always do coming in from the cottage, through the kitchen door, and noticed a plate of what looked like dinner left for me on the table, covered with foil. The kitchen was quiet; the kids sounded as though they were upstairs. There was no evidence of Colleen or Graciela down here. At my feet was the plastic recycling bin, filled with newspapers. It was garbage night. Before I went to bed, I would carry the bin out to the curb. As I sat down with my plate of grilled chicken and a baked potato, it occurred to me to look again at Robert Golden's wedding announcement before it left the house for good. Maybe I had misread it. It didn't actually say he was a widower. I had invented the line about the grown children. The bride was thirty-four, not fifty-four.

The "Sunday Styles" section was close to the top of the pile. I turned to the back page, where I was certain the notice about him had appeared, but it wasn't there. In its place was a hole in the page, a cutout the size of the article. It had been removed neatly, surgically, you might say, with a scissors.

THERE IS LITTLE more compelling to therapists as a group than the subject of what motivates people, what makes them behave the way they do, and what causes them to change. Rarely can you pinpoint in your own or anyone else's behavior a specific event that provokes an entirely new course of action. But rarely is not never, and what happened that night in our bedroom was the turning point, the pivot, for everything I have done since then. The empty rectangle in the newspaper is what got me going.

Colleen sat at her vanity applying her face cream as I lolled on the bed, pretending to read a popular science book about the chemistry of the brain. The TV was on softly and I did not think Colleen was in the mood to cash in her rain check for our two missed dates. "What have you got lined up for later in the week?" she asked.

"Not much I can think of. How about you?"

"Remember I'm giving a talk at the White Plains Women's Club on Thursday at eight? Will you be able to put the kids to bed?"

"Sure."

"Maybe we can go into the city this weekend. There's a new show at the Whitney I'd like to see."

"Sounds good. By the way, speaking of old sweethearts, I saw an announcement in the paper on Sunday that your ex-husband had gotten remarried."

"Really?" Was that a tiny choke I heard in her voice? "Where was it?"

"In the section with the wedding announcements." I looked up over the book and saw that she looked slightly more alert. She was still looking into the mirror, massaging her neck with some cream. I noticed she was blinking faster and her eyes were not as steady as they had been.

"Who did he marry? Do you remember?"

"You missed the piece?"

"I must've."

Jesus, she was cool-headed. I could feel my heart beating in my knees. "Should I go fetch it from the recycling bin so you can read it?"

"No, don't bother, sweetie. It's not that important. What was her name, do you remember?"

"Rachel somebody. Was that the student he took off with?"

"Believe it or not, I don't remember her name." What a lousy answer. "I've really blocked that, haven't I?"

"It's just as well, then, that you didn't see it. It might have upset you."

"That bastard," she said, but her heart wasn't in it, not the way Bea's was when she called her ex a bastard the other day. I could hear that now, the tinniness in her voice, her accusation. Had it always had that false ring, when she talked about him? I don't think so. But maybe I had never known to listen for it.

It could be that he had hurt her so badly she simply wanted to excise him from her life — as he had excised her and Zoe from his — and had chosen an excision from the newspaper of record as her symbol. That's one explanation. Maybe she was embarrassed at still feeling so wounded by him. That could explain not admitting that she cut up the paper. She might have other innocent, charitable reasons for all of her peculiar behavior. But I didn't know anymore how to tease them out of her, and in the last few minutes I had become convinced that I couldn't depend any longer on her version of the truth. As she continued to smooth cream into her pale, saturated skin, not moving from the vanity, not averting her eyes from her own image in the mirror, she gave off the unmistakable vibrations of a person trying to hide something.

By then we both had secrets. Colleen's was concealed somewhere in the content of the wedding announcement and mine in the fact that I knew she had cut it out of the newspaper.

THE NEXT MORNING I woke up determined to find out what she was hiding.

Between my second and third patients of the morning, I logged on to Google and asked it to search two words: lawyers + Yonkers. I wanted to find the attorney who had called Colleen a litigation freak and a man hater. Sandy had said his name to me at one point, but all I could remember was that it began with an *M*. It was Murphy or Murray or McKay. There were lawyers with all three names in Yonkers, but only Frederick Murray listed himself as specializing in family law. I left a message for him.

I called information in Boston and asked for Catherine Franks, who helped Colleen write her book. There were two, one in Boston, one in Cambridge. I called both numbers but did not leave messages on the answering machines. I then called Northeastern's law school and spoke to a secretary in Professor Golden's office. He would be back on Monday, September twenty-second; his office hours were Wednesdays and Fridays from two to three in the afternoon. I would have to concoct a reason to go there and talk to him, to a city I hadn't visited for fifteen or twenty years.

For the first time since I learned that Colleen was representing Sandy's wife the week before, I felt clearheaded and, ironically, unafraid, now that I had evidence there was something to fear. An unlikely burst of energy inspired me to straighten up my office and go to the village barber for a haircut before my next appointment. In the *People* magazine I read there, I was briefly captivated by Movie Star X's account of her recent stay at a posh rehab and the dramatic intervention that her friend, Movie Star Y, had arranged two months before at her Malibu beach bungalow. A dozen people had come together — including her therapist — to convince her to confront her demons. That was it. My excuse to go to Boston: I had been asked to participate in an intervention for a former patient. Or could I tell Colleen it was taking place in Providence, to keep Boston, *her* Boston — and any suspicions she might have about my sudden travel — out of it?

When I returned to my office, there was a message from Frederick Murray's secretary. He couldn't see me until next week, but she would do a preliminary interview for him over the phone.

When I called back, I explained that I wanted to speak only to him. It was a confidential matter that involved my wife, the attorney Colleen Golden.

The phone rang two minutes later.

By then, I was with a patient and the machine picked up. Just as well. As much as I wanted to talk to him, I realized I didn't know how to tell him that I knew his views about Colleen. I couldn't reveal that Sandy had been my client, couldn't reveal anything he had told me.

But by the time I called Mr. Murray back later that day, I had figured out what to do. Take a lesson from Colleen: lie. I said I was contemplating a divorce from Colleen and asked what he would charge to represent me. It was a trick question because I knew he had told Sandy his usual retainer was $5,000 but that because his wife's lawyer was Colleen, he upped the retainer to $8,000.

He asked what the issues were between us and what I would want in the divorce as far as custody. "Joint," I said. "I would insist on it because she works fifty or sixty hours a week."

He didn't tell me she was a litigation freak or a man hater. He didn't have to. After a long, awkward moment in which he said nothing at all and I imagined we had lost our connection, he announced he would require $25,000 down and that his rate was $300 an hour.

I said that was heftier than I'd had in mind.

"You know why divorces cost so much, Mr. Lavender?"

"Why's that?" Is this when he'd spill the beans about my wife?

"Because they're worth it."

I was so startled he had told a joke, I didn't laugh. I just said, "Thanks. I'll think about what you've said."

That, at least, was the truth.

When I hung up, I went on-line to the Web site Sandy had mentioned, www.divorce.com. Out of curiosity, I clicked onto the link for New York State and read up on child support, the division of assets, and custody arrangements. It led me to a posting site where people asked questions about their own situations and a lawyer answered them as best he could. It was dismal information, a grim public bulletin board shot through with legalese, heartache, and financial ruin. It was not a place, real or virtual, that I had the slightest interest in going.

15

Lipstick on My Hard Drive

I AM NOT a casual liar. Or, I should say, had never been one until a few weeks ago. Never thought up a winning excuse if I needed faster service at a doctor's office or restaurant or the time I was stopped for speeding. My tendency in my personal life is toward the bitter truth, silence, or apology, by way of explanation. I didn't cheat on my girlfriends, didn't lie to them when things went sour, and never thought of concealing money from the IRS. But by Tuesday afternoon, after my scorcher phone call with Fred Murray, on top of the previous five days of matrimonial dissonance, my scruples had taken a beating.

By Wednesday afternoon, I had planned a trip to Boston for the following Wednesday, September 24, when I knew Robert Golden would be sitting in his law school office from two to three o'clock. Pru and Bea, advising me by phone, said I should show up there unannounced, given his volatile temper. "He'll hang up on you if you call him," Pru said. "But if you're physically there, at least you have a chance. Be sure to bring photographs of Zoe."

I had also studied the articles by Catherine Franks posted on the Internet and phoned a publication she seemed to write for regularly, an alternative paper in Boston. The receptionist said she was there several afternoons a week but didn't know her schedule. She gave me Catherine's e-mail address and I put it aside, unsure what I would do with it.

By Thursday at noon, I had perfected the presentation I would make to Colleen. It was the most premeditated lie I had told her until then; the others, in the days before, were white lies that fell from my lips without much thought or design. This one was a piece of handicraft, a useful object that was also handsome and well made. I dreaded having to deliver it. Pru suggested I phone it in, my office to her office, to underscore that it was an ordinary professional matter and we were an ordinary professional couple.

"Hi, it's me," I began on her voicemail. "Just got an interesting invitation for next Wednesday, to go to Providence to participate in an intervention with a former patient, a kid from Scarsdale High who's having some problems adjusting to college. It sounds like a one-day trip, I'd be back late that night. Check your calendar and let me know if that's a problem. And think about whether you still want to go to the city this weekend. Maybe Pru can baby-sit while we go to the Whitney."

Once I left the message, I turned on my e-mail and fiddled with an approach to Catherine Franks. It seemed to me that Colleen and I had papered over our recent run-ins and were getting along as amicably as the parents of two small children can — or slightly better because we were trying to pretend things between us were normal. But I was careful not to go overboard with my geniality, like a guilt-ridden philanderer who is so nice that his wife suspects him. What I wanted to learn in Boston was that Colleen's secret was a trifle, an old transgression that she had buried and tried to forget. I wanted then to be able to persuade her that it loomed larger in her fears than it had any reason to; I would remind her of the man who walks around for decades feeling shame over a homosexual encounter. If Colleen's secret past was a version of that, if that psychic distress had encouraged some of her extreme behavior — the litigation mania, the pregnancy trick — I could help her work it out, talk it through, *process it*. I'd find her a first-rate therapist. My fingers started tapping out this list:

<u>Possible secrets:</u>
Murder.
Role in suicide.
Gave up child when young.
Incest. Victim? Perp?
Family tragedy. She got blame?

None of these were the trifles I had fantasized might have burdened her. I deleted the list, as though getting rid of it would eliminate the possibilities, and started an e-mail:

> Dear Catherine Franks —
> I don't have a clear idea of how to approach you but I am coming, by myself, to Boston next Wednesday afternoon and hope we might be able to meet. I am the husband of Colleen Golden. I know you helped her write her book. I will be at Northeastern U. between 2 and 3, but free afterward and could meet wherever it's convenient.

When I reread it, it seemed obvious to me that Colleen didn't know about my trip, but I added this line, just in case: "From what Colleen has told me, you and she are not in touch. In the event you are, I would appreciate your not mentioning this e-mail or my visit to her."

I wondered if I should explain why I wanted to meet her? Wasn't that obvious too — to talk about Colleen? The fact was I knew nothing about her relationship with Colleen except that it was over. Maybe that *was* all I needed to know. I hit SEND and the e-mail disappeared. I was beginning to think that my sister was right, even in this. Colleen is unknowable. Even to me. Especially to me. It was this feeling that Pru was right that lured me back into the house and upstairs, to the little office off our bedroom. To the computer Colleen used. To the e-mail account I couldn't get into three days before. In the "Password" box, I typed in the kids' names, Colleen's birth date, her birth date backward, the kids' birth dates. Nothing. But oddly, I didn't feel agitated, just baffled. Becalmed.

Such a lovely-sounding word, *becalmed,* I have to remind myself that it describes a perilous state. Years ago in New York a patient came to see me six months after returning from a trip to Tortola, where she had gone sailing with her boyfriend on what was to have been an overnight trip. The outboard motor broke and they were becalmed twenty or thirty miles from shore. It was four days before they could move. They ran out of water. Ran out of flares. Sharks circled the boat. Her skin blistered until it bled. Soon after she and this man returned to New York, he broke up with her and she fell into a depression. The two of us talked on and off for months about whether she might try moving to my massage table while she talked. I said I sensed that she had repressed the real trigger for her depression. She admitted that as long as she could sit up straight, she could hold herself together, but the prospect of lying on the padded table reminded her of those nights on the sailboat, trying to sleep on the cushioned fiberglass banquettes and fearing she would be eaten alive. She was so sunburned that ocean water stung her skin. So did her tears. She had not cried since she had returned, even when the man left her. One day she did it. Without saying anything, she stood up from the chair in my office, walked across the room and climbed onto the massage table, lay on her back and wept. It was not a cure, but it was the beginning of her realizing that she could emerge from her depression.

A phone ringing, like an alarm clock, jolted me out of my becalmed reverie. My cell phone. In the breast pocket of my shirt.

"Is this Zoe's house, is this her father?"

"Yes, is she all right?"

"She's fine. Is someone coming to pick her up? School ended half an hour ago."

I drove the eight or ten blocks to the school talking to myself, issuing orders to my unruly daydreams: Get a grip, Eric. Suck it up. Don't wear your obsessions on your sleeve. Don't forget to pick up your daughter at school. The last thing I wanted was for Colleen to have any reason to suspect my behavior as I plotted my day in Boston. The second-to-last thing I wanted was for Zoe to feel abandoned. How many more days until I took the trip, got through this swarm of lies, and came out on the other side? Too damn many.

I LOOK UP at the ceiling from the hard bench and count on my fingers. That was last Thursday. Then Friday. Saturday. Sunday. Monday. Tuesday. Wednesday. Seven days. Today is Wednesday. It's late Wednesday night. I was supposed to go to Boston this morning after my second patient left, but Colleen and the police had another destination in mind for me. I'm on my back on this polished plank that is my bed. Like the fiberglass banquette on the ill-fated sailboat. I'm waiting for the sharks to get me. I'm remembering what happened when I got into bed with Colleen last night. That was Tuesday. So what day did she start snooping? What did I do that led her to suspect me? Was it right after I forgot to pick up Zoe — a fact that Zoe reported to her mother that night at dinner? I blamed a patient for staying late and a phone call that came as I was walking out the door, and Colleen seemed fine with the explanation. But later on, she might have looked back on my lapse and wondered if I was covering something up, like a girlfriend in Providence I was going to see. Could that have prompted her to go looking on my computer for telltale signs — lipstick on my hard drive? When could she have sneaked into my office? Must've been when I took Zoe grocery shopping over the weekend.

Last night as I got into bed, Colleen cuddled up to me and made herself a spoon, wrapped her front against my back and grazed my pubic hair with her fingers. "Big day tomorrow," she whispered.

"In what sense?"

"The intervention. Have you ever participated in one?"

"No, but I won't have much to do. I'm not leading it, which would be intimidating. I'm just going to chime in and talk about the boy when it's my turn. I've been reading about what happens at them on the Internet." That part was not a lie, though the purpose of my reading was to know what I would tell Colleen when I returned. I had decided I would spend the drive back to Scarsdale making up a proper story for her consumption.

Her fingers moved one way and another, and for a minute or two, maybe even three, I worried that my nerves, my suspicions, and my own lying, would interrupt the blood that always flowed to my penis when she touched it this way. How would I excuse my member if it failed me? I need not have worried. I performed. Appropriate word. Did what I needed to do. We had a routine. First this, then that, then this. Before long, we became the beast with two backs, pumping and pressing in a way that was achingly familiar and that I used to feel was sweet and tender and a little raunchy. She called me "Baby" when she came.

At least I thought she came. Here tonight in my solitary cell, it occurs to me to wonder: Was she faking that too? And did that mean she had been faking the others for these four years?

I HAD JUST said goodbye to my second patient and was unplugging my laptop to take with me to Providence — I mean Boston — when I heard a knock at the cottage door. Two uniformed cops. Had they come to tell me something about Jason Cummings? Was this a follow-up call? Or was he in trouble again?

"Hi. Can I help you?"

"Eric Lavender?"

"Yes."

They stepped into the door and circled me, one in front, one yanking my arms to my back and clamping cold metal on my wrists. "You're under arrest." They whisked me out of the cottage and pushed me across my lawn and down the driveway, one gripping each elbow. Were my kids watching this? I craned my head back to the house. "What's going on here? You have the wrong address. What on earth could I have done —" Offended a patient? Hit a child without knowing it as I drove down the street?

"Why didn't you think of this *before,* asshole."

"Before what?"

"I bet you liked it. It felt good, didn't it?" Had I touched a patient on the massage table in a way she didn't like? Was it Susan Reed? Last week she was so agitated, she told me to do the relaxation exercise we've done a dozen times, in which she lies on the table and I cradle her head in my hands for three or four minutes. Did my hand slip?

"'Course it felt good," the other cop said. "These guys are perverts. Who else gets off on their kid?"

"My kid? What are you talking about?" By this time, they'd shoved me across the lawn and into the back seat of the patrol car, a half cage that kept me from being able to flail my body across the seat or bang my head onto one of their heads. "My kid?" Which kid could they possibly think that I had . . . ? "My four-year-old or my two-year-old? Who the hell told you this? My wife? How could you think for a minute that I would —"

"How *do* you guys think? I never understood that."

"You know who I am, don't you? Last month, when Jason Cummings —"

"Yeah, we know who you are."

"You have the wrong address. The wrong guy. This is a big mistake."

"You bet it's a mistake."

IT DIDN'T OCCUR to me until now that Colleen had planned last night to be my goodbye fuck. Thank you, dearest, for sending me to jail with a fresh memory of your nipple in my mouth and your mouth on my cock. I wondered why you insisted on that, and now I know.

Could Colleen possibly have suspected me of anything illicit? Maybe she simply wandered into the little office off the bedroom to use her computer three or four days ago, to catch up on e-mail or pay some bills, and she went looking for a Web site she'd gone to before, and there were my excursions into her past. She could see I had Googled her ex-husband and her coauthor in Boston. And she might have figured out that my upcoming trip to Providence was more likely a trip to Boston, to find out what she'd been hiding from me. Why hadn't I remembered to delete those foolish forays? Once Colleen saw them, she might have waited for me to leave the house — even sent me to the grocery store for a list of things we didn't need — so she could snoop through the laptop in my cottage. And there she'd have found the e-mail I wrote to Catherine Franks. She'd have seen that I had gone to divorce.com — to the entries about custody. I remember now there was an FAQ I found with this title: "Do Fathers Ever Get Custody?" She must've read that page and thought I was planning to leave her and fight for the kids. And that something I was going to find out in Boston would give me an advantage in court.

I'm imagining these events, these computer revelations, but they are entirely plausible. I'm not sure I can come up with other explanations for what motivated Colleen to do this to me, to our family.

In these scenarios Robert Golden and Catherine Franks have plenty to tell me, plenty Colleen does not want me to know. The only certain way she knew to stop and discredit me was accuse me of being a pedophile. That's how badly she wanted to keep me away. If I close my eyes and sleep I will not see the shark as it circles the boat. My head hurts. The generator hums. All of me aches.

*   *   *

"YOUR LAWYERS are here." They've woken me from my wooden mattress and I am still locked up. Morning is here and this is no dream. "Both of them," the cop says.

"What?"

"Here's your breakfast." Through the food hole in the bars he shoves something round with a shiny wrapper that might be a Mc-Donald's hamburger. I'm the only prisoner in the place. There's no kitchen. No porridge. No prison food. It's an Egg McMuffin. A sign of life. Something resembling sustenance. I'm groggy and sore and too tired to rage.

As I cross the cell to pick it up, I see two people, civilians, not cops, coming down the hallway toward me, a petite woman with butterscotch skin who must be Lily Lopez, and a tall, bulky, big-eyed man in a gray suit carrying an oversize briefcase. A Perry Mason lookalike or else I am hallucinating.

"You must be Eric. I'm Lily Lopez and this is my partner, Bernie Rosenberg. He's done a lot of cases like this."

The moment sounds like the setup for a joke: there are three people in a plane that's going down — a Puerto Rican lawyer, a Jewish lawyer, and a confused shrink — and only two parachutes.

But right now I have no idea what the punch line could be.

16

ROR Me

Here's what I had going for me, according to Lily and Bernie: "no priors" and "a rap sheet with nothing on it" — except for this misdemeanor complaint of sexual misconduct. "What about the fact that I didn't do it? Does that count for anything?"

"Yes," Lily said.

"And no," Bernie said.

"What he means —"

"These days, these cases, you're guilty until proven innocent."

My eyes shot from one to the other and landed on Lily, who I had hoped — fantasized, as though she were a pinup and I a lonely teenager — would rescue me. I had half expected Wonder Woman, Madonna in concert with pointy, gold-plated volcano breasts, a hot-blooded Latina version of my unyielding wife. That was not the case. She was ordinary, organized, and more deferential toward Bernie than I had expected. Somewhere between thirty and forty. Her fingernails bitten to the quick. But no shrinking violet: she had arranged to have us meet in my cell, where my hands were free, instead of in the nearby conference room, where they would have to be cuffed to a chair. She had brought me a clean shirt to wear and an electric razor, which she mumbled "might not work so hot" because it had not been used since before her husband "split." She had even arranged that the guard would be stationed outside the steel door, so he could look in at us through the small rectangle of glass but not hear what we were saying. I wasn't a major security risk, though the video camera was still trained on my cell, in case I mauled my attorneys or tried to drown myself in the toilet.

"I'm guilty until proven innocent?"

"In the situation you're in," Bernie said, "with an allegation of sexual misconduct in Westchester County, in the early years of the twenty-first century, you have, essentially, no rights. However, Eric, the facts of your case —"

"How is that possible?"

"Have you had enough to eat?" Lily said. She was sweet-looking, a little plump, and I remembered that she was here because my sister had saved her son's life. "Did they give you dinner last night? I asked if they read you your Mirandas and if they questioned you, but I forgot to ask about that."

She had seemed so combative yesterday on the phone; now she was playing cuddly mother to Bernie's full-of-bad-news father. "The food was adequate, but I want to know if he's serious that I have no rights."

"You have to look at the whole picture of the atmosphere now," Lily said. "They're making up for lost time, for the old days when this stuff was never reported, when it was swept under the carpet with the dust balls. They want to protect the kids. When you know the particulars, you can't blame them. I once heard a cop say, 'We don't suspend the Constitution, but where kids are involved, we err on the side of caution.' When it looks like they *have* suspended the Constitution, we call them on it."

"I'm going to try to strike a deal with Rick Maxwell, the assistant DA," Bernie said, "before we see the judge. I want them to ROR you."

"To what me?"

"Release you on your own recognizance. All they have is a sworn statement from your wife. No witness, no eyeball. At this point, it's just an unverified complaint. Child Protective Services was supposed to interview your stepdaughter yesterday afternoon, but I haven't heard anything about their report yet."

"Interview a four-year-old? What if she makes up a story because she's coaxed in a certain direction? What if she feels pressure to say one thing or —"

"They interview kids all the time. They've got a good team of social workers and psychologists. They're very sensitive to —"

"Eric, listen —" This was Lily, with her hand on my arm. "Let's go through what's going to happen in the courtroom. Everyone understands that the child can be coached. They know what the signs are. They know what to look for."

"Before the arraignment," Bernie said, "I'm going to try to reach an agreement with Rick Maxwell. Your wife has to go along with it. The deal would be ROR, you agree to vacate the house, and we come back for another hearing in two weeks. We'll have time to develop our case. We'll get character witnesses and our own expert witness, Marsha Rogers in Yonkers, to interview your stepdaughter and do the doll business with her, so she can find out if she's been molested or coached on what to say. As soon as I leave here today —"

I interrupted. "Do you know my wife?"

The energy in the cell changed. Perry Mason shut up. Lily's eyes swerved to look at him. "By reputation," Bernie said finally.

"What's her reputation?"

"She's tough," Lily said. "But so are we, Eric. That's the name of the game."

"What else do you know about her?" Maybe, like Fred Murray, they knew more than I did.

"She fits a type," Bernie said. "Women in the matrimonial bar. Not all of them but enough so you recognize it fast."

"Which is?"

"They're smarter than the men," he said, "and they don't play fair. But let's not get bogged down in that right now. I want to go through the motions with Maxwell anyway, to see what kind of case they've got and what issues she balks at. Is your position that her allegation is completely unfounded?"

"Completely. She's knows I've never laid an inappropriate hand on the child."

"Do you bathe her?" Lily asked.

"About once a week."

"Is there any way she could have said to her mother, 'Daddy touched me here'?" Lily said. "Did anything happen recently that might have made her —"

"No. No way. Yesterday morning Colleen took her to school. I kissed Zoe goodbye in the foyer. I told her I was going to go away for the day and I would see her tomorrow. She kissed me and said, 'I love you, big bear.' You tell me. Is that a molested kid? I don't know what my sister told you, but for the last few weeks Colleen and I —"

"What your sister said doesn't matter," Lily said. "You're our client. You tell us what's going on."

"This has nothing to do with the kids. We got into a conflict of interest with clients whose cases overlapped." I explained *Higgenbotham vs. Lefkowitz* and its aftermath, including the pregnancy trick, and presented my theory: "I happened on some kind of secret from Colleen's past and was going to Boston to find out what it was. I invented a story for where I was going — I said Providence — and she must have suspected I was lying. It might've prompted her to search my computer and find out I was going to see her ex-husband and that I'd checked a divorce Web site. She must've thought I intended to divorce her."

"Did you?" Bernie asked. He was paunchy, looked about my age, Sandy Lefkowitz's age, and somewhere between the two of us in his clothing and personal habits. Not as wrinkled, in his pinstripe suit, as Sandy, and not as starched as I usually am, although that morning I must have looked like a vagabond.

"Hell, no. I was just trying to find out what she's hiding from me. I had this wacky idea it could help save the marriage. You guys do divorces too? Could I get a two-for-one package deal?"

"Let's work on one problem at a time," Bernie said.

"We don't do divorces," Lily said. "I don't have the stomach for them."

"That's quite a statement coming from a criminal defense lawyer. Tell me, is my picture on the front page of the *Daily News* yet?"

"Eric, listen," Bernie said, "we've only got a few more minutes. Lily and I do this all the time. We're pros, and, frankly, when you cut through all the hot-button headlines here, I don't think they have a case that'll hold up at trial unless they've got documents I haven't seen. But I don't want to get your hopes up. The fact that they didn't charge you with a felony — this is a misdemeanor complaint, you know that, right? — says to me they have a weak case. Let's see what the CPS report says after they interview your stepdaughter. Your wife isn't claiming she was a witness to the incident. We have to make sure the judge understands that. That's our job today."

"What do I have to do?"

"If you're called on, speak, tell the truth. That's it."

"You ready?" Lily said.

"Do I have a choice?"

She shook her head. "I'm sorry to tell you, *bubeleh,* that at the moment, you don't." Something about the resignation in her eyes reminded me that her son had ended up in the ER yesterday. Her secretary had written it in her note to me.

"How's your little boy?" I said.

"You know, you think they're going to crack in two, but they're sturdier than we are. Ten minutes after we got home, he was fine. He's got a bump on his head and a bandage on his knee. Thanks for asking."

THE SCARSDALE TOWN HALL, a short walk from our house and the village center itself, is a boxy, mid-1960s-style, two-story brick building that I always thought of as benign, even quaint in its local ambitions. It's there, on the first floor, that you go for a dog license, a pass to the community swimming pool and the tennis courts, and information on recycling. I thought of the courtroom one flight up, which I had never had occasion to enter, as traffic court. When the police car pulled into the parking lot at the side entrance, I imagined that we were making a stop on our way to the county courthouse in White Plains, where I expected to meet up with my lawyers. The back door opened, and one of the cops grabbed my elbow.

"We're here? I'm going to traffic court?"

That was when he exercised his right not to answer me, his right to consider me guilty until proven innocent. He and the other cop settled for escorting me into the building, one at each elbow, and it was this moment, this brief march up an outside flight of stairs and through a set of double glass doors, a distance of no more than fifty feet, that felt more humiliating to me than any of the last twenty hours: my public debut as a handcuffed criminal. *Alleged.* Let's not forget that. If this place was traffic court as well as child molester court, there was a fair chance I would run into a patient, a neighbor, or a teacher at Zoe's preschool. For the first time in my life, I yearned to be one of those guys you see on the local news, who yanks his sweatshirt up over his face as he's marched past the cameras.

A speck of luck: there wasn't a camera in sight. I saw Lily and Bernie through the second set of glass doors. They were huddled against a far wall of the lobby with a man I had never seen, a little man with wire-rimmed glasses — and my wife, in a narrow jet black dress, shaking her striking head of strawberry blond hair as she pointed repeatedly at a piece of paper in her hand. Her lips seemed to be saying: "No, I don't think so." Or was I imagining that? She was in widow's weeds already, a prim dress, quite unlike her, which she had bought a few months before for an aged neighbor's wake. In this outfit, she could suggest to the judge that my crime left her a widow, and she could send me a backdoor message, now that I knew that the court system was her favorite way to communicate in both her professional *and* personal life: Welcome to your own funeral, dearest. What did Robert Golden know that would have made it worth her while to destroy our family over? It had to be something that would have destroyed us anyway, or else her calculation made no sense at all.

I was not paraded before her or the others; I was detained in the vestibule inside the first set of doors. Detained, that is, by two cops who handcuffed me to the bench between the potted plant and the standing ashtray. Lily noticed me and slipped away from the crowd. When she approached, she said to the cops, "I'm one of his attorneys. I need to speak to him privately."

Maybe she had information about the CPS report. Poor Zoe, having to be interviewed about this. Poor me, having to rely on whatever she said. Lily trotted over to my bench without waiting for their permission and sat down. "The CPS report is 'inconclusive,'" Lily whispered. "They tried to interview Zoe, but she had a fever. Not severe but enough so she was groggy and not very responsive to anything."

"She was fine when she went to school yesterday."

"The social worker met with her. She verified the fever. They're going back this afternoon. If they think Zoe's in any danger, they'll remove her from the house."

It was all I could do to keep my anxieties on my own dismal situation in check. Hearing about Zoe being sick, Zoe being prodded by these bureaucrats, made me tremble with anger. "What does that mean for me?"

"An inconclusive report is better than a conclusive report that says you did something. Bernie knows what to do with it."

"Did he make a deal with the DA?"

"The DA was fine with it. Your wife balked."

"That's a surprise."

"She says no to everything. She wouldn't agree that today is

Thursday. Listen, Bernie is going to do most of the talking. I'll back him up if I need to."

"Do you know the judge?"

Lily shook her head. "She's an alternate, fills in for the regular guy."

She stood and turned to me, hunkered down and grabbed both my shoulders, staring into my eyes with gung-ho, coachlike intensity, her face six inches from mine. "Don't get sidetracked with her *mishegoss*. Keep your cool. Don't let anything piss you off, and don't attack her, whatever you do." A pint-size woman prepping me for a heavyweight match.

"Where did you learn so much Yiddish?" I asked.

"My ex-husband. He was the only Jewish cop in the Bronx."

An instant later, the non-Jewish cops in Scarsdale grabbed my elbows, unchained me from the bench, and led me briskly away, through one doorway and another, into a chamber that was unmistakably a courtroom. A wood-paneled auditorium with seats for thirty, uninhabited except for a small woman at a raised desk facing us, her black gown's shoulder pads on loan from the NFL. Short blond hair, flared nostrils, a pronounced birthmark over her lip. She was a stylish sixty- or sixty-five-year-old. JUDGE ROBINSON. A plastic nameplate on the desk. Here's to you, Mrs. Robinson. I stood, handcuffed, at one end of a long wooden table, cops on either side of me. Everyone else — I turned to the right — was lined up next to me along the edge of the table facing the judge: Lily, Bernie, the man with specs, and my darling wife. Legal pads, briefcases, and manila files came down on the table, accompanied by coughing, the rustle of papers, whispers, and suddenly a loud voice calling out my name. "Lavender!" A disembodied man's bellow.

"I'm here," I said.

The judge looked at me. "That was not a roll call, Mr. Lavender. The bailiff was announcing the case. Counselor, proceed."

"Your Honor, my partner, Lily Lopez, and I represent the defendant, Eric Lavender, a respected psychotherapist in Scarsdale. We waive a reading of the charges and rights, and request copies of accusatory instruments. I note from the documents provided that this complaint is based on conversations with the natural mother, who was not a witness to the alleged misconduct. It does not appear there is substantiation from anyone. I've just learned that the CPS report is inconclusive because the child had a fever and was unresponsive in the first interview. I understand CPS will attempt another interview today. As to the facts of each and every element of this alleged crime, the People will not be able to proceed with a trial. All they have is hearsay. Therefore, I want to enter a plea of not guilty, but I do not waive prosecution by information. We want to request a continuance of two weeks, and we'd like to be heard on the question of bail."

"You may proceed."

"Your Honor, Dr. Lavender received his Ph.D. some twenty years ago from Columbia University. In addition to his private practice in Scarsdale, he works on a pro bono basis with the psychologist and guidance counselors at the Scarsdale High School and specializes in counseling teenage boys. Last month, Dr. Lavender was called upon by the Scarsdale Police Department to resolve a life-threatening emergency, a situation where a fourteen-year-old boy was holding his father at gunpoint. Because of Dr. Lavender's sensitive work in connecting with this boy over the telephone, the boy released his father and surrendered to the police without harming himself or anyone else."

At that point, the judge's eyes swiveled from Bernie Rosenberg to me. But what could I read in them, in the heavy lids of middle age, the chin, the sagging cheeks? What I usually imagined I saw on people's faces, when they heard the story of my triumph with Jason Cummings, was respect, a glimmer of approbation. I often saw people actually sigh at the end, which I read as a cosmic sigh of relief that sometimes, somehow, something goes right. But no one who had heard it up to now knew me as an alleged child molester, and I had a feeling that made a difference. This face that held my fate was unreadable but focused intently on whomever was speaking, and occasionally on me, the accused, the defendant. It was the studied look of an old-fashioned Freudian analyst, blank, inscrutable, trained to reveal nothing so that any emotion could be projected onto it. But what did she see on my face? Guilty until proven innocent? Did she interpret my exhaustion as remorse? My intense gaze as evidence of defiance or lunacy? What could I do with my eyes to signal that my wife had made the whole thing up?

"He is the husband of Colleen Golden and the devoted and engaged father of two-year-old Sarah Rose Lavender and stepfather to Zoe Golden, whose natural father has apparently abandoned her. I understand that my client and his wife have talked several times about the possibility of his legally adopting Zoe. As you see from his rap sheet, Dr. Lavender has no prior arrests. In his twenty years of practice, he has never been sued or had a complaint filed against him through any of his professional associations. Your Honor, he tells me he hasn't had a parking ticket in three years." The judge did not smile. "But more to the point, he also tells me that he and his wife, who is a member of the matrimonial bar, have had some friction recently because of a conflict of interest involving one of his adult male patients. His patient's wife is being represented by Colleen Golden in her divorce from Dr. Lavender's patient. Once Dr. Lavender learned of this conflict of interest, he ended therapy with the husband and insisted that Ms. Golden cease representing the patient's wife. My client informs me that this conflict of interest has created animosity between the defendant and his wife, and that this discord is the motivation behind Ms. Golden's accusation, not any behavior of his toward his beloved stepdaughter. Because this charge has appeared literally out of nowhere and been thrust upon the defendant, we seek a two-week continuance on this hearing.

"On the question of bail, Your Honor, there is no reason to fear that Dr. Lavender will ignore his commitment to this court. Bail is used to make sure that a defendant shows up for his hearing, not to punish him before the facts of the case are advanced. Dr. Lavender is an integral member of this community. Dozens of people in the village and surrounding towns rely on him for their emotional and psychological well-being.

"Your Honor, my client has agreed to vacate the family house pending consent to an order of protection, without conceding anything. I'd like him to be able to leave the state for business purposes. I ask that you ROR him and revisit the case two weeks from today. Given that his place of work is a cottage in the backyard of the marital home, I would also ask that he be permitted to see patients there two days a week."

The judge's eyes swiveled down the row toward Colleen's end of the table. "Let's hear from the People." The People, she meant, of Scarsdale. The People whose secrets I keep and whose pampered wives and children I coddle and care for.

The little man with the spectacles, Rick Maxwell, had a much lower voice than his size would indicate, and he looked young enough to be a recent law school graduate. "Your Honor, the defendant is clearly a threat to his family and to the community. These are harrowing charges. Forcible touching. A violation of Section 130.60 of the New York State Penal Code, sexual abuse in the second degree, a class-A misdemeanor. According to the mother's sworn statement, the defendant inserted his finger into the child's vagina repeatedly." My head spun to Lily and my knees began to give way. I had not heard these details. Had she and Bernie? She did not turn to me, and I understood she was attempting to be poised and professional. "As Attorney Rosenberg said, the child in question, Ms. Golden's four-year-old daughter, will be interviewed again, later today, by Child Protective Services, and of course we await their report. There is a recommendation in all cases, including this one, that the defendant have no contact with the child. Nor with Ms. Golden's other child, a two-year-old female."

"Your Honor," Lily said, "I'm going to have to object to that characterization. The two-year-old is the defendant's natural daughter, not simply Ms. Golden's child."

"Point well taken. The People may proceed."

"Your Honor, while we don't know when the crime actually occurred, it was discovered yesterday morning when Ms. Golden took her daughter to school and the child complained of pain in her groin area. Yes, as his attorney claims, the defendant has no prior arrests, but I would remind the court that sexual misconduct, particularly of this nature, is often a silent crime, a crime that goes unnoticed.

"I have in court, standing next to me, the mother of the child, who strenuously objects to the defendant's release."

"Your Honor, I have to interrupt here" — this was, astonishingly, Colleen's voice — "though I know I haven't been called on to speak. It's true my husband is a psychotherapist, but what his lawyer left out of his biography is that he practices an alternative therapy with a massage table — I believe his clients have their clothes on, at least that's what he tells me — but in any case, he actually, as part of the therapy, puts his hands —"

"Your Honor" — this was Bernie, caught completely off-guard by this new twist — "this is *not* a hearing on my client's therapeutic techniques, which *no one* has objected to." And which Bernie knew nothing about.

"I want to hear this," the judge said, looking at Colleen — looking, I couldn't help but notice, with more curiosity than she had looked at me.

"Thank you so much, Your Honor." In those six words, she sounded demure and grateful, like a southern belle buttering up a gentleman caller. Did I hear her sniffle? Was she going to pretend to cry? "As you've heard, my husband has his therapy practice in a cottage in our backyard, which I myself had built for him, though his attorney didn't mention that fact. It was a supreme act of trust on my part, that I let this man into our lives, my daughter Zoe's life and my own, let him in so thoroughly that I encouraged him — no, made it *possible* for him — to work in close proximity all day long to *both* of my children. He explained his unusual therapy to me, and I found it, well, curious at first, but he seemed so enthusiastic about it. It never occurred to me in a million years that his technique would spill over onto —"

"Your Honor, with all due respect," Bernie said, "my client's therapy practice is not on trial here. No one in this community or in this courtroom has raised an objection to *anything* Dr. Lavender does with his patients."

"That's precisely my point," Colleen shot back — but in a dulcet voice quite different from her usual. "You see, he seduced me into thinking that everything he does, whether it's therapy or taking care of my children —"

"Your Honor," Bernie said, "the two-year-old is also Dr. Lavender's natural child."

I stared at the judge, whose eyes leaped from speaker to speaker, as though this were a doubles tennis match. Couldn't she slam a gavel and dam up this flood of lies and innuendoes? Or was this so much more entertaining than traffic court that she preferred to sit back and watch the show?

"Your Honor, if I may, when I met the defendant, I was still reeling from a crushing betrayal by my ex-husband, and I can only think now that my judgment was impaired, that I was so fragile and eager to have a new father for my daughter, that I overlooked —"

"I object," I shouted. "This is nonsense, slander, libel, fantasy, pick your label. She tricked me into having a child, she tricked me into moving to Scarsdale, and nothing she says about my touching the child has any truth to it. Nothing!"

"Mr. Rosenberg," the judge said, "please advise your client to remain silent."

"Your Honor," Bernie said, "he is stunned by these accusations, which have *no* bearing on the groundless accusations that have *already* been made against him. I apologize for his outburst, and yet the turn this hearing has taken —"

"Your Honor, my husband told me he touched my daughter inappropriately. He admitted this to me yesterday morning."

"What?" I cried. "This is a complete fabrication! She doesn't know the difference between the truth and —"

"Your Honor, please." A man's urgent voice, louder than all the others. It was Rick Maxwell. "I would ask you to post bail of fifty thousand dollars. Given the extreme nature of these accusations and the —"

"I must object," Bernie said. "In the last two minutes, with no evidence whatsoever, this esteemed member of our community has had his business conduct impugned. And now his wife wants us to believe he admitted misconduct to her that he denies having any part of! Charges like these can't be hurled around as though they have no bearing on —"

"He may be esteemed in the eyes of" — this, of course, was Colleen — "people who don't know him, and that seems to be his specialty, pulling the wool over the eyes of —"

"That's enough, Ms. Golden," the judge snapped. Had she reached her breaking point? Had it taken this long for her to see through Colleen's impersonation of a betrayed woman?

"I just need to make sure you understand —" Colleen said, before she was scolded again.

"I said, that's enough. Counselor, your client referred to his being, I believe the word he used was 'tricked,' into having a child. Could he elaborate?"

Bernie turned to me, his eyes bright with relief, or was it worry? I needed to deliver on this unfamiliar story. But once I let it out of the bag, the evidence would be gone: Colleen would go home and toss out the clomiphene. Then she might take off with the children, take revenge that would last a lifetime. But unless I said it, I'd be on the next train to Valhalla. "Your Honor." I had gotten the hang of that part. But this part — showing my hand and trashing my wife in public — would take gumption. I had to take my lessons from her: ingratiate myself, play the victim, the abused. That wouldn't take much acting. "This is difficult to talk about in public, but that's where we are. When Colleen and I were first dating, in the first three or four months, she told me she was using birth control, a diaphragm to be exact. When we conceived a child, she insisted it was an accident. Several weeks ago, I learned she had been taking fertility pills. This doesn't take away any of my love for my daughter, but it puts a dent in my trust for her mother."

Colleen's response was breathless: "Your Honor, this is a lie and it's irrelevant to the fact that he molested my daughter!"

"Ms. Golden, I will permit no more outbursts in this courtroom from you or anyone else. Mr. Rosenberg, do you have anything further to say?" The judge scribbled something on a pad in front of her and looked up to Bernie. Did she believe me? Had Colleen finally gone too far?

"Yes, Your Honor," Bernie said. "Clearly there is strife in this marriage, but I hope the court will not allow Ms. Golden to continue to abuse the criminal justice system or slander her husband's reputation. I would emphasize again that all we have is an unsubstantiated allegation, no witnesses, a defendant with no priors, and an inconclusive report from Child Protective Services. Rather than punish Eric with exorbitant bail, I request that he be released on his own recognizance. He's agreed to vacate the marital home and return here in two weeks to respond thoroughly to the allegations."

Would Colleen defy the judge again and cry out? From the other end of the table, I couldn't see her, but I could almost feel her thwarted energy, the effort it took to keep her mouth shut when it looked as if I had scored a few points. The judge's eyes veered from Colleen to me and down to her desk. She tapped the point of her pen on a piece of paper, raised her eyes, and ran them down the lineup, lighting somewhere in the middle, on Bernie or the DA. "I've heard the arguments and I understand these charges are extremely serious." Pause. Beat. "Yet I'm inclined to grant Mr. Rosenberg's application to ROR his client. This defendant has no prior arrests, no history of complaints, and from what I —"

"But Your Honor," Colleen cried, "I see I haven't conveyed to you the kind of deception my husband —"

"Mr. Maxwell, instruct her to be quiet as long as she's in my courtroom."

I was home free. Or was I? Was the judge allowed to change her mind, to reconsider?

"I am adjourning this proceeding for six days, until next Wednesday at nine-thirty in the morning in this courtroom. I'm issuing an order of protection for one week, barring Dr. Lavender from contact with either child and from entering the marital home, except once, to get his clothes and personal effects. He may *not* use his cottage for work during this time period. He will have to see patients in another office." Her eyes landed on me. "Dr. Lavender, if you are not here next Wednesday morning, I'll issue a warrant for your arrest and bail will be set at fifty thousand dollars. If you violate the order of protection, which says you cannot set foot in your house once you get your belongings or have any contact with your children, you will also be arrested. Do you understand?"

"Yes, I do."

"I'm putting you on a very short leash. When do you intend to vacate the house?"

"As soon as he's released, Your Honor," Lily answered for me, "as long as the children aren't home. I trust Ms. Golden will see to that. I'll accompany him."

"Officers, remove his handcuffs."

There was an audible gasp from Colleen.

The slam of a gavel on wood. My hands unlocked. Smiles from Lily and Bernie. Quiet chaos. Out of the corner of my eye, I saw my wife race out of the courtroom as though she were being chased. When I turned to watch her go, a face I hadn't expected came toward me. My sister. Her girlish bangs, her radiant smile. How did she? — that's right. She knew Lily. Lily must have called her or she called Lily. I could feel the blood flow again in my hands and my shoulders. Real blood. Real family. Pru threw her arm around my waist, and I could see her eyes were wet.

Lily said, "Good going," and squeezed my forearm.

Bernie said, "Touchdown," and handed me a business card. "Be in our office in an hour, and we'll talk about what's next. Lily wants to go with you to your house."

I tried to smile, to imitate everyone around me. This was a victory, a celebration. This was not the patrol car to Valhalla. I draped my arm around Pru's shoulder and held on tighter than I had meant to. Her sturdiness surprised me until I remembered that it almost always surprised me when I hugged her; she was lean and strong. She and Lily guided me out of the courtroom. I gazed around the lobby — looking for who? for what? — and tried to remember to be happy, to be grateful. But by my reckoning, forty-eight hours ago, I was in my cottage talking to a patient about how she could improve her relationship with her grown daughter after a lifetime of discord between them. I'd never get a Nobel Prize for it; it wouldn't change the course of history; our words evaporated the instant they were spoken. Yes, I know, it's women's work, not the Lord's work that my sister does and Colleen's ex-husband does, helping refugees and political prisoners. But all I wanted was to be back in my cottage again, instead of where I was: homeless, childless, wifeless, terrified.

❧ 17 ❧

They Can't Take That
Away from Me . . . Can They?

THERE WERE FOURTEEN CALLS on my office answering machine and eleven on my cell phone, representing three and four tries from the clients I'd stood up Thursday morning, during my jail time and arraignment. One suspected she had the wrong day; one was indignant. Only one had it right — she feared something had happened to me — and the last caller startled the hell out of me: "Hi, it's Sandy Lefkowitz. Just got your message. I mean, the person said he was you, but it didn't sound like you, and I couldn't understand — you said they *came* for you. I couldn't figure out, who would have come for you? And *me*? Your wife and my wife already have me by the balls, so who's left? There must be a merry prankster out there with your address book. Or something."

Jesus, that's right. I'd called Sandy from my cell — I don't mean my phone — and forgotten completely about it. A small mercy: I sounded so strange he hadn't recognized me. Another mercy that I didn't realize was mine until the end of the last message I listened to: my story must not have ended up on TV or radio because no one mentioned it, and there were no calls from the press.

"Are you ready?" Lily, my chaperone, peeked into my office from the waiting room. I could see she had a legal pad under her arm, and the top page was covered with script, the dark ink of a sure hand. The blueprint for my release.

"One minute." I dropped my laptop and address book into a carrying case and, as I left the cottage, I taped a note to the door, in case there was a patient I couldn't reach in time: DR. LAVENDER HAS A FAMILY EMERGENCY. HE OFFERS HIS APOLOGIES AND WILL CALL YOU ASAP TO RESCHEDULE. It seemed best to refer to myself in the third person, as though I were out of town and someone had to write the note in my absence. Why hadn't I asked Lily or Pru to do this yesterday? Having been separated from my patients, and having heard their aching phone messages — even the angry ones — I felt a wave of tenderness for them. I would call each as soon as I was finished meeting with Bernie and Lily at their office in White Plains.

"I had some ideas about strategy sitting in your waiting room," Lily said as we walked to my car parked on our pebbled, circular driveway. No, not *our* driveway anymore. Was it hers now, or was it marital property subject to division? I could finally understand people going off their rockers and fighting over who would get the driveway in the settlement. Or was I simply trying to distract myself with silliness, with trifles, because they kept my mind, and the rest of me, from giving in to crushing sadness?

"I hope you didn't rule out homicide," I said to Lily. Keep up the patter, run the joke machine, even if they come out lame. "Hop in. My suitcase is already in the trunk." After the meeting with Lily and Bernie, I was moving into Pru and Bea's guest room on West End Avenue, not many blocks from my former life in the city. This was not going to be what you'd call a heroic homecoming.

Even in the state I was in, it was impossible not to notice that it was an acutely beautiful fall day on this acutely beautiful Scarsdale street. I exulted in the panorama until I realized it was not *ours* anymore. The stone mansions, the manicured gardens, the shadows of my children everywhere. Sunlight poured down on us through the antique trees, and the grass on everyone's lawn had an emerald sheen. Perhaps because of the real estate taxes we paid — we? they? she? — it grew preternaturally green.

Before she got in the car, Lily tapped the roof to get my attention, uncertain what to make of my wisecrack. "Eric, I never heard you say homicide."

"I'm just blowing off steam. Don't worry, I'm a peace-loving guy. I take after my wife."

"And I'm a criminal defense lawyer."

"Should we take the parkway to your office?"

"*Sí, cómo no?* It's just two exits."

As we swung out into the street, I could feel the driveway pebbles that were no longer mine crunching beneath the tires. Did my life in the house flash before me as I drove away, as I was afraid it might? No. My mind was stuck on what had just happened: Colleen had allotted me fifteen minutes alone to pack. Everything I touched in the house felt radioactive, except my children's dolls and marking pens, which littered every room. I had tossed a small stuffed animal into my suitcase, a loose-limbed dog with floppy ears, one of three or four that are nearly identical, and all named Ralph. Zoe thought the name was hilarious. "Where's Ralph?" was all I had to say to make her dissolve into giggles. "Daddy, I'm cracking up," she would splutter as she laughed. "I'm breaking in a thousand pieces like Humpty Dumpty. You have to put me back together again." I'd swiped a few photographs from the top of my dresser and scoured the linen closet for the bottle of clomiphene. Gone. As I suspected.

When I could see the house in the rearview mirror, when the vast place grew smaller and disappeared as we turned the corner, the wallop of my departure hit me. It triggered the memory of another loss, the call that had come from the Los Angeles Police Department several years before. As soon as the husky voice identified himself as a cop in L.A., I knew my father was dead. If I had been alone in the car, I would have cried, but I couldn't with Lily there, couldn't, as I negotiated my way through the busy village toward the parkway. Out of the corner of my eye I saw she was reading her notes. I hadn't asked what she and Bernie charge, and neither of them had mentioned it. An odd omission. Or maybe not. They had to know that the cost didn't matter to me. This was a fight for my life. I'd become one of those poor bastards Colleen had mentioned a few weeks ago who would hock his house to pay his criminal defense lawyer. But the money that was mine now belonged to Colleen too. It was one for all and all for one. I needed to stop at the bank and get some. Jesus. No. She wouldn't do that, would she?

"I need to stop at the bank." I made a quick right turn onto the last street before the parkway and drove up to the branch Colleen and I used. "What if she emptied out the accounts?"

"Get receipts from the teller that show the activity. She can take out money, but she can't close an account without your permission."

IT DIDN'T comfort me that my wife's behavior was consistent or that I had begun thinking the way she did. She left $5 in the savings account and $50 in the checking. "Why so much?" Lily asked. We were on the parkway, and she was studying the two pages of recent activity. "Maybe they have a monthly minimum. Or maybe she wanted you to be able to buy a bag of groceries. I have to tell you, Eric, she really fucked herself with this move. Pardon my French. She's going to tell the judge she did it because she was afraid you would do it first and leave her with nothing, but you're the one who has to find a place to live, a place to work, and pay a lawyer. The money is marital property, which means half is yours. She got a history of mental illness? Manic-depressive, something like that, because this is nuts. Here's the exit. Go right at the end of the ramp."

Did she have a history of mental illness? Great question for a shrink about his wife. Maybe that's the secret hiding in Boston: she had been to a psych hospital. Did she think I wouldn't understand? "Not that she ever told me, but that doesn't mean much."

Lily put the bank statements into her briefcase and directed me to the parking lot behind her office. We were both somber and stunned by my new circumstances, by this coruscating evidence of how far — how much farther — she would go. "Look, Eric, before we go up to the office, I need to ask you some personal questions." I pulled into a space and turned off the ignition. "About your therapy practice and about your sex life."

"My sex life? A gorgeous twenty-two-year-old was supposed to come to my cottage tonight pretending to be my patient and we were going to go at it on the couch for fifty minutes. If she was very needy, I was going to give her a little more time. But I called her from jail and canceled. How's your sex life?"

She gave me a deadpan look; I could see she didn't know what to make of this. Maybe I should cool the jokes, since I was paying her by the hour. "You're kidding, right?"

"I'm a married guy whose office is in the backyard. I've got two little kids and a wife who works twenty hours a week more than I do."

"What was all the stuff she was saying about your therapy? You do massages and what else?"

"I don't do massages, and Colleen knows it. I'm an eclectic psychotherapist. It's mostly sitting in a chair talking. Sometimes people lie on a massage table and talk while we do relaxation exercises. Everyone's dressed and they sign release forms. People suffering from physical pain and disabling anxiety — what's wrong, Lily?" She was staring at me in a way that suggested intense curiosity.

"Does it work?"

"It's not like taking a pill. It helps people listen to their bodies and integrate physical and psychological conditions. It's subtle, but it can be very powerful and —"

"Who else besides you does this?"

"People all over the country."

"I mean, around here. You have a name you could give me?"

Now I understood. She wanted the name of a therapist for herself.

"Not on me, but I'll find someone in Westchester for you."

"Thanks. And now we get to talk about your sex life. Any hanky-panky since you got married?"

I shook my head.

"Any incriminating letters or e-mails she can haul out?"

"None I can think of."

"You look at porn on the Internet?"

"No."

"Ever?"

"Years ago, when it was a novelty. Just like everyone else."

"How often?"

"I don't know. Three or four times, but I've gone through two computers since then. There's no record anywhere."

"Adults or kids?"

"Adults."

"Men or women?"

"For Christ's sake. Women. Grown women."

"And sex with Colleen?"

"Above average. No pictures. No videos. Sorry."

"*Mira,* Eric, I don't care what you do with anyone. I just don't want surprises when we go back to court. Better to be two steps ahead of her, not two steps behind. One more and I'm through."

I turned to her, feigning annoyance. She was cute and competent and distressed enough to have asked for the name of a therapist. Too bad I couldn't treat her myself. Even if all the charges against me were dropped, we had too many connections to start a therapeutic relationship. If she were my younger sister, this would be a moment I would feel tenderness and concern for her, her deep brown eyes and honey brown skin, the anxiety that radiated from her chewed-up fingernails, the son whose heart problems had been so bad she needed my sister's help. "Shoot."

"When's the last time you had sex with Colleen?"

I didn't have to think long about that. "The night before last."

I undid my seat belt and moved to open my door, but I could sense that Lily hadn't budged. "You mind if I ask how that came about?"

Your Honor, my wife fucked me at eleven o'clock one night and had me arrested at eleven o'clock the next morning. The sex was her idea, just like everything else has been since the moment we met. She stuck her hand into the elevator at the Mondrian to keep our conversation going. She invited me to lunch, to dinner, to Scarsdale, to the high school, the newspaper, the contractor, the architect, the bank. Was there anything that *hadn't* been her idea? For the first time, it crossed my mind that nursing Zoe by the pool at the hotel was a staged event, just in case I came downstairs early for our lunch date. She had to tell me she had a child, because I didn't know from our conversation in the elevator, but she didn't want it to make me slink away. So she bared her breast and let me watch someone else suck it, to lower my resistance, to grab me by the balls before I knew a single piece of the story. Would she have cooked that up? Would she? Oh, no, not my fair-haired, bonny Colleen. I looked at Lily, who could see I had a hard time answering the question.

"It was her idea," I said softly.

"I'm sorry to get so personal, but I'm trying to understand how that twisted mind of hers works, because I want to know what twisted move she might make next."

"I understand."

"Let's go upstairs and get to work."

Lily was gone in a flash, out of the car and headed across the parking lot to the steel back door of a plain three-story brick office building. I was not far behind. But how could I have been anywhere else — desperate, domesticated pack animal that I had become? The unicorn in another sort of captivity, being shuttled from one pen to another.

UPSTAIRS, in their waiting area, was a surprise: Bea Harris, with a bright smile and a motherly hug. "I couldn't make it to the arraignment, but I wanted to help, and Pru knew you'd be here. She had to go back to the hospital. Your lawyer said I need your permission to be included in the bull session."

"Sure. Of course."

Lily said, "Come into the conference room. Bernie and I will join you in a few minutes."

We took seats at a wooden table across from a blackboard, a quaint touch. A modest room, not a glitzy corporate conference center. It was a small comfort that I was not paying for glamour, especially with the money I would have to borrow from my sister.

Bea covered my hand with hers. "How are you holding up?" Could she see I was close to tears? And mortified to have ended up here. My sister: famous for saving children, and I, for molesting them.

"How did you know Colleen was dangerous?"

"What?"

"The day I went to your apartment and Pru called me when I left. You'd told her I should watch out. How did you know?"

"It never occurred to me until after you told us about the fertility pills and your conflict of interest. Pru and I always thought she had a strange affect, something we couldn't articulate. I'm still not sure what we were seeing."

"Where was I, that I didn't see it?"

"Number one, dear heart, she's very pretty. Number two, you're a nice guy whose job is helping people in distress. Number three, she's something of a con artist. They don't call them artists for nothing."

Bernie's voice interrupted the echo of those words in my rattled, addled brain. "Are we ready?" Would there be any more I needed to absorb? Was I going to break down right here, or could I wait until I was alone later that day in my sister's guest room? Lily sat near the blackboard with her ubiquitous legal pad and her bitten nails.

"We have five days to pull together the evidence that says you didn't do it," Bernie said, "but because the child can't authoritatively speak for herself, and because it's impossible to prove a negative, we've got a better chance of proving, one, that Colleen is a chronic liar and, two, that you're a prince." He walked to the side of the blackboard and wrote the number 1.

"But the judge wouldn't have let me go today if she had believed Colleen, so why do we have to go to such lengths to put on this show? And what if the CPS report comes in this afternoon saying I didn't do anything?"

"Because what we saw today is that Colleen will say anything," Lily said, "whether she has evidence or not. For all we know, she may have coached Zoe to say 'Daddy touched my pookie.' Or the judge could be sick next Wednesday and we'd have to start your defense from scratch with someone new. The DA and Colleen *have* to come in next week with a new story or a new piece of evidence. She can't just stamp her feet again and expect to win. But if there's a judge who doesn't know the history, it's her lucky day."

"We take nothing for granted around here," Bernie said and began writing on the board.

1. Marsha Rogers to interview child
2. C's ex in Boston
3. Eric's touching psychotherapy: defense of / explanation
4. Fertility drug — name of pharmacy? subpoena?
5. Character witnesses
6. Timetable

"Anything I've left out?" he asked.

"There's someone else I was going to see in Boston," I said. "A woman who helped Colleen write her divorce handbook. She and Colleen had a falling-out. Catherine Franks."

"The bank accounts," Lily said. "Number seven, or are we up to eight?"

"What about the bank accounts?" Bea asked.

"I'll tell you later," I said.

"Bernie and I can work with Marsha Rogers to set up the interview with Zoe," Lily said. "Colleen will have to go along with this and —"

"What if she doesn't?" Bea asked.

"We issue a subpoena, she'll have no choice," Bernie said. "This gal does some kind of magic with dolls and drawings and figures out if kids have been coached or molested. She's a great witness. Our office will handle that. Eric, can you remember where Colleen had the fertility drug filled? If we know which pharmacy, we can subpoena their records."

I named a place in the village where we got most medicine.

"What about Boston?" Bernie said. "Are you prepared to go today or tomorrow?"

"Why can't he talk to these folks by phone?" Lily asked.

I was about to answer when Bea grabbed the reins. "The ex has a bad temper and if he hangs up on Eric, it's over."

"Are you up to it?" Lily asked me.

Yes, I had the energy to save my life, but I had to call my patients before I went anywhere — all of them, to say my appointments for the next week were canceled — and get some sleep. "I can leave first thing in the morning."

"We need someone," Bernie said, "to counter her charges about your brand of therapy. Who do you know with a string of graduate degrees after his name who can explain this stuff and not make it sound flaky?"

I described Amanda Ritter, whose credentials were identical to mine but included an associate professorship at CUNY in the graduate psychology department. There was general agreement that she sounded like a good candidate; I would call her as soon as the meeting was over. If she couldn't do it, I would ask her for a referral. Bernie scribbled her name on the board and said, "What about character witnesses? Who've we got for that?" He turned to me.

"Can we use Amanda for that too?"

"How long've you known her?"

"Since graduate school."

"Ever slept together?" Bernie asked.

"How come my sex life is everyone's favorite subject today?"

"Because it's your lucky day," Bernie said.

"So our having sex disqualifies her from vouching for me? If anything, she might be more critical of me if we'd —"

"The DA's goal is to make you look bad. If your only character witness is someone you slept with —"

"A few times almost thirty years ago? Richard Nixon was president. The DA was in diapers. What could it possibly mean in the context of —"

"It would be good to have another name or two."

I was aware of wanting to seem nonchalant in the face of his request, but the longer I didn't answer, the more difficult it was to admit that I couldn't think of anyone to ask. I'd lost touch with the few people I spent time with before I got married. They were mostly girlfriends anyway. My work is a never-ending series of intense relationships, but I work, you might also say, alone: no colleagues, office mates, or underlings. Sure, I know other therapists here and there, but I'm not one of the sociable ones, heading off to the APA convention in Hawaii to hear the keynote lecture, "What Dolphins Can Teach Us about Intimacy," or joining the ad hoc committee on agoraphobia. Outside my family, my only meaningful connections are with people who pay me to pay attention to them. When they're better, or when they abandon the effort in

hopeless exasperation, we sever all ties. I couldn't call one with a favor: "Would you mind testifying under oath that you don't believe
I molested my four-year-old stepdaughter? By the way, how've you
been for the last eight years?"

"All we need is a neighbor," Lily said, sensing my discomfort.
"Someone who's seen you with your kids."

"I'm not dying to call up the guy next door and tell him I'm accused of . . . Why not the Scarsdale police? I can't remember their
names, but I was their hero at the end of August when I kept Jason
Cummings from shooting his father."

"We'll mention that prominently in our statement, like we did
today, but if we can get someone who's known you for a while and
can —"

"Why can't I do it?" Bea volunteered. "I'm Pru's partner, but I've
seen you with your kids."

"Business partner?" Bernie asked.

"Domestic. Romantic."

"We should have someone other than a relative," Bernie said.

"On the other hand," Lily said, "if Eric is claiming he's innocent, maybe we make the case that he shouldn't have to admit the
accusation to his colleagues or neighbors. That it could damage his
professional reputation."

"What about a baby-sitter?" Bernie said.

I felt myself wince at the thought that Graciela would be en-
snared in this, forced to take sides — and threatened with the loss
of her job if she displeased Colleen. This would not have crossed
my mind the day before yesterday, but today I could say: if she
testified for me it might make Colleen mad enough to fire her.

"We have a live-in nanny," I said. "She's their only baby-sitter,
and she spends more time with the kids than Colleen does. I can't
ask her to take sides. Colleen might flip out and let her go."

"Maybe we could ask her a few questions about you," Bernie
said, "that are general. How many hours a week you spend with
your kids, what meals —"

"She supports two kids in the Philippines. She sees them once a year for three weeks. I can't do this to her. Or to my kids."

Bernie's beady Perry Mason eyes shifted very obviously to Bea. "The prize may be yours by default."

"Eric, do you have a problem with this?" Lily asked me. I'd been trying to figure out the ebb and flow of Lily and Bernie's partnership. He was quite a bit older and clearly more experienced, more authoritative. He was in charge and she made it run more smoothly. Pilot and copilot. She ironed out his wrinkled thinking; cooked, cleaned, tended the womanly caboose of other people's feelings.

"No," I said. "No problem at all." How could I complain about someone who had tossed me a life preserver? "Bea will do a terrific job." A better job with my life than I was doing with it myself.

"The hearing is next Wednesday. Let's meet here Tuesday at nine-thirty and put together everything we've got. Any questions?"

I had nothing but questions. They were rhetorical. They were Jesuitical. Questions I was too embarrassed to give voice to in the presence of all of these people assembled here to help me out of the colossal mess I was in.

"No questions for right now," I said.

"Good luck," Lily said. "Let us know what you find out in Boston."

Laugh Out Loud

Is there someone I'm addressing here — or is this only the dutiful report of a dutiful son, a devoted father, a hornswoggled husband? Why are all the words for that so hard and angular, so rough-sounding? *Con. Swindle. Hoax. Bamboozle.* You would never mistake them for the names of flowers or synonyms for "hello." *Greetings. Welcome. Shalom. Hey there.* But what's wrong with a report — one thing happened, then another? Better that than the ranting of an angry man or the ravings of a madman, because who would listen to those? Let me try simply to make this a record of what happened after the arraignment so you'll know — ah, then, it's *you* I'm writing to, isn't it? — that I'm not the person your mother accused me of being. Regardless of what happens next Wednesday when I go back to court, I want you to know what happened in the days since I had to leave our house, because there's nothing I can be sure of anymore — except that your mother will not tell you the same version of events that I will.

She won't tell you that Aunt Pru and Aunt Bea took me in and gave me their luxurious guest room; after my night on a jail cell pallet, I slept in a double bed with four down pillows. Your mother won't tell you how tenderly they took care of me, as though I were a wounded bird, or that my feeling of desperation was as heavy as the flu. Or that I slept for several hours late that afternoon and then began calling patients from a small desk in my room, to apologize and cancel appointments for the upcoming week. I simply said I was out of town with a family medical emergency. After the hearing on Wednesday I would know what would become of me. And of my livelihood. I would have to call everyone all over again, but I left them with the impression that things would soon return to normal — an assessment I knew better than to believe.

In a way I hadn't anticipated, the calls buoyed me, reminded me that I had real relationships with people who counted on me, that I had not been led down this forlorn path with nothing to show for it but a rap sheet and children who might be lost to me forever.

"Are you ready for a glass of wine?" Pru asked, knocking on the guest room door.

"Just about."

"How you doing?"

"Fair. How about you?"

"I just made some calls myself," Pru said. "If you want company going to Boston, I can fly up with you tomorrow, for the day."

"You don't have to do that."

"I know I don't, but there aren't too many opportunities to be with you like this."

"You mean with me having fucked up like a wayward teenager?"

"You've just been mauled by the universe. There's a difference. Red wine or white?"

That was as good a description as any: mauled by the universe. Pru disappeared from the doorway and returned a few minutes later with a glass of Merlot and a small plate of cheese and crackers. I thanked her profusely for everything, especially the money she was loaning me. Had I kept my distance from her since I married because I didn't want to impose, knowing she didn't like Colleen, or was it because I didn't want her feelings for Colleen to give me any ideas about what might be wrong with her myself? Wasn't everything that happened proof that I *was* inferior to my superlative sibling?

"I want to come with you to Boston," she said. "What if Colleen's psycho ex does something to you? I'll wait outside his office."

"That's sweet, Pru, but I don't think he's going to assault me."

"I just arranged to take the day off. Bea and I will be gone for the weekend. I told you, didn't I, that we're going to visit friends in the Berkshires?"

"But you're taking the day off? You didn't cancel someone's surgery, did you?"

"Three tiny babies. Sacrificed for you. Or maybe it was four, I can't remember. When you're finished, come join me in the living room."

"When are you going to stop being so nice to me?"

"Tomorrow, at quarter to three."

I connected my laptop and eventually figured out how to check my e-mail. I don't communicate with patients this way, so it's not as vital as it is to many people, but I was hoping for a response to the e-mail I had sent Catherine Franks earlier this week, the one Colleen probably found if she searched my computer.

There it was.

Dear Eric Lavender —
On Sept. 18, you wrote:
>I don't have a clear idea of how to approach
>you but I am coming, by myself,
>to Boston next Wednesday afternoon . . .

Sorry I didn't get back to you before. I had no idea what to make of your e-mail or what you could have wanted from me, since we don't know each other from Adam. I also couldn't figure out why you said you're coming to Boston by yourself. If you've already come and gone, this may be irrelevant.

Earlier today this fuzzy picture came into focus when I got an e-mail from Colleen, unsolicited, announcing that she's sending me a "bonus" for the book I wrote with her 5 years ago — $10,000. LOL. When the vile thing hit the bestseller list, I thought of asking her for $$ but could never bring myself to get in touch with her.

I know Colleen never does anything generous without an ulterior motive and having received your cryptic e-mail last week, I figured out today there must be something amiss between you. Figured she knew you wanted to meet me and that this "bonus" was her way of paying me to shut up. LOL. She thought I could be bribed for 10K. Maybe 100K — "in unmarked bills," as my son says, trying to sound tough.

If you can't believe I've read so much into your e-mail and hers, that's because you may not have an inside track on how she operates. Or maybe you do. Or maybe I've got the whole picture wrong. If so, sorry about that.

Let me know if you're still in Boston and want to meet.

"Prudence," I called out, her full name a signal that this was serious. "I think I know why Colleen emptied out the bank accounts. What time can you leave in the morning?" I had figured out what Colleen was up to, but I needed my trendy sister-in-law, Bea, to translate "LOL" for me. Laugh Out Loud. Yes, indeed, this Catherine Franks would have a thing or two to tell me about my wife.

HIS OFFICE DOOR on the third floor of the law school was closed, but the small handwritten card next to it confirmed this was the only hour he'd be in on Friday. I knocked lightly, not wanting to wake the sleeping tiger abruptly. Pru, standing a few feet off to my side, theatrically held her breath. I had several snapshots of Zoe in the pocket of my jacket and planned to exhibit them early in our meeting: Count Dracula taming the vampire with a cross.

The door cracked open and a professorial face showed itself — round, topped by a full head of curly salt-and-pepper hair and a pair of wire-rimmed glasses. "Yes?"

"Professor Golden?"

"Yes."

"Do you have a minute to talk about a family matter? My name is Eric Lavender."

"Whose family?" His voice was steady, no turbulence yet.

"Yours and mine." Pru had stepped away and wandered off; I was on my own.

His eyes narrowed, the gaze intensified, accentuated by thick black eyebrows, a high forehead. He was trying to see if he remembered me. "I'm expecting a student but come in until he arrives. Take a seat." He held his hand out to a wooden armchair beside his desk, in a space whose every surface was piled high with papers, files, and books. Whatever decorating tips Colleen might have given him for *his* office were long abandoned. He closed the door behind us, the better to raise his voice if I pressed the wrong button. "Have we ever met?"

"No. I'm Colleen Golden's husband." I watched his face. He didn't move but didn't take his eyes from me. He was taller than I imagined he would be, trimmer, more athletic, in a pair of aged corduroy pants and a polo shirt. "I thought you might want to see this. A picture of your daughter." I handed it to him as we sat down.

It was Zoe on the swing in our backyard a few months ago, radiant in a pink top with her mother's strawberry blond hair hugging her cheeks. I studied his face to see if they shared any features — and to gauge his response to seeing the child he had abandoned. But nothing, no smile, no tenderness. As though he were looking at a pile of bricks. "How old is she?"

"Almost five."

"Hardly my daughter." But he didn't pounce, didn't growl. He looked up from the picture and said in a calm, reasoned voice, "I haven't seen Colleen since our divorce ten years ago. My daughter is twenty-four."

I stared at him, thinking I hadn't heard right. Maybe he would recalculate and come up with a number closer to four. No sign of that. No anger either. He was incredibly placid. "Ten?"

He nodded.

"She told me you —" Did I dare tell him? Would that ignite his wrath? What the hell, I had only a few minutes. "That you left her when she was pregnant."

"What a thoroughgoing bastard I am!" He shook his head as though I'd just given him a baseball score that went against all the odds, and suddenly he was animated. "Went out for cigarettes and never came back, something like that?"

"Left her for a student."

"Wow. Even better. I bet she could work up a lot of righteous indignation over that. How long have you known her?" My mind went blank, a delayed reaction to the news about Zoe and their divorce. I had not known her at all. That was the answer. "Where did you meet?"

"A hotel in Los Angeles. My father had just died. We started chatting by the pool. Zoe, your alleged daughter, was a year old." I did not mention the breast-feeding or her garter belt, which seemed out of place for a woman as nervous as she said she was, and as out of practice. Did not mention my mouth to her nipple, or the broken heart that turned out to be a lie. But the breast milk was real — wasn't it? Could she have engineered the earthquake too?

I was beginning to feel like Alice inside the looking glass, gazing at a distorted version of myself in the mirror — and of the last four years of my life, and of everything from here on out, because this news reverberated in all directions.

"How did you find me? What prompted you to come?"

"The short answer is that I saw your wedding announcement in the *Times* a few weeks ago. Things didn't fit with what she'd told me. The next day I went to look at the paper again, but Colleen had cut out the announcement and then denied having seen it."

"That's why you're here?"

"That's the beginning. I came to find out what she was hiding. I think you just told me."

"I haven't told you anything," he said. "Do you and she have children?"

"Professor Golden, before I answer you —"

"Call me Bob."

"Bob, I'm here because Colleen accused me of molesting this child — her name is Zoe — three days ago." I gestured to the snapshot he had handed back to me. "I spent the night before last in jail, in Scarsdale, where we live. The judge ROR'd me, but I have to go back for a fuller hearing next Wednesday. There's an order of protection, and I can't go to our house or see the kids. And" — I had almost forgotten this in the hail of grim news — "yesterday after the arraignment she cleaned out our bank accounts."

"Good God."

"I have two lawyers trying to get the charges dropped. We need evidence that Colleen isn't reliable, because she's the one who filed the complaint against me."

He stood and walked across the office to a tall file cabinet, showing me the lean physique of a jock, punctuated by a pair of running shoes that looked like they'd just come out of the box. With his back to me he was sifting purposefully through the top drawer. "She didn't pull that with me because she couldn't have gotten away with it. You don't haul your law professor husband into court on a false charge involving his own daughter. Even Colleen's not foolish enough to do that. I'm looking for our divorce decree. The date will help you establish that Zoe isn't mine."

"You have a twenty-four-year-old daughter?"

"Colleen was her stepmother for eight years."

"I asked her a long time ago if you had any children. She said no."

"It's not surprising she wouldn't want to talk about it." He turned around with a thin file in his hand, and I realized that his volatile temper must have been a lie too. It helped her explain why they weren't in touch. "I'll make a copy of it for you. Now we need evidence that proves she actually told you that I walked out on her while she was pregnant. Have you seen the child's birth certificate?" I shook my head. "It would be interesting to see who Colleen declared as the father. Where was she born?"

"Boston."

"Call the public records office. You might be able to get an expedited copy." He sat back in his chair and looked at me and closed his eyes for a moment. Two men bamboozled by the same woman. Is that what he was thinking too? When he opened his eyes, he said, "If it's any consolation to you, I got involved with Colleen shortly after my wife died. Natalie was seven. Colleen had taken a class with me and then became a research assistant. My wife was alive. There was nothing between us. After she graduated, she followed a boyfriend to Albany, but she didn't like it there, or didn't like him, and came back and got in touch with me for a letter of recommendation. My wife had just died unexpectedly. Much to my surprise, Colleen made herself available to me. She volunteered to take my daughter here and there. Poured on the sympathy and charm. It didn't take long to decide I wanted a mother for my daughter who wouldn't die. A young, healthy one seemed a good bet. Beautiful, smart, kind. She had gotten it into her head that marrying me would be a good career move. I found that out many years later. Any of this sound familiar?"

All I could do was nod. She didn't need a career boost by the time she met me. She needed a husband as a decoration for the master bedroom and a father for her fatherless child. Was that all it ever was: I had a role or two to play? Sperm donor, escort, schlemiel?

"What do you do for a living, Eric?"

I chortled. It was pitiful to have to admit. I was a soldier who doesn't know how to use a gun. A fireman who doesn't notice when his house is on fire. "I'm a psychotherapist." I was embarrassed, mortified that as a specialist in the vicissitudes of human behavior, in its dark corners and subterranean longings, I had fallen for all of Colleen's charades. But to *see* people, to know them, they have to reveal themselves to you, they have to let you in. If they lie about almost everything, is it a failing that you believed them?

"You must be thinking I should have known better," I said.

"To the contrary, I imagine you're very trusting and empathic, given what you do. Colleen is too selfish to feel empathy. All she can do is put on a show of concern when she wants something. It took me most of the years of our marriage to understand what was going on."

"You mean something specific was going on — or her behavior in general?"

Here I could see Bob Golden flinch, not a dramatic gesture but a tightening in his jaw, a mild clenching of teeth, a noticeable intake of breath. He was not eager to answer my question, and for the first time since I had arrived, for the first time in days, I was thrust into my usual role of he who listens well to people's secrets. "I'll give you the short version. Things were fine for the first few years. Colleen was working at a law firm, one of the few beginning jobs that didn't require eighty hours a week. She was a nighttime and weekend stepmother, and from what I could see, kindhearted and responsible. When Natalie was about ten, my human rights work expanded and I started traveling more, trips of a week or two at a time to Asia, Africa, Indonesia. Fast-forward a few more years. My daughter came to me one day when she was thirteen and confessed that Colleen had boyfriends in and out of the house while I was gone and sometimes stayed out all night and left her alone.

She'd bribed Natalie into keeping the secret with frequent shopping expeditions. I thought they did a little too much clothes buying, but I innocently believed they liked to spend time together."

It was my turn to say "Good God" and compare it to my own Colleen story, as he must have when he heard mine. "What did you do?"

Another layer of this painful wound to peel back. "I knew enough not to leave right away, because she could charge me with desertion, and I needed to collect the evidence — credit card bills, checkbook ledgers — that she'd been spending inordinate amounts of money on clothes and jewelry on a regular basis. And I didn't want my daughter to feel that she had caused an upheaval, because she felt guilty enough as it was. A few days later, I hired the most prominent divorce lawyer in town to write a letter with an ultimatum, that if she didn't leave the house immediately, we would sue for divorce on grounds of adultery *and* file a child abuse complaint with the police and the bar association — and take it to the press. She had no reason to be afraid of the adultery charge, but the child abuse would have destroyed her career. She wouldn't have had to be convicted for it to hurt." Exactly what she was doing to me, except that in her case it was true and in mine it was invented. "It was a bluff on my part; I had no interest in pursuing it, because of my daughter. I couldn't put Natalie through that. I just wanted Colleen out of our lives with a minimum of confrontation and repercussions. It worked. She left."

"How's your daughter?" And how would my own daughter — daughters? — be with her in charge? That was the real question I was asking.

He smiled, what I could only call a bittersweet smile. "She's in a Ph.D. program to become a clinical psychologist. Shrinks have helped her deal with her mother's death, her sociopathic stepmother, and her oblivious father — who is not so oblivious anymore. That's the language she speaks. That's her territory."

"I certainly know that feeling."

"She's pretty damn good, considering what she's been through."

"Colleen and I have a daughter, two and a half. What you've told me doesn't sit well."

"Of course not."

"I don't know what to do now."

"You've got your work cut out for you with this hearing. Once that's resolved —"

I interrupted him when I remembered something she'd said about him that did not involve his terrible temper. "Colleen told me you taught her to speak, to lose her South Boston accent. That you were her Henry Higgins. Is that true?"

"I taught her all kinds of things. What watercress is — me, a Jewish kid from New Haven. Took her to Venice and taught her art history, taught her the difference between a sonata and a sonnet and to appreciate *Pride and Prejudice,* the book, not the movie. Yes, yes, I know, Pygmalion, an ancient story, older than all the poetry I made her read. Taught her to vote for the Democrats. No one in her family had ever cast a ballot."

"You knew them?"

He nodded. "That was one thing she didn't lie about. Her father was a mean drunk and her siblings were mean drunks in the making, and they all started having children when they were fifteen or sixteen, except Colleen. She clawed her way out of there, and I admired the hell out of her for it."

"Do you know why she left Boston?"

"Sorry, I don't."

When we heard a knock, Bob mumbled that it must be the student he was expecting and leaped up with an eagerness that students don't usually inspire. Poor man had had to plunge into this dark well just because a stranger had shown up at his door. "Let me make you a copy of the divorce decree at the machine down the hall." He sounded relieved that our meeting was coming to an end.

"Bob, one more quick question before I go." He turned to me.

"The wedding announcement in the *Times* said you were a widower. It didn't mention your divorce from Colleen."

"My daughter had the idea of leaving it out. It was her little revenge against Colleen, and I wasn't opposed. The announcement was simpler that way."

He left the office without waiting for a response from me. Just as well. I sat with that information until he returned, imagining conversations with my daughters when they were old enough to make sense of their wounds — and to strike back with hurtful silences and omissions.

IT WAS A LOT to absorb and recount to Pru as we traipsed across the campus and scoured Huntington Avenue for a taxi. I didn't know my way around, and my public confusion corresponded to my private crumbling as I felt the elemental narratives of my life with Colleen give way. Her ex was not a bastard, a deserter, or Zoe's father. I had no idea what would take root inside me in the place where those stories had lived.

I gave the cab driver the address in Cambridge where we were meeting Catherine Franks and sat back and tried to collect myself. When we came to a concrete bridge that spanned the Charles River, I could see the water dotted with sculls and small sailboats, and I recognized the red brick buildings of Harvard that stretched along the shoreline and the quaint Colonial clock tower in the distance, and it struck me as a panorama of innocence, a breeding ground of possibility, a place I no longer belonged. If one of those sailboats in the distance were mine, I would call it *Riddled with Regret*.

"Maybe you should have Bob Golden be a witness at the hearing," Pru said. "Call Lily and ask what she thinks about that. He would certainly get everyone's attention."

The next sound that got mine was my cell phone bleating and humming against my chest, in the pocket of my shirt. The number on the tiny screen was unfamiliar. "Hey, doc, it's Sandy Lefkowitz, getting back to you. What did you mean, they're going to come for me?"

It took a few seconds to get my bearings. How had he gotten this number? I must have given it to him weeks ago just after his wife, or my wife, evicted him from his house. "How are you, Sandy? I got your message yesterday and I'm sorry I haven't had a chance to get back to you." And what would I have said? Your wife's lawyer had me arrested for molesting my kid?

"How am I? Between your wife and mine, I'm up against it."

"Is my wife still representing Ursula?" I mouthed an explanation to Pru: *a patient.*

"Far as I know. My lawyer's been trying to reach her. If she doesn't call back, he's filing a motion to get her off the case. Oh yeah, yesterday my son told me his grandmother, Ursula's mother, has lung cancer. Not a big surprise, she smokes like a chimney, but it means my wife's about to come into money. I didn't want to grill Jack about how sick she was, but it didn't sound good. Maybe it means Ursula will get off my case when she inherits the mansion in Greenwich. Listen, doc, are you all right? After I called you so cocky about how it couldn't have been you on my machine, I realized it *might* have been you and you *might* have been locked up like you said you were."

"I was." The two words spilled out of my mouth, but I wished they hadn't the instant I said them. "But everything's fine now. It was a misunderstanding." My reading of Colleen's notes in her file was not, however. Ursula *was* about to be an heiress, and that might dampen some of her zest for the sport of extreme divorce. She might be worth so much, she'd have to share it with Sandy. Or she might not be entitled to so much of his, if she had a big pile of her own. Maybe that's why she wanted to get the divorce going in the first place, when she found out her mother was sick. She wanted to have as little as possible when the judge decided what her settlement from Sandy should be.

"Everything's fine? Then why did you call to warn me? It must have something to do with my divorce."

"No, Sandy, I was overreacting when I called you. There was a misunderstanding in my family that led to —"

"To jail?"

"No, just the police station lockup."

"Glad to hear it wasn't Valhalla. How long were you in for?"

"It was over in a flash, Sandy, and now things are back to normal."

"But what did you mean, that they'll get me next?"

"You know, at the time, I was caught up in the frenzy of the moment. I have to apologize for that. It was a difficult situation. Fortunately, it was only a miscommunication —"

"So now you're okay," he interrupted, "that's what you're saying?" I could sense he found my reassurances as unconvincing as I did myself.

"Yes," I lied.

"And no one's going to come for me, right?"

"Right. No reason they should."

"Uh-huh. Listen, doc, call me if you ever want to talk about what really happened. I know you're not supposed to call me, because you're the shrink and I'm the patient, but there's a piece of this puzzle that's missing, and I think it has to do with me."

He did me a favor by hanging up, so I didn't have to answer his accusation. His conclusion. What would I have said to him? We were way beyond the comforting BS of professional boundaries and deep into a swamp of ambiguities and clouded obligations. We might as well have had a sexual relationship or a financial one, stuff between us was so tangled. The only good news was that I no longer had to wonder whether to tell him Ursula's mother was dying.

"Who was that?" Pru asked. "Your conflict of interest with Colleen?"

"None other. He heard I was lying. His last words to me were

'Call me when you want to fess up to what really happened.'" We were stuck in a knot of traffic on the road leading off the bridge. Not a car was moving. The sidewalks were thick with college students who had come from places like Scarsdale, who believed, with religious fervor, that they would never make messes of their lives the way their parents had, kids who were certain they were inoculated from screwups and tragedies because they were so damn smart.

"If the professor isn't Zoe's father," Pru said, "who could it be?"

"Fuck if I know."

AM I REALLY addressing these words to you, my darling girls? Are you my audience for these sad revelations — these bombshells about your mother's history and your own? How much do we need to know about our parents' lives? In my profession, the prevailing wisdom — the elemental wisdom — is that our parents' history is our own, and is our birthright; we are entitled to know every morsel, the better to understand ourselves. Insight is thought to be essential. Insight is oxygen. But could it be that it's overrated? That it is nothing compared to the raw power of manipulation, prevarication, possession — said to be nine-tenths of the law — and plain old dumb luck, a commodity I never gave much credence to until I saw my own supply run out?

Luck must be there to remind us of the random nature of the universe. That's not something I'm partial to thinking about, because psychotherapy exists to help us impose a coherent narrative on the chaos of our lives. That territory is where I have always dwelled, where I felt I belonged: sifting through the past, listening to its echoes, digging through motivations and connections and meanings that are visible only if you know how to look for them and what to do once you see them. I believed in all of this. I believed I was the master of my own destiny and that I could help other people become masters and mistresses of theirs — until your mother walked into my life. Until she stuck her arm into the elevator where we had just met and said, *If you're talking to the walls, well — I'm better company than that.* Until Sandy Lefkowitz walked into my office.

And my luck changed. Boom, boom, boom.

"We're here," the driver said. "The entrance is right next to the drugstore. See it?"

The problem was that I did see it, and I knew Catherine Franks was supposed to be waiting for me. But I was not ready for more of *The Colleen Show,* not just yet. Would this be a sequel or would it feel more like a rerun?

≱ 19 ≰

"You're a Winner"

FOR HALF AN HOUR she was a no-show. No sign of Catherine Franks in the long, narrow bakery-café near Harvard where she proposed that we meet, no calls on the cell, no answer when I called the number she had given me. While we waited, Pru read that morning's *Times* while I called Boston City Hall for Zoe's birth certificate. It would take two weeks. I could be locked up in Valhalla in two weeks. Or still living in my sister's guest room. Or seeing my patients in a rented office in Yonkers and explaining that my *Architectural Digest* backyard cottage was being renovated — and that was one of the rosier scenarios.

It was from this trough of despondency that I looked across the table to my sister, whose gaze was focused on the newspaper, and whose youthful, unadorned countenance seemed at home in this college town café. I could not mistake this crowd for the stylish women of Scarsdale. Even close to the university, not all the customers were students. It took a few minutes of puzzled scrutiny for me to see what was different about the crowd: there were women's heads of entirely gray hair, women's lips and eyes with no makeup whatsoever.

"What are you reading?" I asked Pru.

"An article about a medical malpractice case in Florida. A plastic surgeon who rearranged this woman's face so badly that her husband left her and now she's suing the doctor."

"What for?"

"Must be alienation of someone else's affections."

"Would you ever do that?"

She looked up, alarmed. "Do what?"

"Retire to a balmy climate and nip and tuck for millions of dollars between tennis games?"

"The short answer is no."

"And the long answer?"

"Maybe." She laughed and that made me laugh. "But I'd go to Hawaii, not Florida."

"How did you ever do it?"

"What have I done now?"

"Get up the nerve to be a surgeon."

"They don't let you cut until you've been hanging around a hospital for years," Pru said. "It's like turning fifty. You get forty-nine years to prepare, so that when it finally comes it's not the kind of surprise you expect it to be from a distance."

"But there were a dozen specialties you could have gone into."

"I did a residency in psychiatry and was totally frustrated with how little I could do to help people immediately. I've told you this, haven't I?"

"Yeah, but not since I've been arrested. Maybe I'll understand something I didn't before."

"What don't you get about my being a surgeon?"

"Maybe I don't understand how you ended up doing men's work while I do women's work."

"Is that what you think?"

"Sometimes. My sister's a big-shot surgeon. My wife is a ball-breaking lawyer. And my job is reassuring suburban housewives that wearing a size eight does not mean they're fat."

"Eric, dear, you've just been eviscerated. The police, the court system, your wife. This is not business as usual. This week is not the template for your life."

"What made you choose surgery?"

"You know this, don't you? There were eleven women in my entire medical school class, and none in surgery. I did it to show all the egomaniac male surgeons that we could do it — we women. It was 1969. It was a dare. But once I started doing it, I loved it. Compared to oncology or cardiology, it was instant gratification. And high drama. Saving lives right before your eyes, being the hero of the day. I got off on it in a particular way because I couldn't control any of the chaos that went on in our household when we were kids, but now it's just what I do. It only took ten years of therapy to figure all that out."

"But you had it in you."

"Mom taught me to knit and sew. I made microscopic clothes for my Barbie and tried not to think about wanting to marry her when I grew up."

"Since we're stuck in the primordial ooze of childhood, can I ask a politically incorrect question?"

"Would I have liked a Gay Barbie, to go with Tennis Barbie and Fashion Model Barbie? Absolutely. Without question."

"I was going to ask about Dad. If you think his meanness put you off men."

"I think it put me off Dad. Did he put you off men? Maybe you'd have been gay if he'd been a mensch."

Pru sounded slightly irked — but not openly angry — that I had waded into the nature-nurture debate, coming out on the side of nurture, coming out on the side of our fucked-up childhood determining our sexual orientation, which I knew was a controversial position. I immediately wondered why I *had* taken this step, why I'd brought controversy to our table of good coffee and croissants, on this day she had taken off from work to be with me. It was my clumsy way of trying to be closer to her, after a lifetime of feeling intimidated and the last four years of feeling that she disapproved of my wife. "I'm sorry," I said. "Don't take my question the wrong way."

"Excuse me, are you Eric?" I nodded. I'd been so caught up in talking to Pru that I'd half forgotten why I was there. "Sorry to keep you waiting. I'm Cathy Franks. I got stuck in some miserable traffic." Her soft voice matched the unassuming rest of her; she presented as though she were a timid graduate student, a few years older than the usual.

A moment later, Pru went to a table in the back of the café and Cathy took her seat. She was petite and dressed in jeans and an outdoorsy vest. A small face, bright eyes, her brown hair ruler-straight and tucked behind her ears. What the hell had Colleen done to her, this woman clearly cut from more modest cloth than the dry-clean-only crowd who paid most of her bills?

"I had no intention of answering your e-mail," she began, "when you wrote and asked if we could meet, but when I got that e-mail from Colleen about the ten thousand dollars she was going to send me, I smelled a rat."

"You have a sensitive nose. Here's the rat for you." I proceeded to tell her why I was there — to find out whatever Colleen was hiding about her past — and what had inspired my journey, including the arrest and incarceration. If I wanted Cathy to tell me *her* secret Colleen story, it would be wise to tell her mine first.

It was a good move.

She had met Colleen in the steam room of a health club in the Boston neighborhood where they used to live. When Colleen heard that Cathy had cowritten several self-help books, Colleen suggested she help her finish a book about divorce she'd been working on for years. By the time they were talking about money a few weeks later, Cathy admitted she wanted to work on the project to learn enough to do her own divorce. She'd been separated for six months but uncertain about how to proceed. Colleen insisted that do-it-yourself divorces were often bad deals for women and convinced Cathy to write the book in exchange for Colleen representing her.

Cathy always felt uneasy about the swap but went along with it, she said, "for the same reason I went along with everything Colleen wanted me to do: because she exuded such self-confidence, it spilled over onto me. She was bold and brassy and had all the answers — and I thought I had none of them. I was thirty-five, had two kids, and a not very lucrative career as a freelance writer. My husband was a professor at MIT with tenure, a pension, health insurance. He hadn't wanted the divorce, but he was good-natured about it — I mean, he wasn't a bastard. He accepted it. But she had me convinced it was a David and Goliath struggle and that I had to fight for my life. Just as all this began, my dad got sick and my mom wanted me to come back home to Baltimore. So I made our leaving part of the whole divorce, because if I hadn't, Philip could have gotten a court order to keep the kids in Massachusetts."

She reached into her shoulder bag and took out a sheaf of papers. "I didn't know what you'd want to talk about with me, but I brought a few things, just in case. I never understood why Colleen wanted to have two different relationships with me, as my lawyer and my collaborator-boss on the book. But I never had the inner resources, the confidence, to say 'no' to her. She's a powerhouse, and she had me convinced she was rescuing me from a terrible situation. I was grateful. Here."

The letter was typed on Colleen's Boston business letterhead, the firm of Duane, Roberts, Golden Associates. "She never sent me my own because we were working together on the book from the beginning, but this was the form letter that went to everyone else."

Dear_____,

Thanks for coming into our office today.

Divorce may be the toughest decision you've ever had to make, tougher than deciding to marry or have children, because there is so much uncertainty involved for you and your children. Here at Duane, Roberts, Golden, we are committed to minimizing the risk to you, maximizing your settlement, and making sure you and your children don't "fall between the cracks."

We will tailor a divorce strategy that's right for you, in your unique situation. All too often, women — and children — are the victims of the male-dominated legal and economic systems. Our goal is to make sure you and your children end up with all the rights, protections, and advantages you have now, and we're willing to stay with the process for as long as it takes to ensure your well-being. (Did you know that for every dollar a man makes, a woman still makes only 68¢! And, of the Fortune 500 companies, only two have women CEOs!) Until the playing field is level, Duane, Roberts, Golden Associates are here to look out for your interests.

Please look carefully over the contract I gave you and feel free to call me if you have any questions.

As ever,
Colleen

I looked up when I finished reading it, waiting for a translation. She handed me another piece of paper, this one not on letterhead. "Once you've signed the contract and paid the retainer, Colleen sends you this and says to memorize it and throw it away. It's like you're pledging to a secret sorority."

SLOGANS —

1. Forget Feminism
2. Quit Your Job
3. "Gaslight" the Opposition
4. Mothers Matter Most
5. Take No Prisoners
6. Victim Victorious
7. Patience Pays

"Anything else?" I asked. I think I was getting the picture. It looked like a bait-and-switch operation; lure the ladies in with reassuring talk about their rights and privileges, then turn them into guerrilla fighters who pretend to be helpless housewives, whether they are or not.

"Those are the public documents," Cathy said. "I mean, everyone who signs up with her gets them. This is my divorce judgment, which came after the trial. Ninety-five percent of all divorces settle before trial. The other five percent are multimillionaires or Colleen's clients. This was a victory. I got everything Colleen asked for."

I skated over the herebys and hereinafters and got to:

CUSTODY AND VISITATION:

1. Ms. Franks may move to Baltimore with the two children.

2. Mr. Little shall visit the children in Baltimore 2 weekends per month, at times agreed upon by the parents, and have a 1-hour video phone call per child per week in weeks when he does not visit them.

3. The children shall spend two weeks of their summer vacation with their father at a place of his choosing and one week of their winter vacation.

CHILD SUPPORT:

Every Friday beginning May 23, Mr. Little will pay Ms. Franks a check that comes to 42% of his gross weekly income, until the youngest child is 23.

Mr. Little is responsible for the children's health insurance, their recreational and sports activity costs, and college expenses.

Mr. Little is responsible for Ms. Franks's health insurance premiums until such time as she remarries, dies, or has employment that offers her health insurance. She is responsible for any health care expenses beyond the health insurance premium.

ASSETS:

Ms. Franks shall retain as her sole property the marital house located at 2712 Elm Street.

Mr. Little's university pension will be divided such that Ms. Franks receives 50% of his pension as of the date of this judgment.

LIFE INSURANCE:

So long as he has any child support obligations hereunder, Mr. Little shall maintain in full force and effect a policy with a death benefit totaling at least $400,000.

Each line, each obligation, caught in my gut. By the time I got to the end, I realized I had stopped breathing. I looked at sweet Cathy Franks, who was not smiling. "Is your ex-husband still at MIT?"

There was a pause before she answered. "No." The discomfort this caused her was evident.

I felt my eyebrows rise. Cathy handed me another piece of paper. Xerox of a news story. I couldn't tell where it had appeared.

Professor Philip Little, Distinguished Professor of Mathematics at MIT, and one of the youngest mathematicians ever to receive tenure at the Institute, was found dead this morning in his apartment on Boylston St. The cause of death is not yet known but an investigation is pending.

"This is a tremendous loss to our community, not to mention Phil Little's family," said Institute president . . .

I stopped reading and looked up. "Suicide?" She nodded. "How long ago?"

"The fall of 1998."

I had met Colleen in December 1999. Zoe was nearly one year old and they had been living in Scarsdale for eight or nine months.

"I'm so sorry. What happened? Are you okay with talking about it?"

"Now I am. The divorce judgment was issued. I never talked to Phil about it, but you can imagine his reaction. His kids are going to move three hundred miles away and he's stuck with the bills and video phone calls. He had to buy a new life insurance policy because all he had from MIT was the amount of his yearly salary. He bought one for three hundred and something thousand. About a month after the judgment, he sent a copy of the new policy to his lawyer, who sent it to Colleen. She sent me a note that said, 'Congratulations. You're a winner.' He killed himself two days later. Bottle of pills. Plastic bag. Very efficient." I could feel my head shaking in disbelief. "He was brilliant. Eccentric. Distracted. Mathematicians at that level have a reputation for being so lost to the real world that they walk into walls and spend their time gazing at the ceiling. Of being so out of touch that . . . He fit the stereotype, a lot of time. But he loved the kids. Colleen told me that when I testified I had to use the word 'interact' when I talked about him and the kids. I had to say, 'When he came home from work, he interacted with them,' because it sounds mechanical. If the other lawyer asked about his relationship with the kids, I had to say that he seemed distant to me even when he 'interacted' with them."

"And that's what you said?"

"I did everything she told me to do. It was like I was drugged. I was a Colleen doll. I was a robot."

"So he wasn't as distant as you said he was?"

"I was lonely and miserable and felt unappreciated, like all mothers of small children when the fathers aren't home as much as you want them to be. He wasn't the most talkative guy in the world. I wasn't making that up. The loneliness you feel in marriage is worse than any other. You're supposed to be connected to someone, and they're sleeping next to you night after night, but they don't say a word." She stopped and rested on that thought for ten seconds, as though it were an island in the middle of a lake. I rested on it too, thinking of how many of my patients complained that they were in lonely marriages but stayed because of the kids, the house, the comforts, an attachment to the phrase "my husband and I," an attachment to the remote possibility that the old spark might ignite again. And I, who'd never thought of my own marriage as notably lonely — look where I'd landed. "We were convinced he was an eccentric space cadet, but he knew exactly what he was doing with the insurance. And what had been done to him. The new policy was worth nothing and he was gone. The kids were devastated. I was devastated. His parents. My parents. The Institute. The students. It was a nightmare beyond imagining."

"What was Colleen's reaction?"

"I called her after the police called me. She was silent for a long time, ten or fifteen seconds. Then she got her story together and stuck to it. 'We knew he was a weak man, Cathy. That's why you stopped loving him. This is the act of a coward.' When I challenged her, she came up with more lines. 'I've argued cases before this judge and no one else killed himself. Philip couldn't roll with the punches.' When I asked her how I was supposed to support my kids without the life insurance, she reminded me that since the divorce wasn't final yet — it takes four months here, after the judgment is issued — I'd inherit the house and his pension, and my kids and I would get social security, you know that provision if a spouse with kids dies? It's complicated and it's a struggle. But I'm working on a few projects. No more divorce handbooks, though."

"Did you talk to another lawyer?"

"Eventually, when I could tell the story without coming apart. This guy listened to the whole thing and he said there wasn't much I could do legally, because I had gone along with her, I hadn't been coerced, technically, and Colleen hadn't done anything illegal. Lawyers get in trouble when they're negligent or if they tell someone to commit perjury. I had willingly presented my husband as a cold, distant guy who wouldn't much care if his kids moved to Baltimore. Colleen made me think that was fair. It convinced the judge to let me take the kids. But no lawyer would sue Colleen for the simple reason that the judge had agreed with her."

"Didn't your husband have a lawyer? Couldn't he defend himself?"

"He had a lawyer, but he was completely unprepared for this, because Colleen's MO is to refuse to negotiate. She keeps saying she's going to present a settlement proposal, but she has no intention of it. She stonewalls and bullies for a year and comes to trial with this bombshell that I want to move to Baltimore and he's a cold, distant guy who doesn't give his kids the time of day. He's not prepared to fight that with no warning. He did his best."

"But doesn't the judge understand that —"

"Judges are prepared to think the worst of men, because so many men deserve it. That's what Colleen counts on. And I went along with it. Don't ask what I was thinking. I used to hear about women who sleep with their divorce lawyers, and I'd wonder why they did something so foolish. But I'd taken leave of my senses worse than if I'd gone to bed with my lawyer."

"So this lawyer said you had no legal recourse?"

She nodded. Poor thing, that's what I was thinking as I listened to her. "But he did something. He called Colleen and told her he was going to make her practice very difficult to conduct in Boston. He said he would call other divorce lawyers and the family bar association and alert them to her practices. If the opposing lawyers all know what she's doing, they can change their strategies. He said he would talk to her business partners about her tactics and about her bartering with clients, which is very unprofessional."

"And?"

"Three months later, she left town. I had finished writing the book before the judge issued the divorce decree, so that part of our relationship was over."

"I must tell you, when the book appeared on the bestseller list, I encouraged Colleen to send you a bonus. I knew of a ghostwriter who sued the guy who'd hired him, when their book became an unexpected hit. At the very least, I figured you would write to Colleen and ask for more money."

"And Colleen knew I wouldn't, because I hadn't been paid to begin with. And because I never wanted to talk to her again."

"Now I understand why you were so stunned to hear from her. Why the bonus money seemed suspicious. I'm surprised she thought she could buy your silence with ten thousand dollars. Do you really think she imagined you wouldn't talk to me?"

"It's bizarre. But so's everything she does. Maybe she never intended to send me the money. Maybe she just said she would, hoping it would dissuade me."

"I'm sorry you had to . . ." For a moment I said nothing, because I had no idea which thread of her harrowing story to pick up. "Sorry about everything you've been through. And your kids. I know I had nothing to do with it, because I didn't know Colleen then, but —"

"I don't believe in guilt by association."

"The judge said you could go to Baltimore, but it looks like you didn't."

"My dad died sooner than we thought he would, and my mom decided to move up here instead. After Philip died, I didn't want to take the kids away from everything they knew. We had a lot of people around who helped us through it."

"And how are you now?"

"I'm a different person from the one who met Colleen in the steam room. If you subscribe to the credo that everything happens for a reason, I needed to change and not be so easily persuaded. I needed to believe in my own confidence instead of hers."

"Do you now?"

"I'm getting better."

"The e-mail you wrote me was confident. Your reading of the situation was too. I appreciate it." It was Colleen who lured me out of bachelorhood, Colleen who had the chutzpah to trick me into marriage. Cathy Franks would have been better for me, but she never would have swept me off my feet. If I subscribed to the idea that says everything happens for a reason, and I'm not sure I do, maybe this happened so that I could find a way to fall in love with a Cathy next time instead of a Colleen, with a woman who had less razzle-dazzle and more . . . more sanity.

"Speaking of mental health," Cathy said, "I have a shrink appointment I'm about to be late to. Would you e-mail me and let me know how your hearing goes? I bet you'll be okay. Should I leave these with you?" She handed me the papers she had brought.

"All except your divorce decree. I'll send them back."

"Don't bother. I doubt I'll need them again. If I don't hear from you, is there someone I can get in touch with, to find out —"

"My sister." She'll know if I've been sent to Valhalla. "Here's her number."

I remembered I had one more question. "Do you happen to know who the father of Colleen's child is? She always said it was her ex."

"She told me she was separated, that she and her husband had some things to work out before the baby was born."

"She has an answer for everything, doesn't she?"

"It sounds like you'll have the advantage this time," Cathy said — with confidence that sounded genuine, not borrowed, not on loan from my wife — before she turned to leave.

Pru must have been watching us closely, because she was back at the table before I'd had a chance to signal her. "Well?"

It was my turn to do show-and-tell: the form letter, the slogans, the obituary. Helluva story. Too bad I had just learned it was a footnote in the story of my life.

20

Maladaptive Patterns of Responding to Stressful Circumstances

B y the time we were on the six o'clock shuttle from Logan to LaGuardia, I was wiped out and talked out, having repeated to Pru — and Lily, on the cell phone — both of the day's tortured conversations. When I closed my eyes and let my head fall back against the reclining seat, when I urged my brain to quiet down, two pieces of news kept coming at me, like cougars threatening to pounce: Colleen's bribery of her stepdaughter and her heartless response to Cathy's husband's suicide. Would she go so far as to coach Zoe on what to say to Child Protective Services? My mind drifted to diagnoses. Until now, I had always painted her with adjectives: selfish, short-tempered, bitchy, resilient, hardened, hurt. I wasn't her therapist, hadn't thought of her as someone who needed my professional attention, and things between us had been more or less fine — so I was content to file away the adjectives and carry on with the privileged pandemonium that was our domestic life.

It had been news to me that she was a pathological liar. I had suspected nothing; that's how good she was. Gifted. Diabolical. A+ for effort, energy, inventiveness. The trick with the fertility drugs was rudimentary compared to fabricating the volatile ex who'd left her for a student and her heartbroken move to Scarsdale, when in fact she'd been run out of Boston. The characters we used to call psychopaths and sociopaths dissembled like this. Now we say they suffer from antisocial personality disorder, but I rarely see them, whatever you want to call them, in my practice. No one does: they avoid and resist treatment. They blame everyone else for their miserable lives and insist that no one understands them. Standard estimates rate sixty percent of the people in jail as sociopaths. Could it be that high? And could my wife really be so low?

Had I missed the symptoms before now because I'm not a jailhouse shrink, skilled at spotting these folks from forty paces? No, not a jailhouse shrink *yet*. Or was the darkness in which I had dwelled more of a tribute to her artistry than to my own limitations?

I opened my eyes to see our high-tech jailhouse in the sky, carrying us to New York at five hundred miles an hour, and to feel my sister's upper arm brush mine in the next seat. She was reading a paperback novel, as entranced in that story as I was in my own. It was as though I had woken from a dream, and I was slightly disoriented. "Pru?"

"Yeah?"

"Do you and Bea ever fight?"

She turned to me. "Not often."

"What about?"

A quizzical look over her half glasses. "Why do you want to know?"

"It just occurred to me. I can't imagine it. You're like puppies together."

"I have to cancel a lot for emergency surgeries. She's usually good about it, but I almost didn't make it to her daughter's wedding. I'm usually the one who screws up. And I'm more of a slob than she is. Once or twice a year she blows up about that."

"That's it?"

"Since you asked, we had a fight the Saturday you came for brunch about how crazy your wife is."

"Really?" My best deadpan. Not an answer I had anticipated.

But the subject of Colleen's mental health was understandably on many minds. "Whose side were you on?"

"The sanity side. As soon as Bea heard about the fertility pills, she had Colleen pegged. I, on the other hand, just thought she was a first-class bitch until I heard her outbursts in court."

"What was Bea's diagnosis?"

"A serious nut case. That's what we fought about. She insisted I call after you left our apartment and tell you to watch out. I thought Bea was overreacting, and I didn't want you to panic."

"But you called me anyway."

"Bea is very persuasive."

"You didn't change your mind about Colleen even when she had me arrested? It took her outbursts in court for you to be convinced?"

"I knew you would never molest your kids —"

"Thanks, Pru. That's a vote of confidence."

"But I thought there was a very outside possibility — minuscule but real — that she interpreted an innocent gesture of yours as molestation, and she flipped out."

"You can't be serious."

"I said 'minuscule.' But I no longer believe that."

I was flabbergasted, if that intense an emotion were possible in my sorely bruised state. Even my sister had to be persuaded that I was innocent. The plane banked sharply as we circled for our descent, and my insides lurched — or had they been listing since the cops showed up at my door? The lights of the city unfurled beneath us, the city I should never have left for the manicured lawns of Scarsdale. What *had* I been thinking? She was pregnant, and I was tired of being the selfish prick Gaby Goldberg had identified wearing my clothes. I had been doing my version of the New Age say-yes-to-the-universe crap. And look where it had gotten me.

But when I barreled down this road of regret, I immediately thought of the children, not just Sarah Rose but Zoe, whom I thought of as mine, even though she was not. Nor did she belong to the man whose last name she bears. She was a fatherless child. And I was a childless father.

"My ears are popping," Pru said as we began our descent in earnest, dropping hundreds of feet in a matter of seconds.

"I thought they pop going up, not down."

"What can I say? They're popping."

A tender moment, that exchange, a trill of lightness against all the dark, almost as though we were swapping lyrics for a frothy musical — instead of slogging through the sinister story this had become.

IT WAS DUSK as we waited in the taxi line outside the terminal at the end of that bright fall day and the beginning of my first weekend alone since I had become a father. My cell phone rang, and when I saw an unfamiliar Westchester number, I feared it was Sandy Lefkowitz. But maybe it was Lily Lopez. Turns out it was neither.

"Mr. Lavender, this is Graciela." She must have been calling from a friend's house or her cell phone, not the home number I would have recognized.

"Is everything all right?"

"No. I am walking fast to the village for milk, and then I go back home. My visa will expire in one month, and I need Colleen to sign the papers." For a few seconds, I thought she was talking about a Visa card, but no, she meant her immigrant visa. "Today I ask her to please fill out the forms and sign them, but she got angry, so angry, and said to me, 'Don't bother me with your problems, I have enough of my own.' She never talks this way to me, so I poured all the milk down the sink, so I had to buy more, so I could leave the house and call you. She is angry about the milk too."

"Is she yelling at the children?"

"Yes. She is cooking angry. She bangs the pots, and the girls are scared. I'm scared too."

I was speechless. Did Colleen know where Pru and I had gone today? Was that the reason for her rage? It would have been a good guess, my first day free, with next week's court deadline looming.

"If she doesn't sign my forms, they will deport me. Will you sign them, Mr. Lavender, please?"

Could I, in good conscience, say "yes" to this simple request and be able to carry through on it? And what the hell was going on with Colleen, that she was so angry and dismissive about something as frightening to a poor immigrant as her visa?

"Graciela, don't worry tonight. Colleen is upset. I'm sure she'll sign them tomorrow or Sunday. She's always good about that. I would sign them myself, but I can't come to the house right now. I'm not allowed." As I began to say all this on the taxi line, I walked toward a cement pillar where no one stood, so I would have some privacy. My legal troubles and my nanny's expiring visa were not for public consumption.

"I know. The children are so sad. They ask me all the time when you are coming."

"Really?"

"Especially the big one."

"Do you know what happened to me?"

"Yes, but I don't believe it. Because the family before this, they had sex abuse and I saw it for my own self. I saw the girl's down-there parts, and it made me cry. I think there is a mistake here. Zoe says to me, 'If my daddy comes home when I'm sleeping tell him to kiss me right here.' Her nose. She has no fear."

"Graciela, I've never asked you this before, but did you know Zoe's father?"

She took a minute to answer, an awkward minute. "No."

"You never met him when you were working for Colleen before Zoe was born?"

"It was only for a few months." A sharp silence followed, as though she had slammed the door at the end of her statement.

"He was never there?"

Another silence. Another "No."

"Are you sure?"

"Maybe he was there when I was not home."

"She never introduced you to him?"

When I heard the next silence in response to this simple question, my fight-or-flight response mechanism kicked in, and I did something I would never have thought of before today. "You know, Graciela, I can't come to the house right now, but I have two lawyers working for me, and I can ask them about how I can sign your visa. I can call them later and ask if I can meet you somewhere —"

"Oh, Mr. Lavender, that is *very* good. Thank you. Thank you."

"But if there's something you want to tell me about Zoe's father, I need to know what it is. It's very important now. If you want me to help you with your visa —" Was I really doing this? Had my wife's villainy begun to rub off on me? I couldn't bear to finish the sentence, couldn't bear to complete the bribe.

"It's a secret," she said softly, "and she said I cannot tell anyone. She made me promise."

"I'm Zoe's stepfather. Colleen and I have talked about my adopting Zoe. If I'm going to adopt her, I need to know who her father is." What I was doing was called abusing my authority, or maybe it was old-fashioned bullying. Whatever it was, I was determined to find out what Colleen was hiding from me. "The court won't let me adopt her unless —"

"There is no father."

"What?"

"He is from the bank of sperm."

It is only because I'm a therapist, trained to listen to people's secrets, that I heard this without letting out an exclamation. But not long after I heard it, it made perfect sense, and it was my turn to be disquietingly silent. There was no corporeal being who would show up and make a claim on Zoe. Ever. She *was* a fatherless child.

"She will be angry with me."

"I won't tell her anything, Graciela. You don't have to worry about this."

"What if —"

"There's nothing to fear. I'll talk to my lawyers about your visa and what we need to do. But I think Colleen will change her mind and sign for you before then. If she doesn't —"

"Thank you, Mr. Lavender. I will tell the girls —"

"Don't tell them anything about me, please. I don't want to confuse them right now. But if something bad happens tonight and Colleen is out of control or she scares you or the children, call me again. Okay?"

"Okay, Mr. Lavender."

I heard a click in my ear and then nothing. The screen flashed "END."

The next Yellow Cab was ours, and we had something to talk about on our way back to the city in addition to how crazy my crazy wife was: what it meant — legally, emotionally, philosophically, medically, in the long- and short-term — that Zoe's father was an anonymous sperm donor.

At their apartment, we ate dinner, drank good red wine, and told Bea the stories we had heard that day. "Colleen's finished," Bea said over and over, filling our glasses, filling our plates. "She's toast, burnt to a crisp. They have to let you go next week, and then you can figure out how to deal with the rest of this effing mess."

Bea meant my children. My career. My reputation. My marriage.

She was so insistent, so wise, I chose to believe her. But Colleen was not finished yet. Not toast yet. When desperate characters are cornered, we keep thinking they'll give up and be reasonable, because that's what most of us would do. But they astonish us time and again by not doing *what any sane person would do in that situation*. In clinical jargon, we say that they exhibit maladaptive patterns of perceiving and responding to stressful circumstances. When their backs are against the wall, instead of giving up and negotiating, they go another ten rounds, destroying self and others before they call it quits.

But there were a few blissful hours that Friday evening and into the next morning when we were relaxed and giddy with feelings of triumph at all we had uncovered; a few innocent hours from one day to the next when it seemed that Colleen had no possible way out of the mess she had created — until the Visa people called me several hours after Pru and Bea left for the weekend. Not the government agents Graciela was so afraid of. No, the other Visa people, who are sometimes just as fierce.

"THIS IS VISA with a courtesy call for Eric Lavender or Colleen Golden." It came on my cell phone at noon on Saturday, and at first I thought it was Graciela's government visa people. I was sprawled out on the couch with a pot of coffee and the newspaper, trying to imitate the carefree bachelor I used to be. "We're just calling to make sure you actually made the purchase that's in the process of being charged to your account, because it's somewhat out of the ordinary for your spending patterns."

"Which account?" I had gotten a call like this a year ago, when Colleen was at the store buying two expensive leather chairs and a couch; the company wants to make sure the card hasn't been stolen, isn't being used by thieves. The woman rattled off a card number that I knew was Colleen's and my joint Visa. "What's the purchase?"

"A one-way plane ticket to Manila on Cathay Pacific Airways."

"The Philippines?"

"That's what it looks like. The charge is for four thousand two hundred twenty-six dollars."

"Good Lord. Leaving when?"

"Let's see. This evening at five-fifteen. Flight 621."

Had Graciela been deported? Or had Colleen fired her? Or had — ? "No, I didn't buy the ticket, and I don't know anything about it. Please don't charge my account."

"Do you want to report the card stolen?"

"Not yet. Let me check with my wife. I'll call her as soon as we hang up."

Of course I didn't. I called my lawyers on their cell phones. Left messages. The person I really needed to call was Graciela; she would likely be with Colleen and the kids, and my call would get her in trouble. But she must already be in some kind of trouble. I paced the living room, looked at my watch every other minute. It was twelve-fifteen, twelve-thirty, twelve-thirty-two.

At one o'clock Bernie called, and I explained what had happened. "I don't know what's going on at Colleen's house, but it doesn't sound right."

"I'll call the police and have them send someone over there. We scheduled an appointment with Colleen for one o'clock today with Marsha Rogers, the therapist who's going to interview Zoe. Marsha should be at the house right now."

"Can the cops go there without a complaint?"

"Absolutely. They're following up on your arrest and on the welfare of the kids."

"Bernie, one more thing. Graciela told me last night who Zoe's father really is. Colleen always said it was her ex-husband. Actually, it's . . ." I was hard-pressed to say, but was that because I had been duped or because I imagined Zoe's eventual embarrassment at having to admit her father's name was Anonymous? "A sperm donor."

"That means Colleen is a completely unreliable witness. Good. Excellent work. Let me call the cops. Hang in there."

Good? What was wrong with lawyers? I tossed the phone onto the couch and seethed. But a few minutes later, I got it and settled into his strategic mindset. Zoe's loss, in this case, could be my gain. It spooked me to be thinking in such a coldly calculating way about her troubles and my own, but there it was, and here we were. I knocked back the rest of the coffee in my cup and decided to drive to Scarsdale, even if I couldn't go to the house. I couldn't hang around Pru's apartment for the rest of the day, not with the threat of a one-way plane ticket to Manila hovering overhead. There was something seriously wrong with this picture.

21

Flight Risk

I THREADED MY WAY through weekend traffic on the Bronx River Parkway with brewing anxiety. Everywhere in the village I could think of to go — diner, park, library — were places I might run into my wife and children, and that wasn't my motivation for going. I simply wanted to be in the vicinity in case something went awry, even though I had only a vague notion of what it might be. My fear was more like the musical score for a suspense movie: it offered a soundtrack of foreboding, not a recipe, not a script — until I got a call from Bernie when I was four or five exits from Scarsdale.

"There's no one at your house right now," he said. "Marsha Rogers waited from one to two o'clock and overlapped with the police, who rang the bell and peered into every downstairs window they could. Where else would Colleen be on a Saturday afternoon?"

"Her office, shopping, a kid's party." I gave him Colleen's work address, but he hung up before I could tell him I was on my way. By the time I arrived and found a parking space near the train station, Bernie called again with a gravity in his voice, even on the scratchy cell, I hadn't heard before. "She wasn't at the office, but her partner was. I think it's Patty Donlon. Eric, you still there?"

Not a promising introduction. "I'm actually in the village, parked at the train station."

"Patty told her yesterday afternoon that she intended to file papers to dissolve their partnership. The Westchester Bar filed a complaint that Colleen was suborning perjury —"

"What does that mean?"

"Telling your client to lie under oath. Plus Patty had gotten two or three letters from lawyers in town — opposing counsel in divorces — that accused Colleen of instructing women getting divorced to do all kinds of sleazy things. The police weren't clear on the details. It seems Patty had given her a warning or two, but when the complaint came from the bar, she'd had enough."

"Jesus."

"Patty gave her this coming week to settle her affairs with another lawyer in the office. Told Colleen she would get a restraining order if Colleen didn't leave. So maybe she's in town. Maybe she's at the supermarket. But maybe she panicked and took off. Any family she would have gone to see?"

"She's got people in Boston, but she doesn't see them."

"Any place that's a refuge for her?"

"Besides Saks Fifth Avenue? Not that I can think of."

"I'm in Westport right now. It'll be an hour before I can get there. Call Visa back and find out what she's charged lately. Does she have a location satellite in her car?"

"All we've got is an E-ZPass in the window. It'll tell if she's paid any tolls, but it shows up on the computer, and I don't have my laptop with me."

"Check the credit card first. See whether you come up with anything. If she's at the dry cleaners, we have to back off."

"Should I call you or the police?"

"If it looks like she's in motion, go to the police station and talk to Detective Lawson. I'm sure you can use his computer to track the E-ZPass. But if you go, watch what you say. You've still got this accusation hanging over you, and I don't want you to do anything to compromise your defense."

*   *   *

DETECTIVE LAWSON was a tall, lanky guy, about forty, with a good head of black hair combed with brilliantine and a heavily pockmarked face that distracted me every now and then from my own troubles. A wide band of skin from his chin to his right ear was stretched and shiny, as though it had been burned and something new grafted onto it. I wondered what the disfigurement had done to his psyche — made him meeker or tougher, angry or more empathic? There was a gold band on the appropriate finger and a pack of Marlboros in the breast pocket of his suit jacket.

This was the man who talked me through getting Jason Cummings out of the house across the street from Sandy's, but that day had been such a whirlwind, I hadn't focused on him. Today he was going to talk me through what looked like my wife's disappearance. In three days, I had gone from the stark cell upstairs to the inner sanctum of Lawson's chaotic office in the basement of the building that he shared with another detective. The desks were back to back, the ceiling was low, the light fluorescent. I sat in a straight-backed chair beside his desk and we swapped information, questions, likely and unlikely scenarios.

Her credit card trail revealed that at twelve-thirty she had filled the gas tank at a Mobil station in Newark — which could mean she had deposited Graciela at Newark Airport and was on her way back to Scarsdale. The more comforting image was Graciela and the girls in the car, the little ones in their car seats in back, alternately fussy, tired, confused, sad, and boisterous, and Graciela attending to them because their mother was so distracted. But where were they going if not to the airport?

"Technically speaking," Lawson said, "you can't report anyone missing for twenty-four hours. But because of your arrest and your ROR, we've got a heightened responsibility to protect the kids. When's the last time you checked her credit card?"

"Twenty minutes ago."

"Try again. It might tell us if she's headed back here."

While I was on hold with Visa, a uniformed cop delivered a few pieces of paper to Detective Lawson that looked like they'd come through on a fax. He read them studiously. The woman at Visa said that Colleen had just withdrawn three hundred dollars from an ATM on the New York State Thruway. When I hung up, Lawson turned and looked at me. I told him about her latest stop, but he didn't react. His gaze and his silence made me study his distended skin and the pocks that made little craters across his cheeks. "Is something wrong?" He had that look, and it was that kind of day. "Is it about my family? Is that the follow-up CPS report?"

"You didn't hear this from me." His voice went low. "The report only goes to me and the DA."

"And?"

Lower still. "There's nothing to worry about from CPS. But the hearing goes on as scheduled. If the DA has any other evidence, he presents it. Don't get overconfident."

It was difficult to feel overconfident in these circumstances, but I took a few seconds to digest the official conclusion. It seemed to guarantee my freedom — an indisputable treasure, but not one I wanted to swap my children for. "Looks like Colleen's heading north, maybe upstate New York."

"She have family up there?"

I shook my head.

"Friends?"

"Not that she's ever talked about."

"You still have a house key? Let's go over."

"But there's an order of protection. I'm not allowed —"

"If you're with me, you're allowed. For all we know, the kids are in the house. It's unlikely, because we'd have heard them when we were over there. I can get a search warrant, but if there's anything there that tells us where she's gone, I'd rather know now than in two hours."

*   *   *

ASIDE FROM a few open dresser drawers in all the bedrooms, there was nothing much out of the ordinary. But on the kitchen counter next to the phone, the Westchester yellow pages was open to the "Real Estate" listings, and the number 3 was blinking on the answering machine.

"It's your house," Lawson said. "Why don't you do the honors."

"Hi, Colleen. It's Matt Parker over at the *Inquirer*. We spoke about six months ago when you were representing the wedding caterer being sued over the food poisoning episode. Thought I might find you home. Had a quick question on another matter. I'll try you later."

"Maybe he wants a divorce," Lawson said.

"He probably found out about my arrest."

"Hi, Colleen. It's Yolanda from Coldwell Banker in White Plains on Saturday, calling back. You left a message about wanting to sell your house, and I'm happy to come by any time it's convenient. *Love* the street you're on. If I don't hear from you, I'll phone back. Have a great day!"

The third call was a hang-up.

Lawson tapped his fingers against the countertop, a tiny gesture I read to mean that he didn't know what to do next. "Is there a computer here connected to the Internet?"

"Upstairs."

I waited for it to boot up and remembered that last week Colleen had no doubt learned from this machine, maybe inadvertently, what I was up to — going to Boston to see her ex and Cathy Franks. Today the computer's memory was my last best hope for information on where she might have gone.

The answer was Albany. Last night and this morning, she had looked up real estate offices and hotels. Of course. She had lived there after law school, before she had taken up with Professor Golden. In this desperate flight from failure, from being exposed, she returns to a place she used to live. But she has to understand —

doesn't she? — that she can't drive off as though she's twenty-one and the children a pair of tennis rackets she can toss into the back seat and forget about.

"What's she doing?" the detective asked, looking at the Web sites over my shoulder. "You're the shrink. Is there a name for it?"

"I think it's a case of panic. It looks like a weekend trip, an overnight. She's scouting Albany." Did he want my clinical diagnosis? Probably best to keep that to myself. I was hardly the court-appointed shrink, and I had learned long ago that it was unwise to toss off diagnoses as though they were weather forecasts.

"What's that building in the backyard?" Lawson was looking over my shoulder and out the window.

"My office. Colleen built it for me when I moved here from the city."

"I didn't think it was zoned for something so big."

"Colleen worked it out, like she worked everything else. This morning she went to MapQuest and printed out a map of suburban Albany."

A moment later, my cell phone rang — Bernie calling from White Plains. He wanted to know where we should meet. I was getting the hang of this detective work, the scheming and counter-scheming, the interplay among lawyers, cops, social service agencies, the perps, the victims, and the poor schmucks like me who get tossed around like beach balls. One day we're the local hero, next day the villain, and the day after that, the cops' best friend. "The police station," I said after only a moment's hesitation.

"ALL WE NEED NOW is patience," Bernie said as we sat around a conference table in a small room near Lawson's office. I had taken him aside when he arrived and told him that the new CPS report cleared me but that Lawson was not supposed to have told me about it. Bernie said we should treat it in our conversation with him as "an open secret."

I wasn't sure how to do that, but I took my cues from him.

He sat at the conference table with a legal pad and half a deli sandwich that brought the odor of garlic pickles into the windowless room. Lawson drank from a New York Yankees coffee mug, and I noticed I was biting my nails. "Colleen took off and she'll probably find her way back in a day or two," Bernie said. "In the meantime we need to put her whole Boston history into four or five sentences to present at the hearing. I've taken some notes based on what Lily told me last night. Here's what I've got."

My phone rang again, and I recognized the number. "It's Graciela's cell."

She was crying, and it was difficult to understand her through the sobs. She was at Newark Airport, scheduled to fly to Manila in an hour. She hadn't called earlier because when Colleen dropped her off, she had threatened to call the Immigration Service if Graciela told anyone. But now she realized Colleen's threat was hollow. How would she know if Graciela made a phone call?

"I had no idea this would happen," Graciela said. "She told me this morning we are going to Atlantic City for the weekend, and I must pack. But she took me here, gave me my passport and visa, and told me, 'Say bye-bye to the children.'"

"But why? Did she say why?"

"She spies on my phone. She says I am a trader."

"A traitor?"

"Because I call you last night. She spies on my cell phone. I tell her I am only upset about the visa, that is why I call to you, and if she will sign the visa forms, then I am okay. She says, Okay, I understand, and I believe everything is normal and we are going to Atlantic City. But to the contrary, we drive to Newark. 'How come,' I say, 'how come?' She is picking up a friend, that is what she says. I am so innocent, I think everything is normal, but she parks and gives me my suitcase and tells me, 'Say goodbye to the children. I hate traders.' And she drives so fast, like she is in the Kentucky Derby."

"Is she driving in a dangerous way?"

"Very fast. In the village, it's not possible, but on the highway today, yes."

"Did she pay you the money she owes you?"

"One hundred twenty-five, half week. Yes, but I did not deposit in my U.S. account. And so many belongings still in the house, including eyeglasses."

"Do you want to return to your country?" I looked at my watch, at the clock on the wall of the conference room. It was a little after four. I had prevented Colleen from charging the plane ticket to our joint card, but she found another way to buy it. My quandary over what to do came down to this: Was dear Graciela marital property — or was her fate entirely in Colleen's hands? I wanted to return the decision to Graciela.

"No, I want my job," she said, starting to cry again, and the irony and tragedy of her situation — that she took care of my children so she could pay her sister to take care of hers halfway around the world — nearly made me cry too.

"Graciela, go outside the terminal and get a taxi for Scarsdale. I'm at the police station."

"But I have only twenty dollars."

"I'll pay the cab when you get here. Call me when you're ten minutes away, and I'll go to the entrance to meet you."

ONCE WE HEARD Graciela's disquieting news about Colleen's state of mind, Bernie and Detective Lawson abandoned the plan to wait for her return and devised an intricate strategy.

The point was to get the kids out of Colleen's erratic clutches. She was doing exactly what desperate characters do in the desperate situations they create for themselves: blowing her problems sky-high, not solving them. Speeding instead of slowing down.

Lawson's idea was to put out an arrest warrant for Colleen for the only thing she had done that was against the law, because taking your children on a trip and firing your nanny are not. But "offering a false instrument for filing with intent to do harm" — that is, her swearing in an affidavit that I had molested Zoe when she knew I hadn't — is a class-E felony. "We don't arrest people for this very often," he said, "but we don't like it when people lie to us and make us use resources chasing phony criminals. I can't think of another way to intervene at this distance and get her off the road."

If she were stopped for speeding in New York State, the highway patrol would run a check on her and learn there was a warrant. If she wasn't stopped for speeding, we could keep following her credit card tracks and find out where she was spending the night. With the name and address of a hotel, Lawson could alert the local police.

None of us wanted to see her behind bars, but we had a fervent desire to protect the children as her behavior grew increasingly unpredictable. Secondarily, Bernie explained, to get the molestation charge against me dropped, it would help to show the extent of Colleen's irresponsible behavior. "But before we get to that," Bernie said, "I want to get the order of protection against you lifted, so you can take care of the kids if she's arrested."

WITH CRAZY PEOPLE — more so than the rest of us — it's always best to expect the unexpected.

Colleen didn't get picked up for speeding, and for the next forty-eight hours, she stopped charging on our joint Visa card, making it impossible to know specifically where she was. All we could tell from the E-ZPass account was whether she crossed a toll bridge or exited the Thruway, both of which she did on Sunday and Monday. But for all her travel, she did not appear to be slouching toward Scarsdale. These were difficult days for Graciela and for me, and I could not bear to think about what they were like for the children. We stayed at a modest hotel in White Plains — neither of us had the right to be in Colleen's house — that was within walking distance to Bernie and Lily's office, where we used the computer to check the E-ZPass and our cell phones to check the credit card activity.

First thing Monday morning, Bernie filed a motion to get the order of protection against me lifted, based on significant new information.

Monday afternoon, Judge Robinson agreed to hear the motion, and we went through a fifteen-minute presentation in the same courtroom, with roughly the same cast of characters, minus Colleen, and including Rick Maxwell, the assistant DA, who looked as if he had just begun shaving, though I remembered Bernie said their sons played baseball together. Bernie presented the arrest warrant against Colleen, the complaint from the Westchester Bar accusing her of suborning perjury, the divorce decree Bob Golden had given me, Colleen's list of slogans from Cathy Franks, and the $4,000 one-way ticket to Manila that Graciela never used. Rick Maxwell presented CPS's follow-up report, based on a second interview with Zoe, concluding that she had not been molested.

"The sum of this evidence is most disturbing," the judge said.

"It's disturbing to us, Your Honor," Bernie said. "My client is deeply concerned about the children's welfare."

"So am I," she said.

"Your Honor, based on this evidence and what Attorney Rosenberg has said about his client," said the DA, "I'm inclined to lift the order of protection if his wife is taken into custody. But my concern is that if we lift the order right now, Mr. Lavender will take matters into his own hands, hunt down his wife, and there will be some kind of showdown that ends badly. I know that sounds melodramatic, but I don't want to put these children in a more precarious position than they're already in."

"Mr. Lavender," the judge asked, turning to me, "do you think your wife is violent?"

I had been concerned about this since Bernie had the idea to arrest her. "I haven't seen evidence of that, but in the last few days, she's exhibited some irrational behavior. I don't know how scared or desperate she feels now."

"How mentally unbalanced do you think she is?" the judge asked.

The term was too vague to be of much use, but I wasn't about to criticize the person who controlled my fate. "It's impossible to gauge without being in touch with her. Sending our nanny back to Manila because she was angry about a phone call suggests she's not making good decisions. I don't think she's violent by nature, and she's generally a good mother. I didn't understand this until recently, but I've learned — the hard way, you might say — that she has a diminished conscience. She can conceal it for long periods when things are going well, but it starts to show when she's stressed, even if she's brought the stress on herself."

"What does this mean for the children at this point?"

"Again, Your Honor, it's impossible to predict what anyone's going to do, much less someone —" No, steer clear of absolutes. "In the last few days, several people have told me that she has no qualms about being cruel to others when she wants something. The good news is that she probably experiences her children as part of herself. The bad news is that if she's making lousy decisions for herself, she can't separate the kids' needs from what she misperceives to be her needs."

I hadn't intended to give a speech on my wife's psyche — and knew it wasn't kosher to hold forth as though I had made a formal diagnosis. I know how imprecise diagnoses are and how much overlap there is between different disorders as they're defined in textbooks. And how many *other* distinct problems we carry around in addition to the ones that can be neatly labeled. There was a lot I didn't know about Colleen. But if the judge was going to make me the resident expert, and if it made me look like the more responsible parent, I wouldn't turn down the role.

The judge's eyes dropped to her desk, and she seemed to be

looking over the documents Bernie had presented. We stood at the long tables where we had stood the other day, and I could hear Rick Maxwell breathing because everyone else was so quiet. The accusation against me that the judge heard last week was straight-forward; it fit our standard stereotypes of men as predators and children as victims. Stepfather Crosses the Line. Stepfather Betrays Family. Man = Brute. But the accusation against Colleen that she heard today had to be just as troubling, maybe more so, because the elemental stereotype of the good mother, the ultimate protec-tor of her children's welfare, had been turned on its head and spun like a top.

The judge's eyes rose and locked on mine. "You've asked me to rule on lifting the order of protection, and that makes my job eas-ier than if I had to rule on custody for your children or whether your wife committed a class-E felony or a class-B misdemeanor and what her sentence should be." I had not expected such a per-sonal statement, not expected to hear her internal deliberations. "I take Mr. Maxwell's concern seriously. I don't want you to take the law into your own hands and perform a rescue operation. It doesn't sound like that's your inclination. I'm going to modify the order of protection so that you can be with your children inside and outside the marital house *only* if their mother is taken into custody. I know that's a little unconventional, but it fits the situation for the time being. I still expect to see you in this courtroom on Wednesday at nine-thirty — that's the day after tomorrow — about the charges against you. I hope your wife and children are back by then."

"Thank you, Your Honor. I do too."

ON OUR drive back to Bernie's office, he explained that even with the exonerating report from CPS, the DA couldn't drop the charges against me today, and the judge couldn't yet dismiss the case, because the disturbing circumstances around Colleen's disap-pearance continued to make the children vulnerable. The authorities seemed to want to keep a close watch on all of us. "If something unexpected happens," Bernie said, "Maxwell and the judge can say that they acted cautiously, not precipitously."

"You mean they're covering their asses?"

"And they're putting everyone on notice that this is still a volatile situation. That the danger to the kids isn't over, even though the source of the danger may have shifted from you to her."

As soon as we returned to the office, Graciela, who had been monitoring the E-ZPass and credit card use, said she had some good news. "She used the Visa card an hour ago at a drugstore in Kingston." Half an hour later, we learned she had gone to a grocery store in Newburgh, which meant she was traveling south.

I knocked on the door to Bernie's office. "It looks like she might be heading back this way. Do we still want to have her arrested? Do we have a choice anymore?"

"It's up to the police."

"But the point of arresting her was to intervene when she was on a tear and we had no control. If she comes back and the kids are fine, I'm not sure I want to wreak more havoc in their lives. Can the detective discard the arrest warrant?"

"I'm not sure it's so simple, and I'm not sure you want him to. I heard you talk about Colleen in court today, and even if she comes back and everyone's fine, she's still the person you described today. She's not going to become more reasonable or rational. And she'll probably take off again with your kids. She's what they call a flight risk, which means that she has the means and the inclination to take off. Excuse me." The buzzer on his phone had rung and he picked up. I turned away and looked down the corridor at the other four or five office doors, some open, some shut. The secretary, Rita, told me that Lily was in court today and wouldn't be in until much later. I realized that I missed her voice, her motherly attention, the diminutive hands that held all of her angst.

"Eric, you still there?" I stepped back to see Bernie sitting at his desk stacked with files and ringed with cardboard boxes of paper clips. "That was Detective Lawson. They picked up Colleen outside Newburgh. Her car was on the shoulder of the highway with the hazard lights on. She had run out of gas and was waiting for someone to stop and help her. The cop did a routine check and found the warrant. She's okay. So are the kids. They're holding her at the police station until they can transport her back. We can go up in my car and you can get the kids and drive back in Colleen's car. How's that sound?"

"Where will they take her?" My voice caught in my throat, and I could feel a rush of tears jam the corners of my eyes. She had run out of gas. The woman who had engineered everything from her pregnancies to Sandy Lefkowitz's divorce had forgotten to go to the gas station. Or maybe — here's the shrink in me, looking for hidden motivations — she had run out of plans and wanted to be stopped in her tracks. Not that she would ever have that insight — or admit it if she did.

"Probably the same place you spent the other night."

I turned away to wipe my face but could not work fast enough. The tears were sadness. They were relief. A cascading release of all the tension of the last days and weeks. They're alive, I said to myself and shuffled away from Bernie's door to a place down the hall where I could be alone. A sigh forced its way up my windpipe, and I realized I had been practically holding my breath since we discovered them missing. That part was over, but what was to come hurled me into another black hole: Colleen behind bars, disheveled, despairing, and enraged, behind the same bars that had imprisoned me. I could see her raising her fists against the world's cruelty, but I could not bear to envision her all alone in the dark, pissing into that miserable little pot. Who on earth, who on this vast planet, would she name when they told her she had the right to make a phone call?

22

A Perfectly Happy Marriage Until

D<small>EAREST</small> —

The psychiatric literature is divided. The psychiatrists are divided. The vast medical libraries housed at Google and WebMD do not speak with one voice. I have consulted a good number of them and my own heart too. It's surprising, isn't it, that so many people believe we therapists possess real wisdom, that we can be trusted to dispense good advice? Or maybe no one believes that. Maybe they look to us in desperation, more as oracles who will tell us what will happen in the future and what to do in the meantime. But we both know that shrinks stumble and blunder and screw up just like everyone else does. I am Exhibit A.

One fifty-year-old mother I found on the Net said her children had grown up visiting her in prison. It became such a commonplace that it didn't shock her when all three of them ended up doing time themselves. And being visited by their children.

But what becomes of the children who don't visit their mothers in jail? Who are their role models? What nightmares are branded onto their psyches? There are as many answers as there are prisoners in the nation's jails. What's the latest number I read in the *Times*? Two million. Two point four. Forgive me for digressing and going macro on you, dear heart. I do it often these days when I find myself on a random walk in a spare hour between patients, when I try to determine the probability that we could have ended up where we are today. And that our fates and our futures — yours, mine, the children's — are now bound up with two million men and women who live with rap sheets, prison records, another meaning of the word *time*, new definitions of *inside* and *outside*. And there's this: as a convicted felon, you are automatically disbarred. As your lawyer Mickey Silverman said when pleading for clemency in your sentencing, for the crime of falsely reporting an incident to the police, a class-E felony, "Your Honor, Colleen has lost everything that matters to her. Her career. Her children. Her position in the community. I urge you to give her credit for time served and allow her to serve out the balance of her time on probation."

By then, you'd already done three weeks, what with the postponement of the first hearing and your appeal of the $500,000 bail, which you lost. Lily explained to me that the DA would probably have dropped the charges against you for having had me arrested on a made-up charge, but your taking off with the children made you a flight risk for a court appointment, and your unpredictable behavior — falsely charging me, coercing Graciela to leave the country against her will — was harassment that could be prosecuted and might endanger the children's welfare. Mr. Silverman presented as good a case as he could, given the mountain of evidence against you and your refusal to accept responsibility for anything. In the halls of justice, they call that "lack of remorse."

"If the court could only see my point of view," you kept saying, no doubt against your lawyer's advice, "you'd understand my only concern was protecting my children from harm." I suppose you actually believed what you said, or convinced yourself that you did.

You were well advised not to plead insanity or temporary insanity; it would have prevented you from ever getting custody of the kids. When the court-appointed psychiatrist testified on the state of your mental health, his conclusion was good news for both of us. "I believe Ms. Golden has a clear understanding of the difference between right and wrong," he said. "I also believe that when she takes an action that she knows is illegal or morally questionable, she reflexively underestimates the consequences to others of her actions, leading to damaged relationships both personally and professionally." He sliced it right down the murky middle. You know the difference between right and wrong, but you keep choosing wrong because you don't have the capacity to care when you hurt someone. If this is mental illness, it is also behavior that must be contained and restricted so as not to harm others. If this is illness, compassion must be offered with reservations, with limitations. It is difficult to warm up to someone whose only name for me during the trial was the Predator. The Predator who takes care of the children and the house.

You got off easy. The judge bought a good chunk of the silver-tongued Silverman's plea. Only three more weeks in Valhalla. Then you're on probation for a year. I know it doesn't feel that way to you — "only" three weeks. It isn't the blink of an eye to the children either. I imagine that time passes as slowly behind bars as it does to small children who are deprived of their mother. They do their own sort of time, kids like ours. Do you know that there are one point five million kids with a parent in jail, our two girls among them?

I am imagining you reading this letter. You couldn't know that every day I check the mail for the letter you said you would write me — or have you forgotten? It was our first visit, and we sat at our assigned table and you peppered the girls with questions about school, friends, and birthday parties. They were shy at first but devastated when the hour was up. I barely took my eyes off you, but you kept yours resolutely on the children, avoiding mine. Would you rather I not remind you? Would you prefer to hear about our three new goldfish and the broken clothes dryer?

When we got up to leave on our first visit, I said, "We miss you.

Every day." I was saying it for the children's sake and because it was true.

I shivered when you mouthed these words, speaking them so softly only I could hear you: "Then why did you do this to me?"

"I had nothing to do with it," I whispered back. "The police, the DA . . . You can't pull a switch and call everything off just because . . . I don't need to explain that to you." In a more audible voice, I added, "We'll be back next week. Won't we, girls?"

They were crying, softly, then louder, and we were told again that the hour was up. "I'll write you a letter," you called out as they ushered you away. I thought at first you were talking to the children, but they know nothing of letters. And so I have been waiting all these weeks for a private message, an apology, an explanation. I want you to tell me that our life together wasn't all a charade. That I wasn't only a sperm bank and an escort, a bedmate and a lawn ornament. All I find in the mail are bills and overdue notices from the library.

But if I read my textbooks again, I will be reminded that people like you have shallow emotions and fractured intimate relationships. You entice people with your charm and confidence, but you experience connections differently from the rest of us. You find it impossible to maintain closeness. You don't know what to do with love. You insist that you love your children, and we are all touched by your tender feeling — until we remember what you did to their father.

Then why did you do this to me?

I was not quick enough to throw your question back at you, but I could just as easily have asked, "Why did you do this to *me?*"

I am supposed to be the expert in emotions, but I find my own swinging wildly, from self-pity to rage, from vulnerability to sarcasm. I want to touch you and I want to shun you. Want to scold you and want to cry, I who barely shed a tear when my father died, until the night you held and suckled me . . .

It's been a rough few days. That's why I'm writing. I'm pecking out this letter on the old computer in the office off our bedroom while Sarah Rose sleeps in our bed. Zoe is in her room down the hall, and I hear Graciela watching the big TV downstairs in our TV room. She loves AMC, loves all movies with Katharine Hepburn in them, especially *The African Queen*.

After what happened yesterday on our way home, I won't be bringing the kids to see you again. The other two visits were difficult too; so is the flow of daily life between them. If it were not for the continuity and devotion of Graciela, I imagine the girls would be slumped in preverbal childhood despair. But we have kept much of the structure of their lives intact. We are in the same house, I am working out back in the cottage, and Pru and Bea have been spectacular. They invited us to the city and took the girls to *The Lion King* and the Big Apple Circus in the blue tent behind Lincoln Center. Last Saturday, Bea gave each girl a Matisse puzzle from the Museum of Modern Art and pajamas that glow in the dark, which they wear every night.

There is no easy way to explain to them where you are. The experts suggested I say you're in a place that's like a hospital, because you're sick and you have to get better before you can come home. The explanation is fine for Sarah Rose, but Zoe seemed to understand yesterday that there is something sinister afoot.

I've tried to make it as playful as I could, our waiting on line at the entrance gate, sometimes for an hour, going through metal detectors, being searched, being frisked, going through one creepy locked door after another, and I have felt like the clowning father in that Italian movie about the Holocaust, trying to pretend to his son that it's all a game. But what can I say instead? "Mommy's in jail because she's a bad girl"? Does that mean all bad girls go to jail?

In the visiting area, with the other female inmates and their kids, you've done a nice job of explaining that the yellow shirts and pants are your costumes, and you are all on the same team, the

Mommy Team, you call it. Yesterday, I gazed at the other families as we sat at our visiting table and Zoe fired those hardball questions at you, one more exacting than the next. It must have been your courtroom training that got you through such a grilling. "Can we see your room?" "Do you take a lot of medicine? Are you getting better?" "Are there any children in this hospital?" "What happened to your hair?" — because it is no longer the vibrant, smooth strawberry blond that it was a month ago. It's frizzy, unkempt, unglamorous. I can't help noticing the threads of gray that multiply exponentially with every visit. And can't help noticing how much weight you've lost. You're starting to look like those beanpole Hollywood girls I remember from the Mondrian Hotel, where your womanly fullness caught my eye. Your hips are gone, your cheeks are sunken. You do indeed look sick; a hospital might be the right place for you.

The hour was up before I knew it. Both girls looked at me as though I might be able to reverse the decision. Was I going along with their banishment? "All the kids are leaving so their mommies can get better," I said. "All the kids are sad. The mommies are too." Acknowledge the difficulties, name the feelings. Who the hell knows if it does any good?

You were led out of the room waving, smiling, and blowing kisses as you went back to do your time, which must be even harder after seeing the kids. We were near the end of the line of families leaving, so it took longer to get outside than it had before. And it was so cold. Late October. Sarah Rose was in my arms, Zoe's mittened hand was in mine. We were quiet and sad, surrounded by other sad children and their frazzled aunts and grandmothers. Hardly any men. I think I saw three. Sarah's head grew heavy against my shoulder, the unmistakable dead weight of sleep.

When we were finally outside — yes, now I know the new meaning — the sunshine was bright, the sky such a wintry, crisp shade of blue, so different from the overly bright fluorescent room in which we'd been visiting. We had a long way to walk from the building where you live to the gate, to the vast fence that surrounds the grounds. Zoe complained all the way about having to walk, but I decided it was better than her crying all the way. The natural light reminded me of the private darkness tunneling through all of us. It must have taken fifteen minutes to get back to the parking lot. Another five to get into our car and watch everyone else pile into theirs. This was not the Scarsdale Mercedes SUV crowd, not quite. The girls scooted across the back seat, Sarah Rose into her car seat, Zoe beside her, waiting for the seat belt to be clipped at her waist.

It's a few miles of winding narrow country road until you get to the turn for I-287. I was concentrating on the traffic, not paying attention to Zoe's murmuring in the back seat. I think she was saying "Mommy is a bad girl" under her breath, but I couldn't be sure. Just as I accelerated onto the highway, there was a bloodcurdling shriek from the back seat. Instantaneously, I looked into the rearview mirror and saw Sarah Rose's lips open, her tiny head thrown back, the piercing sound shooting from her mouth for no reason I could tell.

"Zoe, what's wrong with your sister?" I shouted, the only way to be heard.

The shriek continued, but I couldn't keep looking in the mirror. I was gripping the wheel and looking to my right to take the first exit. Why hadn't I taken Graciela? She offered to come, but there was no reason I needed her. Was it stomach pain? Was it gas?

"Zoe, talk to me. I can't stop the car right now."

No answer. The endless shriek. My exit, in one-quarter mile.

I flipped on my hazard lights so cars would stay away from me and found an opening in the right-hand lane. "Zoe? What's going on?"

"Nothing."

The shrieking stopped, but Sarah Rose began crying hysterically. In the rearview mirror her hand was at her mouth and it was red. "Sarah Rose, honey, are you okay?" Had Zoe done what I thought she did? Bite her sister's hand and break the skin? Where was the nearest hospital?

I drew a blank, but twenty seconds later I remembered: back where we had just been, on the hill with the prison — the Westchester Medical Center, about a quarter mile down the road from the jail.

SHE DID NOT need stitches. The blood was plentiful and deceptive. Zoe's teeth did not break her skin, but they punctured a recent scab, which reopened and enlarged the original wound. The bite marks were ferocious. The doctor cleaned everything and gave us Tylenol and antibiotics. Sarah Rose slept in her car seat on the drive home. I decided Zoe should sit up front with me instead of beside her sister, and for a long while neither of us spoke.

"She was hitting me," Zoe said for the fifth time. "She was pulling my hair."

"I know that's what you said."

"That wasn't Mommy's hospital."

"What?"

"Why didn't we go to Mommy's hospital?"

How much longer could I keep this up? "Is that why you bit your sister, because you wanted to go back to Mommy's hospital?"

"No, I bit her because she was pulling my hair. Are you going to tell Mommy?"

What was the right answer? "Do you want me to?"

"No."

"Then I won't tell her. But I want you to apologize to Sarah Rose and tell her you'll never do that again. And I don't want you to do it again. Ever, to anyone."

Colleen, should I tell you I don't believe her? Should I tell you that for the rest of the drive home I wondered if she would grow up to tell stories like yours?

263

I put Sarah Rose to bed early and sat with her until I could hear the regular breathing of sleep. Then I went to Zoe's room, where she was doing the Matisse puzzle of "The Dance." As I got down on the floor with her, intending to talk about the day, she said, "Daddy, I don't want to go back to Mommy's hospital."

"Why not?"

"It smells funny. It hurts my nose."

"Do you like seeing Mommy?"

She nodded and pressed a puzzle piece into its place.

"But it makes you sad, doesn't it?" She nodded. "And angry?" It was one continuous nod. "Does it make you want to scream?"

I needed to phone Marsha Rogers, the therapist we'd planned to use as an expert witness, the woman who was going to do play therapy with Zoe to determine if she had been molested. No question about it, the child needs help.

If I stop taking them to visit you, in Zoe's child mind it will be because she bit her sister. But if I keep taking them, her rage will be stoked with the anticipation, the chaos, and the sadness spilling everywhere. Either way there will be consequences: anxiety, trust issues, separation issues, mother issues. But will they be more or less severe if we keep visiting? I don't know.

The truth, dear heart, is that *I* can't bear to go there again. Can't bear to see what it does to them and what it does to me. My nightmares, my own sadness, my adult despair. I will spare you the details, not that you would care to hear them — you who have been so aggrieved, the victim yourself of such injustice. *How could you do this to me?* How else would a con artist tell it? *We had a perfectly happy marriage until my husband turned on me, and now look where I am.* I've never heard you say it, but I bet that's the line about yourself that you peddle inside, just as you peddled the story of Zoe's temperamental father to me.

If I stop taking them to see you, you'll call me cruel and coldhearted. You'll blame me. The truth is I wish you weren't there. I wish the judge had given you what I learned is called "shock probation," where you're so shocked by the indictment that a year of probation is thought to be enough of a deterrent, even of a punishment. Even with shock probation, you'd be out of a job. If you were still practicing, you'd still be coming after the Sandy Lefkowitzes and the Professor Littles of this world, in the guise of saving women and children from the depredations of deadbeat dads. Abusing the system just because you've figured out how to do it doesn't balance out the injustice in this world, even though it must feel as though it does to you — for a few blissful minutes as you savor your latest victory. It must feel like winning one for your side — our side — the side of all the divorced women who are penalized, impoverished, neglected, made to suffer, scrimp, and worry the way my mother did, burning out her brain synapses with excess adrenaline and insufficient income. Never mind who loses. Never mind what's lost.

I realize I haven't mentioned the article about our troubles that came out in the *Scarsdale Inquirer*. It provoked Sandy to call me, and I invited him to come in, on the house, to talk. "I'll make us a pot of coffee," I said, remembering Louise Wallace, who sometimes made sandwiches for hungry clients. It wasn't that I dropped my guard entirely with Sandy, but I told him that what he'd read in the newspaper was largely accurate, and I was sorry I could not have been franker when he last called. He was appreciative of the situation and had some good news. No, he and his wife had not reconciled. But she had not hired a new lawyer *and* she had a boyfriend. Sandy relished the prospect of getting his revenge by suing her for adultery, which apparently he could do even if they were separated. We had a good laugh over that. It was most unprofessional, but what the hell? We deserved it.

Do you wonder about the rest of my patients, what their responses were to our sordid story in the local paper? You should wonder, now that I'm the only breadwinner in the family. It helped that I had a heads-up on the article. A week before I knew it would appear, I called each patient and invited her to come in for a session, so I could discuss "something personal." Everyone knew I had been away and wondered what was going on behind the sign on the door that said FAMILY EMERGENCY. I scheduled almost three solid days of sessions, to make sure people heard the story from me before they read it in the paper. I prepared an informal script that covered the facts I thought would be in the paper, how I thought it would or would not affect the therapy, and why I believed this experience could make me better at what I do. I laid it all out and then invited each one to decide for herself whether to continue our treatment. I meant every word I said. I was fighting, after all, for my life.

At the end of the first day of such speeches, I was walking the fifty feet from the cottage door to the kitchen door, asking myself why I felt so strange, so light-footed. It took some time to decide that what I felt might be happiness. What did I have to be happy about? I opened the back door and saw a sandwich on the countertop with a note from Graciela. "For you, Mr. L." Smoked turkey on rye with a dill pickle on the side, a thick slice of bright red tomato shining between the slices of bread. What a kind, wifely thing to do. I didn't hear her in the house. She must have been out with Sarah Rose. In twenty minutes I would pick up Zoe from nursery school. In the meantime, I could sit at the kitchen table and wonder what on earth I had to be so damn happy about.

It did not take long.

I wanted to keep my patients. I needed them. If I didn't win them over, I'd sink, I'd drown. Not just financially, but emotionally. I need continuity in my life and my kids needed me to have continuity. I ate slowly. Graciela had slathered Dijon mustard on the bread, which I love, and a thin slice of red onion, and the tomato was one I had bought for four dollars at the fancy market the other day when I'd felt sorry for myself, and now its seeds and juices dripped down my hand. I noticed that my inner sneer was gone. I wanted Susan Reed to trust me again with her secrets and wanted her not to worry about the welfare of my children. I wanted to reassure her that we could still work together even though she sometimes feared I might be more focused on my problems than on hers. "I don't *feel* distracted," I told her honestly. "To the contrary, I feel like I'm concentrating acutely these days. But I would certainly wonder, in your situation." The truth was that I was grateful I had the distractions of other people's problems to dwell on.

I was happy *because* I had stopped taking my patients so lightly. I had stopped scorning those I had found shallow, because I had so much in common with them now: I was as scared and lonely as they were, stuck in their expensive houses, in their loveless marriages, devoted to their kids but desperate for a grown-up's kiss, a grown-up's body to hold in the night. Do they feel me listening to them differently? Can they tell I've changed?

But you didn't mean it, did you, Colleen — that you are going to write me a letter? It was another of your enticements, to keep me coming back to you, to keep me waiting. Jesus, you're good. You're positively brilliant. You manage to seduce me even when you're in jail.

SO MAYBE I won't send this letter to you, either. I'm not above a little revenge, a childish expression of hurt. Tit for tat. Isn't that what divorces are all about? Isn't that the basis of your business? When I started writing, I intended this letter to be a courtesy, to tell you we wouldn't come to visit again. And, I admit, I wanted to be close to you again. I wanted to see what it felt like to talk to you, to imagine talking to you. What have I learned? It's a mirage, our closeness. An illusion, a fantasy. I am writing to someone who's not there. I am talking to the walls, just as I was the day we met and you seduced me in the elevator. *If you're talking to the walls, well — I'm better company than that.* You sure are. No two ways about it.

You'll find out the hard way that we're not coming to visit. You'll wait and wait and wait, as I have been waiting for your letter. It will dawn on you slowly that we're not coming, and you can blame me for that too when you get out. Don't get me wrong, Colleen: It's not that I *want* to inflict pain on you. It's just that I don't care if that's how it works out. Do you deserve what's come to you? I could argue both sides of that one. But there is no way I deserved what I got. And the children — they're the big losers here.

Speaking of pain — there'll be plenty more for us to inflict on each other when you get out in three weeks, and sadly, some of it will trickle down to the girls. Let us hope it doesn't pour down on them, doesn't cascade down on their bruised little bodies. Your release date is the Monday before Thanksgiving. Pru, Bea, and I are planning a family day at their place, and I hope you'll see fit to exercise your superlative acting skills and join us, for the sake of the children, at least until you and I decide what our next move should be. I've got my ideas and I know you'll have yours.

One thing I must do before you get out is find myself a good divorce lawyer. While we're still on speaking terms, dear heart, I might as well ask you: Is there anyone nearby you'd recommend?

© EMMA DODGE HANSON

Elizabeth Benedict is the author of *Almost,* which was selected as a New York Times Notable Book and a Best Book of the Year by *Newsweek,* the *Washington Post Book World,* and National Public Radio's *Fresh Air.* She is also the author of three other novels and *The Joy of Writing Sex: A Guide for Fiction Writers.* She has taught writing at Princeton, the Iowa Writers' Workshop, MIT, and the Harvard Extension School. She maintains a Web site at www.elizabethbenedict.com.

ALSO BY ELIZABETH BENEDICT

ALMOST

"Tremendously engrossing . . . smart, painfully
funny and, at times, deeply moving."
— *Newsweek,* "Best Books of the Year"

The forty-something Sophy Chase has just begun an
adventurous life in New York City when she learns that
her almost ex-husband has been found dead on the
New England resort island where she left him just
months before. Lured back to the island by feelings
she thought she had left behind, Sophy must navigate
treacherous emotional terrain involving her grown step-
daughters, a former lover who is now a celebrity lawyer, the mystery of her husband's death—and her own
darkest impulses.

ISBN-13: 978-0-618-23161-4

ISBN-10: 0-618-23161-7

LOOK FOR THE READER'S GUIDE
AT www.marinerreadersguides.com.

Visit our Web site at www.marinerbooks.com.

AVAILABLE FROM MARINER BOOKS